THE DASHING STRANGER

Araminta could not remember her name, who she was, how she had come to the strange band of gypsies. The gypsies knew, but to reveal the truth was to condemn her to a fate worse than death. Within their camp she was safe from the evil designs of her insidious guardian, Lord Robert Eddystone—outside, mere prey.

Unaware of her wealth or her jeopardy, Araminta adapted to gypsy life, warming the hearts of those who shielded her and catching the eye of the dashing stranger who visited the camp only at night . . . a man she'd never dream was the most admired aristocrat in the finest London circles. . . .

THE
WICKED
GUARDIAN

Elsie Lee

A DELL BOOK

For Phebe, Celeste, and Tania

Published by
Dell Publishing Co., Inc.
1 Dag Hammarskjold Plaza
New York, New York 10017

ISBN: 0-440-19801-1

Previous Dell Edition #9801
New Dell Edition
First Dell printing—July 1979

CHAPTER 1

The heavy traveling coach rocketed around a rutted curve in the road, throwing Araminta Surtaine painfully against the far side and waking her from the light doze that had overtaken her after the dinner at a posting inn. Blearily, she grasped the hand strap and peered from the window. It was full moonlight, the horses going at a gallop, but she recognized no landmark. Where were they? It was many hours since Lord Robert Eddystone, her guardian, had taken her from the London house to drive north to her family home.

In explaining the need for the visit yesterday, Lord Robert had smilingly turned aside all objections from Mrs. Hobson, Minta's *dame de compagnie*. "No, no, there is no need for you to disarrange yourself, madam —no need for a maid; there will be plenty of them at Surtaine Manor; I mean to travel light and fast, and my ward will require no company but her guardian, Mrs. Hobson."

"Yes, of course, milord, but all the same . . ." The chaperon fluttered uneasily, but was unable to withstand Lord Robert's command.

Nor could Minta refuse to obey her guardian's order, although she was at a loss to comprehend the necessity for such a trip. "It is not as though I had ever resided there since nursery days, milord. I know no one in the locality, and it seems a very long way to travel in order to sign some papers."

"I am sorry for it, child, but there is no alternative. You will shortly be in possession of your income, and I would fail in my duty to your dear parents if I did not make certain all was in perfect order." He patted

5

her hand. "Mrs. Hobson, please have Miss Surtaine's baggage packed, and order her carriage ready for noon tomorrow, when I will take her up."

When he had nodded himself from the room, Minta said, "I don't trust him; I wish I hadn't to go, Hobby."

"Oh, dear, I don't like it, either—but there's naught to be done." Mrs. Hobson sighed. "And it is true that on May 28 all must be turned over to you, Minta. I suppose he cannot be blamed for wishing to ensure there is no irregularity to cause a whisper—for you are very rich, you know, and it would be a matter for immediate gossip that his lordship would find distasteful."

"Well, I find *him* distasteful," Minta said flatly. "He reminds me of a sleek white pussycat—and his son is a slimy snake. I can't *bear* Francis Eddystone, and even if Lord Robert refuses consent to my marrying anyone else until I am twenty-five, I will *not* have Francis. I would rather be a spinster!"

Mrs. Hobson tittered faintly, "Oh, there's no likelihood of *that,* my dear. So pretty as you are, and so much money as well—why, you'll have all London at your feet next year when you make your curtsy. I declare, we're all looking forward to it—with my sister, Lady Urbaugh, to present you with her own daughter." Mrs. Hobson sighed dreamily. "So fortunate you and Jane are good friends, and yet quite distinct—your black hair, and her blond . . . mmm, the gowns and frocks, the vouchers for Almack's completely assured, with the presentation to follow, and all your mama's jewels . . ." Mrs. Hobson sighed again. "So it is only to finish these few months, my dear Minta, and everything lies ahead."

"If I never have to see Francis again, it would be enough," Minta muttered. "There are times when I wish I had no money, Hobby."

"I own I cannot like his lordship's attempts for a

betrothal," the chaperon admitted. "You are far too young to be tying yourself to anyone, even if you felt a partiality. But as for money, you will be very glad you have it in time to come!"

Swaying back and forth by the hand strap, Minta's mind was suddenly fully, most suspiciously, awake. This was no main coaching highway, but a rough country road of potholes and jolting stones. Little as she knew of the terrain, she yet knew Surtaine Manor house was no more than ten miles from the great turnpike and that this approach wound through two villages. Beyond the coach window were no houses, no indication of human habitation. Darkened they might be at this hour, but there should be dwellings visible in the moonlight. Araminta saw only trees tossing spring leaves in the breeze, and when she had unfastened the window, she could distinctly smell the sea!

The fresh air further sharpened her wits, despite a dull ache in her head. The route to Surtaine Manor led directly up through the center of England, not within twenty-five miles of any coast. "Where am I?" she wondered wildly. "What has happened to Lord Robert? Am I being kidnapped?"

Leaning to breathe deeply from the window, she forced her hazy mind to recall events: they had left London punctually at noon, with Lord Robert sitting beside her in the coach; four hours later, they had stopped to change horses and refresh themselves with tea; and two hours after that they had stopped at a posting inn for dinner. To that point they had been on the main highway, with the postilions blowing up for the tolls, but at dinner's end, Araminta was yawning uncontrollably.

"Poor child," Lord Robert said sympathetically. "Indeed I am sorry for your weariness, but it is not much farther. Why do you not make yourself comfortable with the pillows, and I will sit beside the coachman to direct him? No, no, the footman will stand behind, and I shall be glad of the air."

She had been asleep almost before he had finished settling her feet on the jump seat and tucking the pillows about her; but now, coupled with her throbbing forehead, Araminta had a terrible certainty that she had been drugged. "The final glass of wine," she thought; but she had taken no more than a few sips while Lord Robert's eye was on her, and the instant he'd turned aside to acknowledge the report that the coach was ready, Araminta had jettisoned the remainder of her wine into the woodbox. As Lord Robert turned back to her, with great presence of mind, Minta had apparently just emptied her glass and was replacing it on the table. "I hadn't had enough to counteract these bumps. . . . But why?" Where could Lord Robert be taking her? What could he mean to do?

Araminta struggled to put her feet down and sit erect, fighting for common sense and self-control. He could not mean to kill her—it would gain him nothing. Despite Mrs. Hobson's mutters that Lord Robert took far more of Minta's income than was justified, if she died unwed before the age of twenty-five, everything went to some distant cousins in the colonies that were now called America.

Bracing herself as firmly as possible, Minta cautiously poked her head from the coach window, and could hear voices from the driver's seat above and forward: Lord Robert's bland baritone and—she stiffened in horror—his son's affected London drawl!

"Oh, I don't mind . . . don't know how Clara will take it . . ." That was Francis, and Lord Robert's suave reply, "She'll take anything for money, dear boy."

"I daresay, but how d'you get the little pigeon to

hold still for the plucking?" That was Francis again. "She loathes me, y'know—can't say I fancy her, either. Flat-chested little dowdy with a devilish sharp tongue."

"Exactly like her mother; never knew why Oliver Surtaine picked her, but that's neither here nor there." Lord Robert's voice floated back clearly in the silent air. "I've drugged her; she'll hold until we reach Crossthwaite—never know it isn't Surtaine Manor; she hasn't seen the place in ten years. Hankins is ready to read the marriage ceremony—and in no case to object if she can't answer distinguishably." Lord Robert laughed evilly. "Tomorrow she signs papers to do with the dissolution of my guardianship; among them will be the marriage certificate."

"Hmmm, well, I trust it works, but I wouldn't depend on it. She's cursed sharp, and she don't like you any better than she likes me," Francis observed indolently. "Be just like her to inspect every paper and ask an explanation."

"There will be two dozen papers, and after the first dozen lengthy explanations, I fancy she'll begin signing more quickly," Lord Robert returned.

Araminta withdrew her head and sank trembling against the rear seat. Oh, she had been right to distrust Lord Robert! How could her father have been so deceived as to place his daughter in such hands! No matter—*what* was to be done to save herself? Crossthwaite? She had never heard the name, but if it belonged to Lord Robert, there would be no help for Araminta among its staff. "I can refuse to sign *anything*. . . ." Useless; if he had drugged her this evening, he would only drug her again, until she was sufficiently dazed that he could guide her hand to sign the marriage contract. "I can cut my hand, and be unable to write. . . ." Useless, again. He would merely keep her at this Crossthwaite until the wound healed.

Mrs. Hobson might be deeply disturbed by a lengthy absence, but what could she do? *"Nothing. I am with my legal guardian; I am wholly in his power, and there is no one who could interfere."*

Unconsciously, Minta was sobbing under her breath, shuddering with revulsion at the mere thought of being forcibly married to that loathsome Francis Eddystone. And who was Clara? His current lady-bird, no doubt.

While her mind whirled frantically in search of escape, Araminta was suddenly aware of a slackening in the pace. Oh, God, were they even now reaching Crossthwaite? No, they were only going up a hill; she could see no sign of light or habitation. The road seemed to ascend between deep side ditches. Almost of itself, her hand quietly reached through the window to unfasten the coach door; and as they neared a patch of deep shadows, slowing even more to gain the top of the gradient, Araminta gathered her skirts together and launched herself full force beyond the swing of the door.

She felt a jolting blow on her ankle that tumbled her over and over; her head was foremost; it hit something, and Araminta knew no more. . . .

The coach continued on its way, picking up speed on the downside of the hill and swerving so sharply that the coach door swung into place and latched itself. Then it was gone, but not without witnesses.

From the depths of the woodland shadows, Joe and Alfie stood open-mouthed, observing an unmistakable body flying into the ditch. "Ooo-errr, I don't like the look o' that," Joe whispered hoarsely. "Come on, leave the rest o' the snares for tonight, Alfie. We've four prime rabbits, they'll do us till tomorrow. I say, cut for home."

Alfie hesitated, "Keeper'll find snares, do we leave 'em," he whispered back. "Means he'll know our run—there's only three more. I say clean 'em out, long as we're here. Else, we'll have to find a new lay."

Joe was reluctant. "I don't want to cross t' road with a deader in the ditch."

"Look the other way, then—a deader can't hurt you," Alfie scoffed. "We got to cross somewhere to make the camp, and the snares is up this end. If you're skeered, go down a piece and come back t'other side to meet me."

"I ain't skeered," Joe protested indignantly, "I just don't want nothing to do with deaders."

"You ain't got to do nothing," Alfie began, and stopped with a gulp. "What were that?"

"It were a groan from the deader," Joe whispered fearfully. "Come on, Alfie, let's get away afore some-one hears."

The body in the ditch groaned again, and Alfie stopped his scramble into the woods behind Joe. "No," he said shakily, "we can't."

"Why can't we? Let keeper find 'un."

"No, it's in the Bible—Ma read it to me—about the good Samaritan. We got to help, if it's alive." Alfie gritted his teeth and crept forward cautiously. Leaning down from the bank, his eyes widened. "It's a female!" he hissed, beckoning to Joe.

In the moonlight, Araminta's face was alabaster white, her black ringlets disheveled beneath the crum-pled bonnet. She lay with eyes closed, moving her hands faintly and moaning. "She's *beautiful!*" Alfie mur-mured, spellbound.

"But whyfor would anyone throw her in a ditch?" Joe asked uneasily. "I tell you: leave her there, Alfie! Milkman'll find her, come morning."

"No, that might be too late." Alfie was already letting himself down the bank, gently lifting the limp form into his arms. "Come on, Joe, help me. It's nobbut a mile to get her home to camp. Ma'll know what to do."

"What about rabbits, then?" Joe objected.

Alfie debated. "Snares are all on the way back—lay her down gentle-like whiles we check 'em. Gives us a rest, and we're always headed right."

It was slow going for the two boys, complicated by their burden's occasional moans that might draw the attention of the game keeper, but Alfie took it as divine approval of their rescue when the remaining snares produced three more rabbits. "Bigger than any of the others," he whispered gloatingly. "And we got away with snares!"

Eventually they staggered awkwardly into the firelit circle of caravans that was their home, "Black Jack's Traveling Circus." The rabbits were festooned from Joe's belt, bumping his legs and backside with every step. They had tried various ways of carrying Araminta, but nothing seemed satisfactory. At last Alfie draped the limp body over his shoulder. "She don't weigh heavy, but she's the wrong shape or something," he panted. "Keeps sliding off me; hold her on, will you?"

Despite the hour, the camp was awake—at least, its human tenants. Laughter, a snatch of song, and boozy voices floated out from the great wooden carts while the boys made their way to the biggest, most gaily painted of all. Clambering up the rear steps with Joe's assistance, Alfie found his father—Black Jack himself—playing cards with his usual cronies. All activity stopped, the dealer's hand suspended in mid-air, while Alfie stumbled across to let Minta slip from his shoulder to the divan bed. She was still unconscious, but breathing.

"Lord bless us, lad, what have you there?" His father stood up in alarm.

" 'Tis a female," Alfie said when he could speak. "They threw her out of a carriage into the ditch top of hill, but she ain't dead, Pa. So me and Joe cleared snares, and carried her back for Ma to see to—like in the Bible."

"It were Alfie's idea, not me," Joe inserted a hasty defense, "but we got seven rabbits."

"Clean 'em up, and fetch Sally—she's over to lion tamer." Black Jack stepped forward to peer over his son's shoulder.

"Ain't she beautiful, Pa?" Alfie's voice was yearning, but even bruised and dirt-stained with a frock crumpled and filthy from the boys' inexpert portage over the fields, Araminta was undeniably exquisite— and the last thing Black Jack wanted at this moment! She lay like a sleeping fairy-tale princess against the gaudy divan coverlet, unaware of the silent inspection above her as the other card players crowded forward to look.

"Aye, she's beautiful," Black Jack agreed heavily. Wiser than Alfie, he knew at a glance she was also Quality, which only compounded his difficulties. "Go along to help Joe with rabbits—else there's too many people, no room for Ma to tend her."

Silently the men resumed their seats, eyeing each other furtively. "Eh, what's to do now?" Ted, the wild-beast tamer, muttered finally. "They'll come searching, asking questions. Yon's a high-bred young female— however she got into ditch, they'll want body, Jack."

"Alfie'd no call to meddle in plans of the gentry," Sam agreed. "Best to stay clear, should have left her in ditch."

"He couldn't." Jack sighed. "Not when she was

alive. Sally's rearing him into a proper Christian—not but what it's demmed inconvient sometimes."

"Be a demmed sight more inconvenient do she die on us here," Ted returned. "Then what'd we do?"

"Put body back in t' ditch," Sam suggested.

"Cross your bridge when you come to it," Black Jack stated. "Might be someone'd be grateful we cared for the girl, come down handsome for our concern. By her clothes, there's money, and we've no call to suspicion any foul play—might have been an accident." He shrugged. "Female swoons in the close air of the carriage, falls against door not properly latched, and ends in ditch." Under the patent disbelief in his cronies' eyes, he shifted uncomfortably. "Could have been that way," he insisted. "See what Sally says. . . ."

His wife was already entering the caravan. "What's this Joe's saying?" she demanded a bit breathlessly. "Alfie's brought home a dead girl? Where is she?"

"Over there." Black Jack nodded. "And she isn't dead . . . leastways, not yet. See what you can do."

Sally bustled forward to lean over the motionless form. "Lord save us!" she said under her breath, reaching for Araminta's wrist and gently stroking back the tumbled black curls with her other hand. "No, she's not dead, nor her pulse isn't too feeble. The poor, pretty child—what can have happened?" She straightened up with decision. "Well, what *you* can do is clear away out! Tell Alfie to bring water, and ask Bess to lend me a hand."

"Yes, ma'am!" The men made haste to transfer themselves to Ted's caravan. " 'Tis best one—Bess is over to Sally, and young'uns is asleep. . . ."

Sleep shortly overtook them, as well, but in Black Jack's caravan the women were doing their best for Araminta. With gentle fingers they stripped off her clothing, raising their eyebrows in silent recognition of their luxury. Finest cambric, delicate French lace, silk hose so badly torn as to be useless; garnet earbobs, brooch, and gold locket with an intricately worked chain they set aside carefully. A tiny reticule embroidered with a design of pansies yielded a chased-silver vinaigrette, a handkerchief with a monogram indistinguishable in the dim light of the caravan, and a leather purse.

It jingled when shaken.

Bess thrust out her chin. "You'll count it whiles I watch, and we'll put it up safely with the jewelry," she stated, "for whatever happens, there's never been no thievery in Black Jack's circus."

"Aye." But when they had upended the purse, they stared at each other, half-frightened. " 'Tis ten Golden Boys," Sally whispered, "and underneath . . ." Trembling, she drew out a folded bank note for a hundred pounds. "Oh, Bess, what shall we do?"

"Leave one guinea in the purse, hide the rest, and say nothing to anyone—not even Jack," Bess urged. "He'd not take it, nor my Ted, but did they know, they might mention, Sally, and so *much* money: it'd be a temptation."

"You're right!" Sally swiftly wrapped the bill and coins together with the jewelry in one of Araminta's torn stockings. "Do you watch me, Bess!" Dragging over a chair, she clambered up and thrust the packet between the two roof joists above the bed. "Now"— replacing the chair—"you know where I've put it. Do anything happen, you can swear to it."

"Aye." Bess nodded tersely. "Sweet little thing, whatever could have happened?"

"I dunno—she's got a terrible lump on her head; broke the skin, it did, with drops of blood, but I've cut away the hair," Sally said efficiently, "and bathed it well. 'Tis that bothers her, she moans when 'tis touched . . . but she's got a great scraping cut on her leg, too."

"Be painful till it heals," Bess observed, "but at least there's no bones broke. I wonder who she is? I can't believe anybody'd want to harm a child—it must have been an accident, Sally."

"Well, if so, we'll know soon enough," Sally said. "I don't like her lying unconscious for so long, Bess; but do she come to herself, she'll tell us all."

"And do she not?" Bess asked after a moment. "What then?"

"It'll not come to that."

"But if it *do?*"

Sally drew a long breath. "There's always . . . the sea," she said evenly.

It was nearly an hour before Lord Robert Eddystone's coach turned through the decrepit iron gates of Crossthwaite, past the untenanted gate house that was slowly crumbling to pieces. Slowly they bumped up a rutted drive and drew rein before the front door. While the horses gratefully stood still with heaving sides from their exertions, Francis surveyed the house in the moonlight. "Good God, you *have* let the place go!" he observed with a sniff of distaste. "With all the Surtaine money in your hands, I'd think you might have spared a bit for repairs."

"The Surtaine money was not in my hands, as you put it," his father returned. "Annual accounts must be presented to the court for widows and orphans. Every item must be substantiated, or the judge will make the orphan a ward of the court. The best I could do was to include certain of my living expenses with Araminta's, and even that was questioned." He snorted angrily. "The judge thought 'the household

16

bills surprisingly large, considering the young lady is not out!' "

Francis laughed maliciously, "A pity you couldn't put your gambling debts into the accounting!" He looked around restlessly. "Have you no service in this dismal hole?"

"Skeleton staff—the fewer people the better tonight." Lord Robert secured the reins and descended stiffly, to stamp the circulation back into his legs, while the main door was suddenly unbolted and opened. "Evening, Martin." Lord Robert went around to the steps, as Francis lazily swung down from his seat. "You had my instructions, I see."

"Yes, milord, and all's prepared," Martin wheezed hoarsely. "Mr. Hankins is waiting in the study—not but what he's been there long enough to fall asleep."

"Drunk, is he? No matter." Lord Robert shrugged, tramping up to the entrance. "We'll have a bottle of the Madeira to warm us, Martin, and whatever's in the larder—cold beef or ham, an omelet and cheese."

"Yes, milord. The missus has something, I disremember what, but she's already in the kitchen."

"What about her?" Francis nodded toward the interior of the coach.

"Let her sleep. It'll go easier if she's just waking and slightly dazed. She'll not be sure what she's saying," Lord Robert said indifferently, striding into the house and rubbing his hands together. "Damme, it's colder than one thinks for driving! I need some wine and a fire."

A few candles lit the hall, casting eerie shadows on the staircase disappearing into darkness above. What Francis dimly remembered as the salon and the morning room were merely closed doors, but to the rear was a strip of light lying across the floor. Following his father into the study, he found a roaring fire and several branched candelabra, which Martin was making haste to light. There was also a man in clerical garb sprawled in a wing chair and snoring stertorously.

"Good God." Francis wrinkled his nose in disgust. "Is that your parson? I doubt you'll get him on his feet, let alone able to say the service!"

"He'll serve well enough," Lord Robert said grimly, swinging the chair away from the fire to conceal the man's flushed face and slack mouth. "Pour the wine, will you? I'm chilled to the bone."

"So am I," Francis remarked pensively, "and in no case to deflower a bride, I assure you."

"You'll feel better when you've eaten." Lord Robert tossed off his wine at a single gulp, murmured, "Ahh-hh!" and refilled the glass. "Martin, as soon as we're served, you can bring in the luggage, and be sure the chill is off the bedrooms." He sank into a chair and stared silently at the leaping flames.

After a moment, Francis also sat down. "I hope you know what you're about, sir," he muttered. "For my part, I think it's demmed risky! What if the girl sets it about London she was constrained?"

"She won't be in London," his father returned calmly. "She'll be here, by her husband's orders."

"The chaperon, Mrs. *Thing?* She's bound to ask questions, and she's got very influential relatives." Francis chewed his lip uneasily. "I didn't bargain for a drunken padre, sir. You may be able to get him to mumble the words, and get her to say 'I do' and sign the certificate . . . but if there's an inquiry, it wouldn't take a second for any court to discredit him." Francis sipped his wine. "That's if you could get him sober enough to stand in the witness box."

"Good God, what a faint-heart!" Lord Robert scoffed impatiently. "Fifty thousand pounds a year—twenty-five for you and twenty-five for me, and naught to do but keep the girl here for a few months! No matter what she says later, no court will believe her, Francis. With any luck, you'll get her pregnant, and I'll handle Mrs. Hobson. She's nothing to live upon, I've only to insinuate she was feathering *her* nest out of Minta's fortune, and she'll keep her mouth closed in order to get another position." He looked around as the door opened. "Ah, Mrs. Martin! Good evening, good evening—and what have you got for us, I wonder?"

"Good evening, milord—'tis only chicken and ham," the woman said apologetically, "with some mushroom fritters and stewed salsify. We'd not know exactly when your lordship was arriving, but I've jelly pancakes to follow, and there's a cold mutton pasty, if you'd fancy it?"

"No, no, this will be excellent. Thank you, Mrs. Martin." Lord Robert surveyed the fireside table she was covering with dishes, and nodded, smiling appreciation. "Oh, you might have some hot washing water in readiness for bedtime."

"Yes, milord."

"Hmmm, hmmm." Lord Robert inspected the contents of the various covered dishes. "Simple fare, Francis, but you'll find it edible. I recommend the fritters, but leave room for the pancakes—she does them very well."

"I'm happy there is something to anticipate," Francis murmured, forking a chicken wing, a modest slice of ham, and two fritters onto his plate . . . and wincing at a sudden explosive snore from Mr. Hankins. "Good God, I don't require Pandean Pipes to entertain my supper—but neither do I wish the grunts from a pig sty!" Francis complained, eyeing his father's ample provender and happy chomping with disfavor. "How you can eat with such an accompaniment!"

"One grows used to minor inconveniences," Lord Robert said indistinctly, "in pursuit of an ultimate goal . . . such as twenty-five thousand pounds a year."

His son's pallid eyes flickered briefly and bent to the supper plate. Lord Robert Eddystone might have his plans; so did Francis—and they did not include an even split of the Surtaine fortune. Once married, Araminta's money automatically belonged to her husband. Francis felt that five thousand a year to his father would be quite sufficient repayment for the effort of working out details in the affair . . . nor could Lord Robert complain without ruining himself. "Thank God I wouldn't sign any sort of contract!" he thought. With nothing on paper, Francis had only to deny all knowledge of a drugged bride, a drunken parson, a tricked signature. "Really, the governor's no brain," he thought contemptuously. "When it comes to money, it's every man for himself."

He would have been surprised to learn that Lord Robert was actually far ahead in the game. He meant to get the marriage performed and consummated, but before his son would get the signed certificate, there would be a legal agreement. If it were not signed by Francis, he would find himself in the difficult position of raping his father's ward in the guise of a marriage . . . and as Francis had said, nobody would ever credit Mr. Hankins.

In reflective silence, broken only by the cleric's snores, father and son ate the jelly pancakes whisked in by Mrs. Martin, hot from the pan. At last Lord Robert wiped his mouth with a sigh of repletion, and settled back in his chair. "A glass of brandy," he said to Francis, "and then we'd best get on with it. Oh, Martin"—as the servant entered—"bring the brandy . . . and our compliments to Mrs. Martin. The fritters were exceptionally tasty."

"Thank you, milord. I've brought in the baggage, and Ben's seeing to the horses."

Lord Robert frowned. "I didn't tell you to send the coach to stable."

"Beg pardon, your lordship." Martin looked bewildered. "But when all was out, I supposed you'd want horses rubbed down."

"All was out?" Lord Robert repeated. "You fool, what about the young lady? Now, we've to get her from the rear yard."

"Young lady?" Martin was thoroughly confused. "You did say to prepare a chamber for a lady . . . but she weren't there, milord."

"WHAT?"

"No, sir, milord," Martin quavered as both men sprang to their feet. "I brought in bags, and Ben—he come along and looked in back, but it were empty, milord. So he took coach away. Would you want it brought back, milord?"

"No, no," Lord Robert muttered, "but she *must* be there . . . where could she have gone? She's fallen from the seat, Ben didn't see her . . ." He strode from the room, with Francis behind him. "Get me a lantern!"

But when they had gained the stable, where a toothless old man was disposing the horses into stalls, there was no doubt: the coach was empty! The only trace of Araminta was the jumbled pile of down pillows that had been placed about her, and a single long French kid glove of palest pink, scented with fresh lavender. His eyes starting from his head, Lord Robert wildly hauled everything out to the packed dirt floor, from which Francis retrieved the glove.

"Give over," he said. "She won't be there, unless she's turned herself into a mouse. She must have roused while we were supping, and gotten out of the carriage. She could easily have come into the house, in search of a proper bed—I'll warrant she's half-dazed from the drug, with a bad headache as well. She'd want nothing so much as a chamber, *any* chamber."

"You're right!" Lord Robert exclaimed. "Of course! With Martin bringing up the luggage, she simply followed him. He'd not have realized while he was distributing the valises."

Hastily the two men returned to hurry upstairs. Three chambers were brave with candles and cozy fires, luggage opened and partially disposed into armoires. Cans of steaming wash water kept warm on the hearths. Of Araminta there was no trace. Lord Robert continued along the passage, opening doors onto unused rooms and flashing his lantern into darkness.

"A waste of time," Francis pointed out. "Were she here, she'd have turned into the first prepared chamber, sir. The alternative is that she's wandered off into the grounds. Summon everyone with more lanterns—she can't have gone far."

"Get the dogs out, too." Lord Robert panted his way down to the hall, bellowing for Martin to rouse the household. "We fear the young lady has become lost in the shrubbery. Turn everyone out to search."

Francis dangled Minta's glove for the dogs to sniff, and baying loudly, they ranged around until one of them found the pile of coach pillows in the stable. "They've got the scent, good! Bring them out to the front drive where the coach was standing, let them pick up the trail to tell us which way she went." Hopefully, they trooped back to the entrance, but the dogs only milled about aimlessly, and as often as he presented the glove, they merely wagged their tails or went back to the pillows.

Now thoroughly alarmed, the men looked at each other. "Call off the search," Francis said finally. "It's obvious she didn't get out of the carriage here, or the dogs would find her. I wonder, sir—was she ever in the coach after we left the inn?"

"Devil take it, she must have been," his father growled. "I packed her in myself and latched the doors. The drug was already taking effect, she was nearly asleep."

"Nearly, but perhaps not quite." Francis frowned in memory. "There was a small time lapse while you settled the landlord's account, and I was taking my place on the box. What if she felt unwell? We had not started—she might easily have stepped out unnoticed, to seek aid from a female servant in the inn. Had she any money?"

"How can I say?" Lord Robert shrugged irritably. "I must suppose a few shillings; more would not be usual in a young female's reticule."

"But the landlord would not know this," Francis reflected, fingering his chin thoughtfully, "and if Minta found the landlady, she might well have been seen to a chamber. We would have been long gone before ever it was realized our passenger was left behind. Nor was there any word of our destination. You paid off postilions, groom, and coachman, to return to London. The mail coach went through while you were dining in the private parlor; presumably the men joined its passengers, but even if they had time to gossip with a hostler, they'd only have said you were bound for Surtaine Manor.

"Yes, I fancy that was the way of it." Francis yawned delicately. "And Miss Minta will be quite safely disposed until you arrive to rescue her."

Lord Robert chewed his lip and grunted. "Damn the cursed wench!"

"Why, as for that"—Francis turned to the stairs—"it would seem the blame is your own, Father. Had all been settled before ever she was assisted into the coach, there would not have been that fatal time lapse—or the most comfortably fruitless journey I have ever endured. Bid you good night, sir."

"Where are you going?" Lord Robert demanded as his son started toward the landing. "We have to go back for her—God knows if the horses can make it after so little rest, but no matter how slow the pace, we must reach her before she wakes."

"Not 'we,'" Francis said gently, continuing on his way. *"You."*

"I?" Lord Robert stared open-mouthed. "Do you seriously expect me, at my age and at this hour, to drive over that miserable cart track alone?"

"Take Martin with you," his son suggested, pausing to look down at his stuttering parent. "If I did not resemble you so closely, sir, I must have suspected my mother had played you false," he observed, "for of all mutton-headed ideas! Return, you must—and as fast as possible; you can scarcely mislay your rich ward for longer than it will take to discover her absence and retrace your path . . . *but* upon ascertaining her safety in the inn, you will have no choice but to bed down until the morrow. To insist upon waking her for instant removal will certainly occasion surprise, and if—as seems probable—she is in a drugged stupor, her sluggish movement may also be noted.

"In either case, you cannot hope to regain Crossthwaite until full daylight, by which time she will have recovered from the effects of your drug and be able to see she is *not* at her own home," Francis finished dulcetly. "I trust you have a plan to cover unexpected contingencies, of which this appears definitely to be one."

"Devil take you, Francis," Lord Robert choked furiously, slapping his hand against the newel post. "I have troubled myself to arrange the most advantageous possible match for you, and because of a trifling hitch, you will throw all into my lap? Damme, I'll take the chit to Surtaine—let her sign a few papers—return her to London . . . and you can whistle for your cozy income!"

"Exactly what I meant to suggest—with a small embellishment." Francis leaned over the upper stair rail with a mocking smile. "By all means take her to the manor, get her signature to everything—*including the marriage certificate;* it can be filled out later. Then plead business here, suggest she'll like to see your home for tea—it's no more than ten miles, after all. 'If at first you don't succeed, try, try again!' or to put it another way, 'Faint heart ne'er won a fair lady's fortune.'

"Surely you can contrive privately to inform her staff that Miss Araminta will be returning from *here* to London? Surely you can contrive to drug her tea?" Francis said coldly. "We will then proceed as originally outlined."

"And what will you be doing?"

"I," said Francis, "will take care to keep out of her sight, and charge myself with the responsibility of getting Mr. Hankins just drunk enough that he can be awakened at the appropriate moment tomorrow night."

"Hmph," Lord Robert snorted, "you have an answer for everything."

"Yes, I rather fancy I have, in this instance," his son murmured thoughtfully. "Good night, Father. Drive slowly, and try not to end in a ditch."

Lord Robert stood shaking with rage, watching the languid figure disappearing along the upper hall. "Damn him, damn him," he muttered, clenching his fists. The soft click of a latch, followed by the gentle slither of a bolt, set the seal on his fury. Whirling, he strode down to the study and crashed open its door, to face the boozy countenance of Mr. Hankins. The minister was only *just* on his feet, teetering with hand outstretched to the decanter, and smiling foolishly at Lord Robert.

"Ah, good evening, milord—expected you long since, must have fallen into a doze," he slurred. "Must beg pardon . . ."

Lord Robert glared at him. "You've had enough liquor!"

"Only hair of the dog," Hankins protested, "be all right in a minute, milord—quite ready for the ceremony, assure you." The man spilled as much as went into the glass, but when he'd tossed it off, before Lord Robert's incredulous eyes, the minister shook himself into complete control. "Where would you wish the service to take place, milord?" he inquired courteously, with no slightest indistinct vowel. "I had thought perhaps the salon, and instructed Mrs. Martin to fill two vases with flowers. There is something about flowers, milord—brides are always partial to them."

"Yes, yes, that is so," Lord Robert murmured, narrowing his eyes thoughtfully in the grip of a new idea. "But as it happens, the young lady has, uh, been delayed by an accident to her coach. We must go to fetch her."

Mr. Hankins looked surprised. "The hour seems very late, milord."

"Exactly!" Lord Robert filled a glass for himself, and blandly gestured to the decanter. "Have another, Hankins—it's like to be a chilly drive, but we cannot leave a gently bred young female alone at a posting inn, eh?"

"No, indeed, milord!"

"So we will go to the rescue, and perform the ceremony there, eh?" Lord Robert downed his brandy with a sardonic chuckle. "Damme, why didn't I think of it before? To the devil with Francis," he muttered under his breath. "I'll marry her myself!"

"I beg your pardon, milord?"

"No matter, no matter," Lord Robert said testily, striding over to jerk the bell rope. "Finish up, man, and get your greatcoat. Martin, have the horses put to, and dress yourself to come with us as quickly as you can."

All that kept Lord Robert from falling asleep on that ghastly trip was the pull of the reins in his hands, and the savor of his son's discomfiture! The journey seemed interminable, made doubly worse by Mr. Hankins' recovery and jaunty reflections on the beauty of nature at night, but at length they were pulling into the posting inn as dawn was breaking. "I'll want fresh horses in four hours; meanwhile, rooms for myself, my companion, and my man. Is the landlord awake?"

"Not yet, 'tis full early—but night barman'll be up, to attend to Edinburgh coach."

Stumbling slightly with weariness, Lord Robert made his way into the inn—to encounter disaster: there was no young lady sleeping alone in any chamber!

"Nonsense, she must be here! She was taken ill as we were about to leave last night, and by ill-luck we had gone without realizing she had left the carriage. The landlady will have cared for her."

"Begging your pardon, sir, but there ain't no females in the house at all this night," the man said stubbornly, and produced his tally in proof. "Number 1, two gentlemen come down from the North; Number 2 and 3, Earl of Penarvon and his valet; Number 4 and 5, vacated at half after four this morning when the mail coach from Scotland come through—and a demmed time I had to rouse 'em!"

"Here, what's afoot?" The landlord came bustling down the stairs.

"Gentleman insists as there's a young female a-staying here, but she ain't on me tally, and so I showed him, Mr. Reddy."

"Of course there's no female, this is a respectable house," the landlord began indignantly, and stopped as he caught sight of Lord Robert. "Eh, 'tis you, milord! Pray, be seated—how may I serve you?"

"By assuring me of the safety of my ward, of whom this fool disavows all knowledge, but I must suppose your good wife has given her a chamber—she was ill, you know. No doubt she stepped from the carriage to seek a woman's help, and in the turmoil of leaving, we drove away . . ." Lord Robert's voice trailed off in the face of Mr. Reddy's blank expression. "Good God, don't say she is not here?"

"She is not, milord." The landlord shook his head worriedly. "Nor she didn't leave the carriage after you'd helped her inside. Me wife was watching too. When you'd left the yard, she passed the comment that little miss was looking far from well; she hoped as the trip weren't much farther. Dear, dear, what can have happened? Did your lordship stop anywhere else?"

"Oh, yes, as a matter of fact we did," Lord Robert improvised hastily, heaving himself to his feet. "I forget the name of the inn . . ."

"It'd be the Dog and Duck, no doubt—fifteen to twenty miles along the turnpike," Mr. Reddy said helpfully, "or did you go farther, there's the Spotted Cow. First-class houses, both; you'll not need to fret, milord. She'll have stepped down, as you say, looking for assistance, but the goodwives in either inn would see to her. Dear, dear, what a shock for your lordship! Barman, a glass of brandy for Lord Robert . . . and I'll have the horses put to for you. By good luck, there's a team rested overnight, milord. You'll soon find little miss."

He bustled away to instruct the hostlers, and Lord Robert sat down heavily, staring into space until the brandy was set at his elbow. "Thank'ee," he muttered automatically, and felt his hand shaking so that liquid dribbled down to his chin when he sought to drink. He wondered dazedly if this were a nightmare from which he would presently wake in his bed at Crossthwaite, but there was a compelling reality about the brandy he was mopping from his lips.

Good God, where could Araminta be? His mind whirled frantically in total confusion: he had the best of reasons for knowing she could not have crept from the carriage at either the Dog and Duck or the Spotted Cow, for they had turned aside from the main highway before either inn was reached; nor had they stopped for so much as a minute anywhere along the back-country road to Crossthwaite. His eyelids were drooping uncontrollably with weariness; there had been nearly eight hours in the coach from London, broken briefly for tea and dinner, followed by more than three hours in which he had driven at least half the way, spelling Francis. An hour's rest for supper at Crossthwaite, another hour of search, four and a half hours to return, and he must still get back to his house.

Lord Robert groaned inwardly, but there was no alternative. If the girl was not here, she must be there, and in daylight they would find her more easily.

He did not push the horses for the return journey. The soft morning air cleared his head somewhat, and Mr. Hankins' sprightly chatter helped him to stay awake. It was a long while since he had driven along this road. Lord Robert noted the presence of a gypsy caravan on the headland. A few farm gigs drew aside to allow passage of his coach, the drivers touching their forelocks respectfully. He made a mental note to write a stiff reprimand to the town council concerning the disgraceful condition of the road. "God knows when last it was dragged," he said irritably, "and the ditches need clearing, as well."

It was after ten of the morning before he reached Crossthwaite again and climbed down from the driving seat. "Put the coach away," he said tersely to Martin, "and set everyone available to a search of the grounds. Hankins, go with them."

He stomped wearily up the stairs; the closed door to his son's chamber was obscurely infuriating. Lord Robert strode over and battered upon the paneling full force, until a languid voice protested, *"Will* you stop that filthy racket! I'm coming. . . ." Lord Robert continued to batter until Francis unbolted and glared at him irascibly. "Oh, it's you. What the devil are you about?"

"I am about to go to bed," his father returned bitingly, "and while I am restoring myself after eight hours of tooling my coach back and forth, you can join the search for Araminta." He observed the glazed eyes with grim satisfaction. "She was *not* at the inn." Lord Robert turned away to his chamber. "Perhaps she has turned herself into a mouse, but if you want any part of that fifty thousand pounds, you can hunt for her."

CHAPTER 2

Bathed, bandaged with basilicum powder, and clad in a clean night shift, Araminta still lay unconscious beneath the covers of the divan in Black Jack's caravan. She no longer moaned, nor moved restlessly, but Bess and Sally felt encouraged. "There's no fever, the pulse is slow but steady," they told each other. "She'll do. 'Tis a natural sleep; come the morrow, she'll be herself again."

"Aye, sleep's the best medicine . . . and I could use a ration!"

"Go home, if you like," Sally whispered. "I can manage now."

"Nay, I'll sit it through. We'll keep each other awake —not that it's necessary with Jack snoring 'God Save the King' behind the curtain." Bess laughed silently.

Throughout the night they dozed intermittently, rising to steal over softly for a look at their patient, but there was no change. With the coming of daylight, Bess went off to her own home on wheels to wake Ted and get their breakfast. Sally waited hopefully for Araminta to open her eyes. First Alfie, then Black Jack came out yawning and stretching. "How is she?"

"Still sleeping. She'll be all right. Alfie, try for some fish . . . a nice bit of sole would do her good."

"Yes, Ma."

Jack was less easily convinced. "Ought she to be so white, Sally? Looks like a little ghostess."

" 'Tis natural for her, with such fine black hair— like silk, and masses of it," Sally returned. "I shouldn't wonder if she was Scottish. Remember that knife-thrower's wife? She looked the same."

"Aye." Jack sighed. "I wish she'd wake, so's we could return her where she belongs. I'll tell you straight: I want no law men asking questions at this moment."

Sally's eyes widened with suspicion. "Why not? What have you to fear, Jack Bickell?" she demanded.

"Nothing," he disclaimed hastily. "I'm just . . . averse to any tanglement with what don't concern us."

"So that's it! I wondered why we were staying so long in one place, *and* close to sea. You're back to the free-trading, don't deny it," she stormed at him. "And after all your promises, your sworn oath to me! Won't *nothing* teach you? Last time was a piece of luck by the grace of God, they couldn't prove a case—which only means they're watching you extra careful. Next time"—Sally caught her breath, anguished—"you'll be transported, if they don't hang you. Oh, Jack!"

"Nay, nay." He hugged her awkwardly. " 'Tis something else altogether. Better you know nothing, but don't fret, lass—this is on the side of the law and would gain me a pardon for anything else."

Sally searched his face with painful intensity. "You're telling me true? Oh, Jack, don't lie to me! If anything was to happen to you, I'd never bear it."

" 'Tis the truth, and pays me well for doing my duty to king and country," he assured her soberly. When she continued to look at him warily, he shuffled his feet and muttered, "Well, I don't say there ain't a bit on the side, Sally, but I'm not actively concerned. I've kept my promise. 'Tis only to look the other way occasionally or turn a deaf ear—nothing for which I could be took up, I swear—and all the time I'm salting away in the funds," he finished eagerly. "It won't be long before we can have us a proper cottage, and set Alfie to a decent trade. Think o' that!"

"I'd like it," she admitted, "but if it's not honest come by, it'll do us no good, Jack."

"But that's what I've just said," he urged. "This time it's the king's money I'm earning rightfully."

"Well," she sighed, "you'll do what you're bound to do, I suppose, and if you do it the wrong way, it's for the right reason. You've always took thought for me and Alfie and the babes that died, but be careful, my dearie!" Sally smiled faintly. "You're the only husband I've got, and money'd be no use without you."

"Ooo-er," he scoffed, to conceal emotion, "you'd not need any money to have a dozen offers in a fortnight, begging you to walk over to parson this afternoon."

"I'd have more than a dozen," she said calmly, "but that don't say there'd be one I'd find in step with me down the aisle." Sally giggled irrepressibly. "Go along with you, Jack Bickell! Let me get breakfast."

But nothing roused Araminta. She continued to lie with eyes closed, unaffected by the pungent odor of frying fish, the clatter of dishes and cutlery, the voices and movements about her. The roar of Ted's lions and prized tiger demanding their feed, the cackling hens and geese in the pen behind Black Jack's caravan, the dancing bear jingling its chains, and the neighing of the prancing horses, the stir of awakening to daily chores throughout the encampment, the inexpert bleating of the musicians endeavoring to conquer a new entrance march, and the joyous barking of trained dogs—all disturbed her not.

By noon Black Jack was seriously worried. "I think we should send for doctor, Sally. You say she's all right, but such a stupor don't look natural to me. One thing to care for her till she tells us who she is—and maybe a reward from her family—but do we take responsibility, and she don't come round from your treatment"—he shook his head—"it'd be bad, very bad! You're no doctor, there'd be questions: why didn't we tell someone she was here? Family'd say she might have been saved with doctor, call you a murderess, Sal!"

"Aye, but she'll not die, Jack. I'll own I wish she'd wake, but pulse and heart are stronger than this morning. And from what Alfie said," Sally reminded her husband, "it might be we'd have saved her to no purpose, did we report. Think: if she was deliberately pushed from the carriage . . . who did it, and why? You'll not get *me* to believe it was anything but foul play! Do we send for doctor, he'll tell constable, and if there's been inquiry—might be we'd only deliver her back into the hands of those who want to kill her, Jack!"

"Aye, but I mislike it altogether. If she's to be killed, I'd rather 'tweren't laid at your door."

"Give it to sundown," Sally pleaded, "and if she's not come round to give us her story, take her down after dark to lie on doctor's doorstep. Ring the bell, and vanish."

"I doubt it'll go so far. They'll already be searching, they'll need body to be sure"—Jack fingered his chin nervously—"and it *could* have been accident . . . in which case we're causing tragic suspense to someone, Sally."

"It were no accident," she said flatly. "Do you tell me that sweet little lady were *alone* in the carriage? Did she fall accidental-like, her maid would stop carriage at once to go back and pick her up. One thing I'll say: our son don't lie, Jack! He told us what he saw, and Joe agrees. I'll not let child go, until I'm sure of her safety!"

"All right, but for God's sake do your best to bring

her to her senses before evening, or I *must* be rid of her." Black Jack tightened his lips. "Tonight I'll want the van empty," he said evenly. "You'll visit elsewhere until I come for you. Understand?" She nodded silently. "It's all right, lass." He smiled reassuringly. "Tonight it's the king's gold . . . and here's my hand on it!"

"I'll bring her round, leave it to me!"

Jack was right that it would not go so far. While Lord Robert Eddystone slept nearly as motionlessly at Crossthwaite as his missing ward in Black Jack's caravan, his son was going over the grounds by inches, growing more and more anxious. Where the devil was the girl? If she had slipped from the carriage while they were at supper, the dogs should have got the scent; but even if the light pressure of her sandal on the driveway had not left sufficient trace, she could not have wandered far, half-dazed as she might have been by Lord Robert's drug.

By noon Francis was forced to the incredible conclusion that Araminta had either jumped or fallen from the carriage. Old Ben produced a small substantiation for this. "Arrr"—he bobbed his head—"doors was latched, but window in off-door were let down and catch weren't truly fastened, just thrust to."

Greatly perturbed, Francis retired to the study and considered. Lord Robert had driven forth, and back, both by moonlight and daylight this morning. Granted he was not precisely inspecting the ditches on either side of the road, he could not have failed to see a female body had there been one along the way; and if he'd overlooked one, surely either Hankins or Martin would have drawn his attention. Could Araminta have been hurt in her fall, and revived sufficiently to crawl away like a wounded animal? Good God, after a night of exposure, she might be dead! A pretty scandal *that* would make!

"Have to find her!" He tossed off his glass of Madeira and made for the stable. "Saddle the cob!" He rode down the country road for the space of an hour, narrowly inspecting both sides and occasionally turning the horse up to the verge to search among the nearer trees. Nowhere was there anything suggesting a wounded girl creeping into the shelter of shrubbery. At length he had come up to the turn-in for a gypsy circus, blazoned with gaudy posters inviting one and all to the show.

"Black Jack's Colossal Display of wild beasts, Prancing Horses, Trained Animals of many sorts—entrance one shilling. Come early and see the performers in their cages!"

Thoughtfully, Francis Eddystone sat on the cob and surveyed the ring of caravans across the fields. This would be the most likely spot. Between here and the join to the main turnpike there were an increasing number of small farms and houses. Had one of them discovered Araminta, the word would have reached the posting inn by now, and the landlord would instantly have identified any mysterious female as Lord Robert's missing ward. He would certainly wonder how she came to be found on this road, and as certainly, would have notified Surtaine Manor.

"The best defense is a good offense," said Francis to himself, and made all speed back to Crossthwaite, where he ordered Ben to pole up a single team to Lord Robert's carriage in thirty minutes. While he swiftly changed his riding clothes for knitted pantaloons clinging to his spidery shanks, a blue superfine coat of Weston's cut, and glossy boots, Francis equally rapidly worked out a story.

Miss Surtaine had become unwell during dinner; Lord Robert had thought best to bring her to Crossthwaite, since he was uncertain what staff there might be at Surtaine Manor. The rest was truth: to his horror, she was missing on arrival . . . grounds searched . . . drive back to the inn and return to Crossthwaite . . . grounds searched again, as well as a minute search of the road. It was not watertight, but served to explain the delay in consulting the constabulary. Lord Robert was now laid on his bed, recuperating from the exertion of driving all night; his son, Sir Francis Eddystone, was carrying on the search.

Should Araminta be found anywhere in the houses of the hamlet, his appearance might well produce sufficient revulsion as to cause question. Francis smiled sardonically, while expertly arranging his neckcloth in complicated folds known appreciatively in certain London circles as the Eddystone Light. He considered it a calculated risk; privately, he was certain Araminta had been found by someone in the gypsy camp. "That's where she'll be, no doubt of it. They'll have stripped her of whatever bits of jewelry and money she had, probably taken her clothes as well. No matter—she can buy more," he said to himself. "Or take along her luggage! She'll be too glad of rescue to object to the rescuer . . . drive her to Surtaine Manor, bow myself out gracefully, and come back cross-country. M' father'll be awake, pole up the other team, and he can join her for dinner.

"Have to abandon the marriage—pity, but there it is, unless he can find a way to allay suspicion. Damme, what a knucklebrain he is! Francis snorted disgustedly, swinging himself into the driver's seat of the coach. But the important thing is to get her safely back."

Tooling gently along the road, following Martin's directions on the location of doctor and constable, Francis passed the circus encampment with an inner smile.

He would have been less happy had he known himself observed—narrowly, and with deep suspicion. Hidden among the trees and crouched low to set his snare, Joe was briefly confused that there was only a team instead of the four horses of last night, but as the coach wound its way down the hill, he knew it for the same.

Abandoning his task, Joe went leaping from hummock to hummock over the field, keeping the coach in view. He drew a breath of relief when it passed the entrance to the circus ground, and froze with terror as it stopped far down into the valley before the doctor's house. Motionless as a hare in its forms, Joe lay on the hillside and watched: a man in London clothes descended and went into the house; twenty minutes later he came out with the doctor beside him; they climbed up to the driving seats and drove away. Joe sprang up and raced across the fields to another vantage point, from which he could see the coach standing outside the constable's office.

He waited not for the emergence of driver and doctor. Joe turned back and loped swiftly for the caravans. "They'm searching for her," he panted. " 'Tis same carriage, but only two horses today. I saw a man, stopped for doctor, and gone on to constable."

Sally stared at the boy, her face going ashen. "God, what'll we do with her?"

There was a slight silence while they all looked at Araminta's placid sleep. "Under tiger's cage," Alfie said suddenly. "Clear out the space for costumes and put her in there, Ma. Nobody won't go near tiger, do we prod him until he roars."

Sally looked at Bess. "Would Ted mind?"

"Not him," Bess said firmly. "In any case, he'll

not know. Go on, carry her over whiles I get her packet."

"Packet?"

Bess was already nipping up to retrieve the money and jewelry. "You never know," she said succinctly. "Best to put it with her. And prop open the door to be sure she's enough air."

Long before Francis was returning, Black Jack's Traveling Circus was ready for him. While there was no one unaware of a visitor in the main caravan, others besides Bess made haste to transfer various small assets to places of safety. In their experience, once constable got a legal toe in the door, he'd poke his nose everywhere . . . in which they were perfectly correct. To Constable Hasty, the request of Sir Francis Eddystone for assistance in retrieving his father's ward was a heaven-sent opportunity for investigating side issues. He dispatched his son on horseback by the rear lanes to request the assistance of Constable Warren from the neighboring hamlet, and was not to be moved by any representations of the urgency in the matter.

"It's a demmed big camp, Sir Francis. Be she there, they could be slipping her surrepshus-like from a rear door whiles we're coming in the front," he said stolidly. "Best to wait for reinforcement."

Privately, he doubted the girl was anywhere in the circus vans. It would not be in character for Black Jack Bickell to conceal a girl. His circus was well known the length of the English coast. There was no doubt of a sideline in free-trading, though he'd never been caught, but equally there had never been an instance of thievery or sharp dealing within the camp. He ran a good clean show; most of his people had been with the circus for years. They were not above snatching an occasional rabbit or netting a trout in private water, but local citizens had nothing to fear. Jack carried his own poultry, bought produce from surrounding farms, or traded picking labor at harvest time. By now, his circus was genuinely welcomed in every village.

Ergo, if Miss Araminta Surtaine had come into his hands, Jack would have sent for the doctor (if she was ill) or notified the constable (if she were dead). In matters of this sort, Jack Bickell was scrupulously honest and law-abiding. Conversely, Constable Hasty was not impressed by Sir Francis Eddystone: he was a supercilious fop with an oily voice, and the constable rated his smooth story as a farradiddle. Fleetingly, Constable Hasty wondered what *had* become of the young lady—run away deliberate, he wouldn't doubt, and if Lord Robert was anything like his son, constable didn't blame her. There was certainly more to the matter than had been told. Howsomever, it was just the chance he and Constable Warren had been looking for. . . .

It proved even better. When Constable Warren arrived, by good luck he'd known where to put his hands on a pair of revenuers!

"Why do we need them?" Sir Francis frowned.

"Every extra pair of eyes does be a help," Hasty returned sententiously, "and any officer of the law is the same as any other, no matter what his partickler duty. Shall we set out?"

From his lookout post, Joe observed the little company issuing from the constable's station: doctor and London driving coach, local constable and three other men on horses. He waited only long enough to verify they were heading this way, and raced up to higher ground, where he signaled to Alfie, who signaled in his turn by means of a piercing whistle that alerted the camp.

By the time coach and horsemen arrived, the circus

was blandly in control, with no least sign of nervousness. Black Jack strolled forward with mild surprise. "Constable Hasty! Good to see you. And to what do we owe the pleasure?"

" 'Tis not exactly pleasure, Jack, but duty. This here's Sir Francis Eddystone—Jack Bickell, owner of the circus, Sir Francis—with a tale of accident to his father's ward, Miss Araminta Surtaine. Seems she somehow fell from carriage last night whiles they was driving along this road to Crossthwaite, which is Lord Robert's estate," Hasty said ponderously. "We've reason to think she might have been brought here by some of your people—meaning to aid her, of course. Sir Francis has brought doctor . . . if you'd show us where she is?"

"Gladly, but she isn't here." Black Jack frowned. "Tchk! What a sad accident!"

"Come, come, my good man, don't lie!" Sir Francis drawled contemptuously. "Of course she's here. If you'd brought her forth at once, I'd have rewarded you handsomely. As it is . . . Constable, do your duty."

Hasty cleared his throat, exchanging covert glances with his fellow. That was no way to speak to Black Jack Bickell! If it weren't for revenuers present, Hasty would have refused to go farther. He sensed Constable Warren would agree: wait for another day. As it was, he'd no choice. Reluctantly, he drew out the legal paper and thrust it at Jack.

"This here's search warrant," he said gruffly, and muttered, "Sorry, Jack," under his breath. He wasn't liking the expressions on the faces of the circus people.

"Why, no apologies needed, constable. You'll go where you like, search to your heart's content," Black Jack returned affably, "and take revenuers with you. That way you'll be through in half the time, and we'll be glad to have our names cleared on all scores." With a wave of his hand, he invited the men into his caravan. "May as well start here, gentlemen."

The two constables flushed uncomfortably, but the revenue officers asked no better than a look into Black Jack's home. They went over it inch by inch, nor were in any way discomfited by his mild observation that, were they hunting for a young lady, she was not apt to be found in the rafters. "Even mouse couldn't hide up there. . . ."

Hasty and Warren contented themselves with going from one caravan to another, making an official request to inspect, and thanking everyone *very* politely for courteous reception. "Let revenuers do the rest, we'm looking for a young lady," Warren muttered, "nor she ain't here—not that I expected it. Bickell wouldn't *never,* nor any of his people."

"Aye," Hasty grunted in reply, "but we got to cooperate with revenuers . . . not but what I think Jack's give it up. Last time was a near thing."

For an hour the search went on. The whole camp was unweariedly helpful in throwing open every door, every drawer. Long before they'd finished, the revenue officers had grimly realized it was a waste of time. Somehow these people had got wind; if there had ever been anything to find, it was no longer here, but having begun, they must carry through. Nor could they give vent to their frustration, for there was no word, look, or smile but was completely cordial. With innocent eyes and limpid voices, the caravan owners invited the officers to " 'ave a cuppa, dearie—'tis thirsty work crawling around in the dust! I disremember when I last did a turn-out, and traveling do seem to build up the dirt-like . . ."

Throughout the circus the men went, not allowed to miss a single spot. As each caravan was completed, the whole company tagged along to the next, to stand around chattily until the officers emerged. Such an amount of motion and voices naturally penetrated to the animal cages, and at length the search was overlaid with the full-throated roars of lions, tiger, and bear, pacing about uneasily. The dogs were yelping, the poultry cackled vehemently, the horses stamped and whinnied, and Bess's cat severely bit the man who inadvertently stepped on his tail.

"God, it's worse than Bedlam!" they said to each other. "There's nothing here. Let's be off!"

At the outset, Sir Francis had found the odor of the beasts distasteful. Covering his nose with a scented handkerchief, he returned to the carriage after the shortest stroll. "Faugh! What a stench!" he observed to the doctor. "Must beg your pardon for exposing you to it, but we'll leave as soon as they find Minta."

The doctor eyed him impassively. "I must tell you I doubt she is here, Sir Francis. Jack Bickell is not liar. In fact, his reputation is better known in these parts than yours or your father's," he remarked, turning toward the circle of caravans. "If you will excuse me? Since I am here, I will employ the time in examining certain of the children who have from time to time been my patients."

"Well, *that* was pretty cool," Sir Francis said to himself, affronted. "Oh, the devil with him! Hold to the main issue: have to find Minta, and never mind the peasantry. Not even the Crossthwaite parish. I should have got our own constable rather than this man who's probably hand in glove with that black rascal." Crawling inside the coach, he propped his legs on the strapontin and dozed . . . until Constable Hasty's voice roused him to the incredible news that Araminta was nowhere in the circus camp.

"But, she *must* be here," Francis protested. "She's nowhere else in the village; she's not at the inn or in the grounds of Crossthwaite or anywhere along the roadside. This is the only place left." He sprang down from the carriage and scowled at the men. "Damme, I should have gone with you," he said petulantly. "I tell you: she *is* here . . . unless they've done away with her."

There was a small gasp from the onlookers, and Constable Hasty asserted himself. "Now, *that* you'll not say about Jack Bickell," he stated firmly. "Whatever became of the young lady, there's four of us law officers has searched this camp *my-nutely* . . . with every help from people here, and a demmed nuisance it were for 'em, but they been open as daylight with us . . . and your young lady *ain't here!*" He glared at Sir Francis. "What's more, I could have told you she weren't. When Jack Bickell said it, 'twas the truth. Jack Bickell don't lie, nor there's no thieving gypsies in *his* crews."

"Then why were you bringing revenue men, answer me that?" Francis snapped.

"Only to shorten the search," one of the officers said blandly, "not but what we'll agree 'twere waste of time. Howsomever, you laid the charge; we lent a hand to satisfy it: *the girl ain't here!*"

Surrounded by impassive faces, Sir Francis felt retreat the better part of valor. He swung himself up to the driver's seat of the coach, seizing the reins and looking down at the assemblage. "So you say," he snorted caustically. "We'll see what Bow Street says." Flicking his whip over the horses, he got them in motion and drove away at top speed, leaving silence behind him.

"Wonder what did happen to her," one of the revenue officers murmured after a moment. "Well"—he swung up to his saddle—"thank you for your assistance, Bickell. No doubt we'll be seeing you again."

In swift succession, the other men were mounted and trotting away, until at last only the doctor was left. "Here, I say," Jack exclaimed, "how are you to get home?"

"I can walk, or you'll lend me a cob as far as the road."

"Send you home in gig," Jack returned irately. "Alfie, harness up. Come you in, sir, and have a drop of homebrew or what you'll fancy. 'Tis least we can do—here's your day wasted, and I doubt you'll get fee for it from yon counter-coxcomb!"

"I'm sure I shall not," the doctor agreed placidly, "but it's no matter. I'll be well repaid if you've a glass of that Madeira." He followed Jack into the caravan and sank into a chair with a smile for Sally. "I had a glance around, and you'll be glad to know everyone's in good health," he remarked, "and now the law has gone, ought you not to bring the young lady back to her bed, Mrs. Bickell? No," as her hand shook uncontrollably in setting out the wine, "I've no reason to make reports. I'll confess I'm curious for the story—it must be uncommon to cause you to protect her so fiercely."

"Aye, it is," Jack agreed heavily, "and it queers us what to do. Nay, doctor's to be trusted, Sally. You said yourself we'd call him, did she not wake by evening. Go and get the lass, while I tell tale." Dr. Alling listened, enthralled at the report, sipping his wine with absent appreciation and murmuring, "God bless my soul!" until Alfie and Sally came in, carrying Araminta to the divan.

"She's still not waken," Sally said piteously. "Pulse and heart are strong; I changed bandages at noon—figured to let her sleep, 'tis best medicine—but mayhap I done something wrong."

The doctor set aside his wineglass and bent over

Minta's still figure, gently examining Sally's bandages and nodding his head. "No, no, you've done excellently—no need to doubt yourself, Mrs. Bickell. The girl couldn't have had a more competent nurse," he said soothingly, "nor is it uncommon to have a prolonged sleep—almost a coma—following a head injury, but I think we may try to rouse her. Alfie, bring my bag?"

It was still some minutes before Araminta's throat constricted to swallow a teaspoonful of Dr. Alling's potion, and further minutes before the thicket of black lashes lying semicircular against her cheeks fluttered faintly. "Ah, she'll do," he murmured with satisfaction, and stepped away from the divan. "Mrs. Bickell, let her see a woman's face first. Whatever the truth of the matter, it was obviously concerned with men: these Eddystones . . . and she will need time to adjust, is bound to be confused for a space."

Thus, when Araminta opened her eyes with a faint gasp from the pungency of the vinaigrette held beneath her nose, she saw a plump little woman, with bright yellow hair owing more to the peroxide bottle than to nature, smiling at her comfortably. "There you are, my dearie! And a lovely long sleep you've had!"

"Yes, thank you," Minta whispered, smiling back. "And who are you, please?"

"I'm Sally, and now you'd like something to eat, I'll wager."

"Would I?" Minta's gray eyes clouded doubtfully. "I don't think so, thank you." The black lashes flickered, drooped once more.

Dr. Alling swiftly poured a little wine into his glass and thrust it at Sally. "A few sips," he muttered. "Bring her around sufficiently to tell us her direction, to permit us to reach the family."

"Aye," Jack agreed in a low voice, "for I'd be rid of her as soon as may be, doctor. Sally's in t' right of it; after a sight of that demmed Londoner, I'd not be easy until she's back where she belongs. He may or may not be guardian, but tale is altogether too fishy for my shilling!"

Dr. Alling nodded curtly, his eyes on Sally, holding the wine to Minta's lips. "Just a swallow, my dearie—and another swallow—ah, that's the way . . . and now we'll put pillows behind, so's you can sit up."

"Yes, thank you." Minta's voice was still no more than a thread, but she sat up docilely while Sally bolstered her erect. The gray eyes traveled curiously about the interior of the caravan, and grew puzzled. "Where am I?"

"You had a little accident," Sally said carefully, "and here's doctor to say it's all right, you'll soon be home again."

Alling went forward to take Araminta's wrist and smile at her. "Can you tell us where you live, my dear?"

The great gray eyes were bewildered. "Don't I live *here?*" she asked, looking from one to another and passing on to glimpse Black Jack with Alfie beside him. Slowly her bewilderment changed to painful concentration. She put one hand up to her forehead. "I can't remember," she whispered frantically.

Dr. Alling flapped an urgent hand to the others for silence. "Never mind," he said easily. "It will come back to you in time. You bruised your head, you know, and that sometimes makes one confused. Meanwhile, you are home with Sally and Jack . . . and here's Alfie who found you after the accident. Another good night's sleep, and all will be clear again." He nodded reassuringly, and turned to search among the vials and boxes in his bag. "A teaspoon of this mixed in a little water every hour," he murmured, "and one pill before she sleeps, which should be no later than ten tonight.

A very light diet: a cup of clear broth, a bit of boiled fish, poached eggs ... whatever you have, Mrs. Bickell, but nothing heavy such as"—Dr. Alling's nose sniffed appreciatively—"rabbit stew.

"Good-bye, my dear." He smiled at Araminta. "There is no need to worry; tomorrow will be a better day." Snapping shut the medical bag, Dr. Alling motioned the others firmly out to the caravan steps. "As I suspected, there is a loss of memory from the head injury," he said in a low voice. "Do not press her! It may return tomorrow, it may take longer— but until she can give us some word of a family member, it will be wiser not to use her name. Loyal as your people are, the less they know, the better."

"The less they know, the happier they'll be," Jack agreed. "They don't seek to know; they'd rather not. But if lass don't come to herself tomorrow, what's to be done?"

Dr. Alling considered. "I've some acquaintance in London; I'll send an urgent request for information on the Surtaines," he said. "There is also her home somewhere in this general vicinity, by what Sir Francis said. I will put about some inquiries as to its location, and while I am about it," the doctor finished, "I believe I shall also inquire about Lord Robert Eddystone and his son. I do not doubt the existence of Crossthwaite, but between us and it lies the property of the Earl of Minchampton. It's a completely different parish, our vicar may know theirs, but I've no knowledge of their medico—if there is one."

"Aye, it'd be twenty, thirty miles or more," Sally murmured. "We never stopped there, did we, Jack? Seems there weren't no proper field—or was it locals were against any show as a work of the devil?"

"No, that were near border. Here there weren't space," Jack said. "When we break from here, we go near sixty miles north afore we reach a good open space on headland of Lord Wainfleet." He fingered his chin nervously. "I hadn't planned a move as yet," he muttered. "Weather'll be better in a few weeks. I tell you true, doctor: the lass is a complication. I'd be grateful if you'd write as soon as possible, and set out any other leads you can think of. I've the blunt for it.

"She may come to herself, but I'd like all set in motion now: an express to town, answer prepaid," Jack said earnestly. "Someone sent up-road to discover this manor, wherever it may be. I don't want lass surrendered to that nasty piece o' work we saw today —nor yet I don't want no bowmen-prigs poking about circus." He fumbled in his pocket and hauled out a leather purse. "If you'll handle inquiries, and do you find safety for her, I've the blunt for a post chaise."

"That's very generous of you," Dr. Alling observed.

"Oh, they'll repay me," Jack said quickly, "but even if they didn't, it'd be worth it. You'll set it about, get it started?"

"I will—but until her memory returns, call her *anything* but Araminta Surtaine!" Dr. Alling warned, climbing into the gig beside Alfie. "I'll not come back, unless there's some desperate need, Jack. It'd be noted and cause question. Send one of the youngsters with a report tomorrow. To the *rear* door. . . ."

CHAPTER 3

Silent in the moonlight, sails furled, the schooner gently rocked at anchor discreetly hidden beneath the grass-covered bluff. With noiseless efficiency, half-naked men passed cartons and kegs from hand to hand, ending in the long boat at the bottom of a ladder. At length they all ran down to settle at the muffled oars, and pull rhythmically for Alfie's fishing cove, where they beached the boat with the minimum of scrape over sand and reformed the line to unload . . . all except one man.

While the cargo was being swiftly transferred to a cave halfway up the bluff, he cautiously followed a separate path up among rocks and sea-warped shrubs until he gained the crest. There he paused to reconnoiter and draw breath. Ahead, the land sloped gently down among the trees to the dip occupied by Black Jack's Traveling Circus. He moved at a crouch to the shelter of a giant oak, but could see no sign of life aside from a few tiny gleams of banked campfires. Very softly, he gave a muted owl's hoot, and slipped forward from one tree trunk to the next. When he stood at the edge of the caravan ring, he repeated the owl's hoot—thrice, with an artistic lapse of time between each.

No light sprang up, but he sensed a stirring within the wheeled houses. Then, his duty done, he made his way quickly to the main caravan and was inside before anyone had emerged elsewhere. A single tallow candle flickered in the draft of the closing door, but the visitor was too accustomed to need more light. He unhitched the jug fastened at his rear, set it on the table, and sank into a chair with a yawning sigh of mingled relief and satisfaction. Removing the cork, he tilted the jug expertly to his mouth, took several healthy swigs, and sighed again comfortably. Finally he struggled out of his boots, chafed his damp feet for a minute, and stood up.

He had nearly thrown himself full-length on the divan when he realized it was occupied. In the feeble tallow gleam, he could just distinguish an unmistakable female form with a bandage on its head. "Good Lord!" He recoiled, thunderstruck, and hastily made his way among the clutter of furniture to reach behind the curtain for an importunate shake of Jack's shoulder. "Pssst!"

The rhythmic basso-profundo snores ended abruptly in a grunt of alarm. "Eh, who's there?"

"Giles! Who's that on the divan?"

"Shhh!" With a flumping heave, Jack came out of bed and stood blinking in the dim light, closing the curtains behind him. "Gor," he muttered worriedly, "didn't expect you tonight, Mr. Giles . . . I had it in mind it'd be Sunday."

"So it was planned, but I dared not wait so long. They nearly got me as it was. What's afoot here?"

"Keep voices down, and light the lantern." Black Jack moved about swiftly, draping cloths and clothing in a makeshift screen over chairs to leave Araminta in darkness. "She'll not wake; doctor left a pill, but if t' boys is out, we dassn't leave caravan for fear of being seen. Hungry?"

"I could use some bread and cheese, or whatever's handy," Giles admitted, closing the door of the lantern and straightening up to grin at his host. "Good to see you, man!"

"And yourself, lad!" Jack returned in a hearty whisper. But indeed it was true. From first meeting, he'd taken a liking to the tall young daredevil with copper-red curls forever tumbling over his impish pale blue eyes. He called the lad "Mr. Giles," suspicioning it was a false name, but with no idea that his occasional night visitor had been christened some thirty years previously with the monumental moniker of Giles Edward Andrew Ormeraux, Marquis of Bishton, Viscount Desmond, Baron Transome and Rushley.

With instinctive understanding, Giles Edward, etc., knew Jack was much happier not knowing. For all Jack's sturdy self-respect, a small difference would creep into their relationship were he to learn "Mr. Giles" was not simply a well-educated government agent, but one of the foremost aristocrats in England, with a fortune to match his titles. No, let Black Jack Bickell be comfortable in the thought of assisting a spy for Wellington; it was nearly at an end anyway, if this trip were any gauge. Giles sat down, propping head on hands and twisting his lips moodily, until Jack put various dishes on the table before him. "Cold rabbit pasty, end of the ham, here's bread and cheese. I've homebrew, or there's still some Madeira from last time . . ."

"There's brandy this time"—Giles nodded toward his jug—"and some of the smoothest Oporto you ever tasted, when the men get it up from the cave." He picked up the knife and attacked the hambone with satisfaction. "Ah, Sally knows how to cook! You can have your French chefs," he said indistinctly. "Not that the food isn't good, but for a steady diet, give me plain meat and an honest English cheese! Well, what's to do here?"

" 'Tis a demmed set-out, but mayhap it's better nor we'd think," Jack said slowly. "We've had revenuers

here, turning camp inside out, and finding nothing . . .
be a day or so afore they start watching again, I reckon, and meanwhiles, boys'll have cargo into safety.
Aye, now I think on it, tonight's t' last moment revenuers would expect!"

"What brought revenuers?"

"Her"—Jack jerked his head toward the divan—
"but if you're bound to London, mayhap you can help.
Listen!" Slowly and carefully, he related the whole
sequence, while Giles made havoc of the ham and
decimated the wheel of Stilton. "So it stands: little
miss don't know who she is nor remember what
happened," he finished, "and here's Sally fighting-
fierce against letting child go—to tell truth, I'd mislike setting her in hands of Sir Francis, myself; but in a
day or two, he'll have law on us, Mr. Giles, and do
she still be here"—Jack shook his head sombrely—
"it'd go hard for me.

"Doctor understands, he'll back me . . . he could
maybe persuade the constables into seeing the rights
of it, they got the measure of Sir Francis themselves . . .
but 'tis revenuers," Jack said earnestly. " 'Tis touch
and go, we all know that. They'm near convinced
camp is clean—*near*, but not entire. If they find I
fooled 'em about the girl, it'd be a black mark I'd never
be rid of. I could break camp, go north to Wainfleet,
but that's farther for you. Anyways, I don't like responsibility."

"Could I have some bread and cheese, too?" a
voice inquired wistfully. "It looks so good."

Jack's weatherbeaten cheeks paled beneath the tan,
but Giles was not a counter-Boney for nothing. He
smiled at the little face peeping over the shielding
chairs. "Hallo! How are you, Meg?" he asked experi-
mentally.

The huge gray eyes regarded him trustfully. "I'm

very well, thank you—except that somehow I hit my head," she confided. "We don't know how, because I'm not remembering very well, but luckily Alfie found me and brought me home. Oh, thank you," as he held out a slab of bread spread with the Stilton. She took a bite and frowned slightly. "Could I come out and sit with you? It appears difficult to eat while you're kneeling, but if I go back, I can't see to eat at all."

"Of course you can't!" Giles stood up, chuckling, and made a long arm to pull aside the barricade. With three efficient movements, he'd wrapped Minta in the divan cover and transferred her to a chair. "There you are! I haven't eaten quite all the ham. Would you like some, Meg?" He used the name for a second time, glancing at Jack warningly, but there was still no reaction. If anything, the girl was more comfortable to know she had a name and to feel this caravan was home, that it was *all right:* even if she couldn't remember, the Bickells remembered her.

"Yes, I should like a bit of ham, please," she decided, "and perhaps something to drink. I suppose there is not any tea?"

"Not at this hour," Giles agreed with suppressed amusement, "but a very small glass of Madeira should serve the same purpose." He raised his eyebrows at Jack, who silently hauled the bottle from its cupboard. Giles poured a judicious tot. "There you are— sip it slowly."

"I know how to drink wine, thank you," she said, affronted.

"Of course—I beg your pardon," he murmured, refilling Jack's brandy tumbler. By the man's glazed eyes, he needed a restorative! "Well—and what have you been doing with yourself since I saw you last, Meg . . . aside from cracking your pate?" he asked easily, lounging down in his chair.

She was not to be flummoxed, though; it was a quick-witted little miss, who'd admit nothing beyond a tiny loss of memory concerning the accident. "Oh, the usual things." She shrugged airily. "And yourself?"

"The usual things," Giles replied with a straight face, wondering how long the game would last. "What an enchanting child," he was thinking, as Sally suddenly emerged from the end of the room.

"Who's here?" she asked, alarmed. "Is anything wrong? Oh," she sighed with relief, " 'tis you, Mr. Giles."

"Aye." He sprang to his feet apologetically. "Did we wake you, Sal? No need for you to stir yourself—Jack's found me some food, and here's little cousin Meg to give me the news."

Sally's eyes widened, but she picked up the cue at once. "Meg, my dearie—you should be abed. Jack, how could you disturb her!"

To Giles's admiration, Araminta was equally swift. "He did not, really. It was only that, when I saw Giles eating bread and cheese, it looked so very good that I suddenly felt hungry," she pleaded, and was suddenly overtaken by a monumental yawn.

"And now you are suddenly very sleepy," Giles teased. "Back to bed, young lady!"

"Well, I think I will," she conceded. "My feet are grown cold."

With a laugh, Giles picked her up bodily and swung her back to the divan. "Sally will tuck you in; sleep well!"

"I shall, thank you."

Jack came out of his silence. "Where are *you* to bed down?"

"On the floor." Giles shrugged, and laughed silently at Sally's expression. "It's safe enough—I beg you to believe I'm too weary for dalliance this night!"

She bit her lip, but could not repress a faint giggle. "That'd be the day!" she scoffed. "No man the likes of yourself is ever too weary! Go along with you, do ... slide in alongside of Alfie."

"Oh, sad stuff!" Giles pouted.

Jack had the last word. "At least he don't snore," he observed blandly.

Long before the occupants of the other caravans were stirring—they were all lying in for an extra snooze to compensate for the exertions of the night —Giles was up and off in Jack's modest farm gig with Alfie holding the reins. Such local residents as were already tending their livestock found nothing surprising in the glimpse of Black Jack's wagon; Alfie would be gone to market, probably stopping at one or another cottage on the way back to buy milk and butter.

Well-acquainted with the coach schedules, Giles swung down a short distance from Mr. Reddy's hostelry and strode forward to speak to the driver emerging from the inn. Alfie loitered only long enough to be certain Mr. Giles would be took up for a vacant place; once there had been none, and it had been necessary to go farther in order to get him completely away from the locality. This morning, however, the coachman was nodding, and in a twinkling Mr. Giles was gone. So was Alfie, taking his time for the return trip and fingering the gold piece he always received for this transportation service. It was understood the money was his, although he always gave it to his father for safekeeping. Today, very daringly, he meant to spend his coin—if anything good enough for Araminta could be found.

Following the standing instructions, Alfie went from one yard to another, procuring the usual goods, until he entered Mrs. Upson's kitchen. "If you please, ma'am, Ma wants butter and some greens, if you've any to spare," he began, and stopped. Piled on the work table were strawberries—masses of fat juicy fresh red strawberries, already perfuming the air. Mrs. Upson's lips twitched, noting his yearning gaze.

"Aye, 'tis time for jam, and a gradely crop this year," she remarked. "Would you like some?"

Alfie nodded violently, dragging out his gold piece. "Could I have some cream, too?"

"Of course." She bustled away to the stillroom, came back with a small milk pan. "Fill that, whiles I get cream and butter . . . and then you can go out to garden and pull some beets. Thin out for me, you know how."

"Yes, *ma'am!*" Joyously, Alfie picked and chose among the berries, dashed out for the greens. Coming back, he saw the family cat waiting for the door to open. Behind her were four kittens. "Shall I let 'un in?"

Mrs. Upson sighed. "May as well. Joe be going to drown kittens as soon as he has time. I could wish he'd drown *her,* and get us a nice tom, for a change."

Alfie eyed the kittens parading past him; one was pure white. It occurred to him that Araminta would like a pet. "If you be going to drown 'em, could I have that one?"

Mrs. Upson looked surprised, but made no objection. "Although what your mother will say!"

In the event, Sally said nothing when her son returned with strawberries, thick cream, and a white kitten. She was a very wise woman. It had been apparent to her at the outset that Alfie was in love; nor was she disturbed. His reactions were entirely normal, and if anything, extremely good for him. Let him worship at the feet of beauty, let him observe a gently bred little lady, let him see how *manners* were used. It was for this same reason that Sally was happy to welcome Mr. Giles on his secret visits. Whatever his business (and Sally had a shrewd suspicion), Alfie was hearing an educated voice and observing courtesy. For as long as Araminta remained with them, he'd see the feminine counterpart. There might be sadness when she left, but it'd pass, and Alfie would never forget what he'd learned of gentility.

Swaying back and forth in the mail coach, the Marquis of Bishton was cudgeling his memory: Surtaine? Was it lesser nobility, or some long-established shire family that eschewed the London *ton?* Better versed in colorations than Sally, Giles thought the combination of black hair, porcelain skin, and gray eyes was more Irish than Scot. Could she be part of the jumped-up peerage created by Prinny to pack Parliament in his favor? Her voice and manners were definitely English, but perhaps she had been educated deliberately to lose any accent.

In his mind's eye he could see her again, kneeling on the divan and wistfully asking for bread and cheese . . . and when he'd brought her to join them, her dignified reproof of his instruction on sipping the wine! Giles smiled to himself. How old was she? The mind that had made him the Most Wanted Man by Napoleon Bonaparte was working busily now. For all her featherweight in his arms, Miss Araminta Surtaine was no child; there had been a definite *shape* beneath the coarse cotton night shift. She was old enough to be accustomed to Madeira, but not old enough for presentation to the *ton,* Giles thought suddenly. Scant attention as he paid to the London season, it was part of his disguise to appear occasionally in the social maelstrom: one or two evenings at Almack's, a few carefully chosen balls or receptions, even fewer accepted invitations to dine, and a half-dozen visits to the various gambling clubs.

London's prominent hostesses had long since given him up, although cards were sent for every scheme of entertainment; it was understood that one asked the Marquis of Bishton, and expected him when he was bowing gracefully over your hand. Similarly, only the most optimistic (or gullible) mamas placed any reliance on the outcome of his favoring a young lady with a request for three dances or sent a lavish bouquet of hothouse flowers from his lesser estate of Rushley, which was within an hour's drive of town.

Nevertheless, had any female with the grace and favor of Araminta burst upon the social scene, Giles must certainly have been made aware of it. If nothing else, his mama and two older sisters would have brought her to his notice, for nothing so far could convince them that the Marquis of Bishton was happy in single-blessedness, had no desire to set up his nursery, and was entirely content that all his property should pass by default to an obscure second cousin, aged twelve and currently rated as incorrigible by the headmaster of Eton.

No, Araminta Surtaine had not yet had a season, but if she had a titled guardian, her presentation to the *ton* must be upcoming. Or was that the crux of the matter? By the time the stagecoach was pulling into Cambridge, Giles rather thought he had the answer. On impulse he abandoned his seat and hired a post chaise, whereby he reached London midway between tea and dinnertime. His appearance caused a severe shock to his butler. Indeed, when Mr. Ringleby opened the door, he had all but closed it again in the face of the unsavory character standing on the top step, when the unmistakeable deep voice of his employer said, "Hallo, Ringleby—send up the bath water, will you? Tell Noakes to lay out evening dress; alert the stable I shall want my carriage tonight; have the brandy brought to the study, and ask Mr. Graham to step in to me, please."

Scooping up the snowdrift of cards and notes on the butler's tray, the marquis strode along the hall while Ringleby was still stuttering, "Y-yes, your lordship." Behind the closed door, Giles was oblivious of the helter-skelter, hurry-scurry, taking place in his household. Rapidly he skimmed through the mail neatly arranged by his secretary, and had glanced at the list of social events before the man entered hastily. "Good evening, milord."

"Hallo, George," the marquis said absently. "I'm back."

"So I observe, milord," George murmured with a grin, for he stood upon the easiest terms with his employer. "Can I assist in any way—of which the most pressing is to inform your chef whether you dine at home."

Giles raised his head with an answering grin. "Set his mind at rest before he kills himself like that Frenchman," he begged. "Not tonight—perhaps tomorrow." Scanning the day's accumulation, "Here's a pot-luck from Tallerton—will it be too late to accept?"

"No, indeed—in fact, I am bespoke to join you."

"Send him word, then. Order the carriage for seven, and get a message to Mr. Fogg: ask him to wait on me tomorrow at ten."

"Certainly, milord." The secretary stepped out to the hall, dispatching the orders—creating calm in the kitchen—and re¹ ʹrned to find the marquis staring into space, with the brandy decanter at his elbow. Silently, George filled a glass and extended it.

"Thank you." Giles downed the liquid and asked abruptly, "Does the name Surtaine mean anything to you?"

"Not personally, if that is what you mean, but there was a Surtaine among the original charters of the East India Company, and I believe another—or it may have been the same—was a moving force in the drainage of the fen country."

"Hmmm, a nabob. Yes, that fits. Hand me the *Peerage*, if you will."

"I don't think there was a title." George brought the volume from its shelf.

"Probably not." Giles was rapidly turning pages. "Here we are: Eddystone, Robert Percival Charles, third baron . . . hmmm, hmmmm, yes . . ."

"Good God, that old court card?" George said, startled.

"You are acquainted?"

"Lud, you may see him in any club," George grimaced, "one of Prinny's set, and a particular crony of York. There's a son—I doubt your paths would cross, milord; he'd be older than yourself, and he runs with Harwood, Bettison, Monty Buford . . . that crowd."

Giles nodded absently, continuing his perusal. At length he closed the *Peerage*. "See what you can find out about the Eddystones, George: where and how they live, what odor they hold in the clubs, any tidbit of gossip . . . but be discreet."

"Certainly, milord."

George bowed himself away in considerable bewilderment, but to the Marquis of Bishton, Black Jack's problem was becoming much clearer in its broad outlines. Given a titled widower with a taste for gambling and an intimacy at Oatlands, where the Duke of York played whist for five pound points . . . add a bachelor son whose friends were Peep o' Day boys on the fringes of society, and top off with a beautiful young ward descended (probably) from a nabob, and Giles felt the story wrote itself. All that remained was to ascertain the exact details, with which Mr. Fogg should be able to assist, although once Giles had the facts, he had no idea what he would do with them.

The central difficulty was Araminta's loss of memory. Until she was in possession of herself, it would be useless to send her home; if her relatives had been unable to prevent what was beginning strongly to look like an abduction, Lord Robert Eddystone would find a second try even easier. Giles had an inexplicable determination to protect the child. On the other hand, she was damnably in the way. Jack did not want a mark against him in the eyes of the law; Giles did not want the law interested in the circus in any way! For a day or two, until her wounds healed, she could be kept out of sight in the caravan, but then she must be allowed freedom.

Equally, the Eddystones would move heaven and earth to find Araminta. No matter what his scheme, Lord Robert could never admit he had lost his ward. The son had threatened Jack with the Bow Street runners, but Lord Robert would try everything else first. While his valet deftly snipped away the excess from his hair, the marquis pondered Lord Robert's course of action.

First, he would roundly have cursed Sir Francis for mishandling the search of the camp, Giles thought with amusement. Next he would have gone to Surtaine Manor, wherever it was, on the chance she had managed to reach it somehow. Depending on the distance, that might have occupied most of today. Would he have dispatched his son independently to Araminta's usual residence while he went to the manor? That was more debatable, unless Sir Francis was not known to have been with his father when the journey began. On the whole, Giles decided Lord Robert would have ordered his son to leave matters alone. Sir Francis might even now be returned to his usual London pursuits, but upon drawing a blank at the manor, Lord Robert would first renew his application for help to Constable Hasty, who would need considerable persuasion, after yesterday's abortive search. Giles grinned to himself.

However, Hasty would be unable flatly to refuse; in due course, he would stop at each house with an official request for information of an unknown young female. Constable Warren would no doubt agree to do likewise in his hamlet, but neither man would push himself; it would be tomorrow before they had covered every place. Lord Robert would also enlist the constable for Crossthwaite, and initiate a bloodhound search of every inch of land in the vicinity. The Earl of Minchampton's keepers would be asked to cooperate; if there existed any lake, stream, or ornamental water, it would be dragged for Araminta's drowned corpse; and it would all take an immense deal of time, thank heavens, during which she'd be safely cared for and might regain her memory.

And if she did not?

The Marquis of Bishton frowned into his dressing mirror, causing the valet to quaver, "I beg pardon—is your lordship dissatisfied?"

"Yes," said Giles, "but not with you, Noakes. I look entirely respectable once more."

"Thank you, milord." The valet bridled slightly. "I could wish your lordship would allow me to accompany you on your sojourns, for the condition of your lordship's clothing is *beyond* what is permissible, even in rustication!"

"Poor Noakes!" Giles sympathized with a grin, "but for all you must labor to repair me, I am better pleased to wallow without any clucking over my condition."

"Yes, milord," Noakes said resignedly. No more than the rest of the household did he understand his employer's sudden predilection for unattended disappearances into the countryside. After twelve years in the service of the marquis—or ever since his inheritance—Noakes found the possibility of a liaison requiring such secrecy most unlikely. His lordship was not one to dally with married ladies, nor one to toy with a rustic miss. Then where had he been going in the past months, to return earth-stained and poorly shaved?

At least, the marquis knew what was due to his consequence in London. Noakes's heart swelled with satisfaction at the tall figure descending the stairs. "Correct to a shade!" he congratulated himself. From gleaming pumps to primrose satin court breeches, walnut-brown velvet coat, and snowy neckcloth, his lordship testified alike to his valet's artistry and his own impeccable taste. Not for milord were shoe buckles of vulgar size, nor any clutter of jewelry. A single sapphire nestled in the lace at his throat, the old-fashioned gold seal ring of the Bishtons was on his right hand, a simple fob indicated his watch pocket, and the gold-rimmed quizzing glass was more utilitarian than a cause for envy. Whatever entertainment he meant to honor this evening, his lordship's entrance would cast all other gentlemen in the shade; there was no doubt of it!

The movements of the Marquis of Bishton in subsequent hours, however, would have compounded his valet's existing puzzlement.

Allow two days, Giles told himself, but then Araminta must be away from the circus. What the devil shall I do with her?

CHAPTER 4

Giles's outline of Lord Robert's endeavors was almost exact, with a trifling difference: he did not have as much leeway as he thought to spirit Araminta away to safety.

Upon his return to Crossthwaite, Sir Francis found his father engaged with a late nuncheon of substantial proportions. "Well, have you got her?" he demanded, throwing aside his napkin and hauling erect with a creak of his corsets. "Minta, my dear child!" Lord Robert hastened to the door of the breakfast parlor.

"Save your Shakespearean anguish," Francis snapped. "No, I have not got her—I believe there's a conspiracy. That rascally constable insisted on waiting for his fellow from the next hamlet, which allowed ample time to warn that blackguard at the circus. Needless to say, when the officers finally arrived to search, there was no trace of Minta. They had two revenue agents with them." He snorted. "I'll be bound they didn't want *that* pair . . . but however, they turned the camp inside out. Looking for evidence of free-trade, of course, but if there'd been so much as a bow from her slipper, they'd have found it."

Lord Robert went ghastly white. "Good God, what can have become of her?" he muttered, tottering toward his chair.

"Oh, she's there, right enough." Francis snorted again. "They'll hold her for ransom, you'll see. In a few days, very roundabout, someone will have seen an unknown girl, and the constable will suggest offering a reward. Make it big enough, and she'll be returned in two hours. These damnable gypsies!"

"Those are not gypsies," Lord Robert said flatly. "It's a well-known troupe that's camped here for years, according to Martin. They'd have been invaluable in helping a search, if you hadn't set up their backs. Damme, what a fool you are, Francis! Do you know nothing of country folk? This is not London, where rank and breeding take precedence. Give these people a tale to enlist their sympathy for our terror, and they would have spread the inquiry faster than a flock of pigeons." Lord Robert was stamping back and forth, pounding fist into palm, glaring at his son.

Francis threw up his head arrogantly and returned the glare. "May I point out that this entire plan was your own, sir," he hissed bitingly. "If you had not seen fit to be rid of the coachman, you would have been *inside* the carriage to keep your ward under your eye. You had only to tell the man it was necessary to come here for the night, you were returning groom and postilions to London. We would get replacements from the manor."

"And what think you the servants would have told Mrs. Hobson?" Lord Robert lashed back. "If you had consented to keep your post chaise instead of saving money by joining our carriage, you would have been following us to observe . . . not that I believe Minta fell out en route."

"That puts us at *point non plus*." Francis shrugged. "She is not here; according to the landlord, she is not there, and apparently she is nowhere in the middle."

"If she ever were, your mismanagement has delayed finding her," his father growled. "No, I fancy we were right in the first place: she got out of the carriage before we left the inn. With the amount of traffic, coaches constantly coming and going, I doubt Reddy or his wife could have lingered. They may have seen us preparing to leave, may have seen us driving away, but I'll wager their attention was distracted—a question from a serving wench, or a new arrival demanding service. It'd take no more than a second's turn of their heads for Minta to climb out, and in the dim light, they'd not have realized."

Lord Robert fingered his lips nervously, "It's possible the drug did make her queasy. I thought her merely drowsy," he muttered, "but she might have wanted to, uh, vomit."

"In the stableyard?" Francis raised his eyebrows. "And then what?"

"Finding we had left, she took a post chaise to follow us—as she supposed—to the manor. That was the *first* place to visit, before you put the cat among the pigeons here," Lord Robert stated superbly. "Good God, the circus has a good reputation, but unquestionably they free-trade on the side, and on top of getting a search warrant, you brought the revenuers down on them!" He scowled furiously at his son, languidly sipping a glass of Madeira. "You may *look* like me, I can't disavow parentage, but I wish I could, for you are as stupid as your mother. There was some excuse for her: she was a woman, and French, into the bargain . . . and a demmed bad one it was!"

Francis shrugged lazily. "I doubt you were any better, sir. One supposes she only married you in order to escape the gathering clouds of Revolution, and I could wish she had thought to bring more of the family assets with her."

Lord Robert flapped a hand irascibly. "We waste time. Tell Martin to have the horses put to; I'll go over to the manor. The more I think on't, the more I feel she is there. She would not have needed money, you know, for the steward would have paid off the chaise when she arrived." Noting Francis' incredulity, he said defensively, "A hostler would have seen her into a chaise, knowing she had been in our carriage; I questioned no one, in view of the landlord's statement, but it must have happened in that fashion."

Within a half-hour, Lord Robert had started off. Some three hours later he returned, looking haggard. Stripping off his driving gloves, "No," he said succinctly to Francis.

In spite of himself, Francis was beginning to share his father's alarm. "What mean you to do now?"

"What can I do but continue the search? Whatever has happened, it began in this locality. She *was* with us at the inn; if the dogs are to be trusted, she did not reach Crossthwaite. In any case, we have searched house and grounds. She is not at Surtaine Manor, and has not been seen anywhere in the hamlets along our way. It no longer matters *how* she vanished from the coach," Lord Robert said somberly. "Depend upon it, there will be some simple explanation that has not occurred to us, but the vital point is that she *must* be somewhere in a radius of forty miles. Every avenue must be mobilized to find her."

"Lud, that will take a week, sir!" Francis protested uneasily. "I cannot stay from town so long at present. I had thought to stay no more than two, at most three, days. To be absent, fail in my engagements without word, is to cause curiosity."

"I do not want you, in any case," Lord Robert said stolidly. "You have already muffed our best chance. I will do my possible to eradicate the bad impression, but go back to London by all means—or to the devil, for all of me. Martin will drive you across to the nearest posting inn on the turnpike tomorrow morning, and with luck, he may be able to get a fresh team. You can take Hankins with you; I don't want him, either."

"I suppose there's no possibility she might have slipped out at the inn and gone back to London?"

Francis murmured. "Even if she voided, some part of the drug might have caused her to forget she was bound for the manor."

"I don't think it. She may have had more money than we knew, but to hire a chaise for so long a trip— even to procure a seat on the London coach—must have been remarked, and the landlord informed. More probably, once out of our carriage, she was sufficiently dazed that she merely wandered off"—Lord Robert sighed—"until the remains of the drug overtook her. You see? She may be anywhere."

"The effect would never last so long, sir. By daylight, she would have no more than a headache; she would go in search of food."

"Perhaps, but I fear the worst, Francis." Lord Robert shook his head. "In the dark, and half-drugged, what if she stumbled? Broke an ankle . . . or fell into a lake or quarry? She may even now be lying wounded, chilled and starving beneath a sheltering shrub, or trying to find her way out of an encircling forest," he said brokenly. "It doesn't bear thinking on!"

Francis eyed his father appreciatively. "A superb rehearsal, sir! Almost you convince *me*."

"You should be convinced! Oliver Surtaine was one of my closest friends, dear to me as a brother! For ten years I have watched over his daughter— watching her grow from childhood into an entrancing young woman. I sought only to protect her by arranging a suitable marriage that would shield her from some gazetted fortune hunter," Lord Robert moaned, sinking his head in his hands.

"Better and better!" Francis laughed mockingly. "Well, I will leave it to you, sir—you are the guardian, after all, from whom explanations will be asked . . . particularly if her drowned corpse is recovered from a mire."

Thus Lord Robert Eddystone was slightly in advance of the schedule the Marquis of Bishton had projected, although his course of action was similar. While his lordship was directing Mr. Fogg to ascertain all the details of Mr. Surtaine's will and the provisions for guardianship of his daughter, Sir Francis was en route to town at the unheard-of hour of nine in the morning. Having already drawn a blank covert at the manor, Lord Robert was equally astir by eleven. Martin had been successful in procuring a fresh team, of which two were poled up and the other pair waited in the stable.

With Martin beside him for directions, throughout the day Lord Robert tooled back and forth: to the Crossthwaite constable, the Minchampton head keeper, the length of the turnpike—stopping at every inn, every hamlet constable, every vicarage. Nowhere was there a clue, a smile of relief, a brightening eye of "There now! I said as little miss'd be looked for!" By the time he'd returned to Crossthwaite, Lord Robert felt he was staring ruin in the face—which was not a new sensation, and exactly why he'd devised a scheme to bring the Surtaine money into Eddystone hands—but the current situation was beyond words frightful.

If Araminta were dead in the course of a journey with her guardian, there would be questions. No matter what the explanation, no matter if it were accepted by the Court of Inquiry, nothing would ever still the whispers in the *haut ton*. Wearied and (he admitted to himself: frightened), Lord Robert ate his dinner of country soup, roasted chicken with stewed mushrooms, lamb fries, and roasted potatoes, removed with a neat's tongue stewed with peppercorns and a dish of fresh green peas, and followed by a plain butter cake with fresh strawberries, but made so little dent in

71

the dishes presented to him that Martin was worried. "He don't seem to fancy nothing."

Mrs. Martin was more calm. "He's too anxious to savor his food. In his case, you'd have no appetite either. Eh, 'tis a terrible thing. What can have happened to the little girl?"

Araminta was having the time of her life! Following the pre-dawn nuncheon, she slept long and dreamlessly, undisturbed by the circus people going about their customary chores. It was nearly noon before she opened her eyes and smiled at Sally, quietly sewing beside her. "Good morning!"

"Good morning to you, my dearie. Well, you've had a fine rest, and look the better for it." Sally laid aside her work to inspect Minta's bandages, nodding with satisfaction. "Just as it should be; you'll be right in no time."

"I'm sure I shall. Oh, *strawberries!*" as her eyes reached the table.

"Alfie brought them for you, and as soon as you're dressed, you shall have some." Sally produced a bright red cotton gypsy skirt and white peasant blouse, borrowed from Bess. Shoes had been a problem, until Sally thought to ask about for children's Sunday slippers. A twelve-year-old's fitted Minta's tiny feet perfectly. In consultation with Bess, it was agreed as permissible to take one gold piece from Minta's coins for clothing; she certainly could not be wearing a fashionable London frock of palest pink-worked muslin in a circus camp.

Araminta had no fault to find with the costume. "How gay and easy it is!" she exclaimed delightedly, whirling until the flounces spread out around her. The berries were equally successful. She ate them slowly and daintily, savoring each one under Alfie's adoring eyes, but the peak was reached with presentation of the kitten.

" 'Tis to keep you company, like."

"Alfie! Oh, how *kind* you are!"

He flushed awkwardly, " 'Tis naught—they were going to drown 'un."

The kitten was behaving in the most exemplary fashion, cuddling into Araminta's hands and purring ecstatically. "How could anyone drown such a sweet little thing! What shall we name it? Snow White?"

" 'Tis a tom," Black Jack observed mildly. "It needs a boy's name."

"Dick?" Sally suggested. "Dick Whittington had a cat."

Araminta shook her head. "He had one, but he wasn't one. No, it should be a name for a knight in shining white armor . . . I know!" she said excitedly, "El Cid! He was a *great* knight. I don't know that he wore white, but he saved Spain from the infidels."

"Sid?" Jack repeated cautiously. "Aye, that'd be a right good name."

Throughout the afternoon, Minta happily played with her kitten, and obedient to Sally's instructions, stayed within doors to prevent strain on her leg bandage. Equally obedient to Black Jack's orders, those who came to the caravan smiled like old friends and called her "Meg," but toward suppertime, Minta was looking uncertain. "I think I ought to be doing my chores," she said, "but I can't remember what they are."

"Never mind," Sally returned authoritatively, "you had not many, and I'd rather you did not risk any more damage until you are recovered, Meg."

"Yes," Minta murmured doubtfully, "but I could do the sewing while I sit still."

Bored with inactivity, Sally thought. "You can," she agreed, "if it does not make your head ache."

"No, no, I enjoy sewing!"

Her stitchery was exquisite, although she frowned at the size of the holes in Jack's socks. "There is nothing left—throw them away!"

"We cannot, until we reach a place with shops to replace," Sally said artfully. "Meanwhile, what is he to wear? Do your best." By the expression on Alfie's face when his goddess began on *his* holes, he meant to wear those socks over his heart!

There was a fascination to Sally in discovering what Minta did, or did not, know. It appeared she had forgotten only her name; her education and accomplishments remained. She spoke casually of making a new frock when fabric could be had. Spying Sally's knitting basket, she evidently thought this might be one of her tasks, and happily appropriated it. Conversely, she was unacquainted with cooking, the making of beds, laundry, or dish washing. She watched Sally's movements covertly, with a faintly puzzled frown: was this something else she had forgotten? Sally worked away briskly, hoping it might stir Araminta's memory of servants, leading to recollection of living in a different sort of home under other circumstances. Instead, Minta simply picked up by observation, and as soon as she felt competent, she lent a hand.

"I could finish the dishes, it won't hurt my leg," or, "I'll finish setting table."

She learned with amazing speed. Faced with whole fried fish for supper, she was briefly at a loss. She must always have had boned fillets, Sally thought—but with only a few glances at the others, Araminta was expertly dissecting her fish as to the manner born! The simple meal must have been far different from her past, but it awakened no recollection of courses and removes. True, she sat and allowed others to wait upon her, but she ate with gusto.

Furthermore, Araminta *conversed*. She asked what Black Jack and Alfie had been doing during the day, she informed them of her own day and the visitors to the caravan, inquired where Alfie had got the fish— small snippets of no moment, but beneath Sally's eyes, Araminta had got everyone talking. Instead of a silent mastication interspersed with terse grunted reports, the table was suddenly at ease in a pleasant exchange of news. It was all the best possible example for Alfie, and to Sally's delight, he was absorbing Araminta's ways: using his napkin, asking that bread be passed instead of plunging his fork across the table to spear a slice. Even Jack was relaxed and comfortable, smiling impishly at Sally while he related an amusing incident of that afternoon.

Over this supper table, Jack was once again the man she'd married when everyone was scandalized that the daughter of a duke's butler could prefer a mountebank to an upstanding young footman with hopes of butler keys in time. She was not aware that she, too, was responding to Araminta's social manners and showing a glimpse of the Sarah Dawkins that Black Jack Bickell had married.

The camp was stirring, preparing for the evening's performance. From the wild-beast cages came deep-throated roars as Ted forked in their suppers. Sam's bear danced anxiously on its chain, adding roars in expectation of its own feed. Sensing the beginning, the horses were snorting, swishing their tails, stamping in their stalls.

"Please, may I go to look?" Minta begged. "I'm sure it will not be too hard for my leg."

Sally consulted Jack with a look, and after a moment he nodded. "Alfie, take Meg around the midway —but bring her back here before the audience arrives." He smiled at Minta. " 'Tis too crowded, you'd perhaps be elbowed aside and break open the leg wound again. You'll see the circus another night, when all's healed."

"Yes, please—it is so long since I have seen a circus," Minta said dreamily, quite unaware of her words. "There were pretty ladies on horses, and elephants trotting in a ring holding each other's tails . . . and a cage of monkeys." She chuckled. "And I ate so much toffee I had a stomachache! Do you remember?"

"I do, indeed," Sally said swiftly, standing up to clear the table, "but we've only two monkeys left—the others caught cold and died—and Tom took his elephants south for fear they'd die of cold, too. Don't *you* remember?"

Minta's eyes widened in uncertainty, but she would still not admit. "That's so," she agreed, "but there's still plenty to see. Come on, Alfie!"

When they'd gone, "Sullivan's circus," Jack said positively. "That's what she's seen. He works up and down the North Road."

"Perhaps, but I think she lives in London," Sally returned. "Wherever she came from, I'm glad to have her, Jack."

"So would I be, under other circumstances," he said after a moment. "As it is"—he shook his head—"keep her as close as may be, Sal. Mr. Giles meant to discover what he could, or doctor may have word from his friends. Until then, she's best out of sight. Gor"— he started to his feet at a piercing feminine scream from the camp—"what's happened?"

Jack dashed from the caravan with Sally at his heels, while the screams soared to hysteria. "Johnnie! Oh, my baby, my baby!" Thrusting through the excited crowd, they soon took in the situation, and it caused a long indrawn breath of horror from Sally. Sam's infant son was inside the tiger's cage! The great beast was lying at the far end, licking its paws and paying no particular attention to the baby crawling toward it, but as the hubbub increased, it suspended its toilette to look inquiringly through the bars.

"Where's Ted?" Jack's deep voice was in command. "Quiet down, everybody—you're making the beast nervous. Sally, get Mary *away,* or there'll be a real accident. Where is Ted?"

"Walked over t' shore, Joe's gone for him . . . take too long afore he gets back, have to get gun and shoot tiger," a dozen voices said.

"Wait a bit," Jack ordered. "Move back from the cage, and stop talking. Try coaxing the baby to crawl back to the door, first." Slowly, the crowd retreated, forming a ring of wild-eyed suspense at a distance, while Sam plunged forward with his gun. "Don't shoot unless you must; that beast is valuable!"

"I've t' blunt to replace 'un," Sam muttered, white-faced.

"You can't replace the years of training," Jack warned quickly. "Hold steady, man. It may not be necessary."

Nor was it. While Jack was withdrawing the crowd and making ready to attempt a rescue, Araminta calmly walked up the wooden steps and into the cage. With no slightest sign of fear, she went forward and picked up the baby. "Come along, Johnnie." The ring of circus people stood spellbound and trembling speechlessly as she turned back to the door. At this second intruder, the tiger rolled over lazily and got to its feet with a questioning growl. Minta looked at the beast casually. "Well, you're a fine fellow." She smiled soothingly. "Yes, you are!"

Then she was pushing open the door. "Someone take the child, please? I don't think I can carry him down, because of my leg bandages." Mary broke away from Sally and tore forward, arms outstretched to take the baby. Minta still stood in the entrance to the cage. "Could someone help me, too? My leg feels stiff."

By now the tiger was padding forward to sniff curiously at its visitor, but Araminta remained calm. "Yes, I'm going," she assured it. "You can have your home to yourself again in a minute."

Amid dead silence, everyone could hear a peculiar deep throaty sound: *the tiger was purring!* One step at a time, Minta came down to the ground, leaning on Alfie's hand, while Jack swiftly swung closed the cage door and latched it securely. He was nearly as white-faced as Sam, but still in command. "All right, everyone—move away, or the beast'll be too nervous to be shown tonight. 'Tis over safely," as Ted came running up breathlessly.

"What happened?"

"Somehow baby got in t' cage with Sinbad. Sam were set to shoot, but it weren't necessary; Meg got 'un out," various voices said. "Arrr, proper fearless she were! Tiger were purring, we heard him!"

"Gorblimey!" Ted muttered, swiftly testing the door bar. "I'd swear all was secure . . ."

"You'll check twice from now on."

"Never fear! Sam, I'd not have had this for any money!"

"Don't think on it," Sam said gruffly. " 'Twas accident, happy ended, and Mary'll keep baby under her eye after this." He turned away to join the crowd about Minta. "God bless you, little miss!"

"Aye, how you *dared!*"

"It was really quite safe," she said, surprised. "Sinbad had just been fed, you know, and the big cats are always sleepy for a while after eating. The keeper at the Royal Enclosure told us so, don't you remember?" looking at Sally.

"That's so." Sally gulped. "I'd forgotten. Well, come away in. 'Tis time to ready for the performance."

While the bear danced, the horses pranced, and Sinbad jumped through hoops; while Lord Robert Eddystone toyed with his dinner; while Araminta knitted contentedly with El Cid curled into a ball on her lap, the Marquis of Bishton was consulting his grandmother.

Mr. Fogg, his man of business, had indeed uncovered all. It had taken no more than a few hours after receiving his lordship's instructions. By tea-time he was able to put Giles in possession of the facts, although these afforded the marquis no satisfaction. Oliver Surtaine had broken his neck in the hunting field ten years past; Lord Robert Eddystone was named as guardian for Araminta, jointly with her mother, but Mrs. Surtaine had survived no more than a twelve-month. This left Lord Robert in full command until Araminta attained the age of eighteen, at which point she would have the use of her income, to be paid directly to her. Thereafter, she could not marry without Lord Robert's consent until she was twenty-five.

The real crux of the matter was that Araminta would be eighteen on May 28—a scant two weeks away.

Clad in his evening dress the previous evening, Giles had dined with his friends, and gracefully excused himself in time to be admitted to Almack's, where he found his sister Louisa, as expected. She was (in vulgar parlance) popping off her oldest daughter this season. As Noakes had prophesied to himself, the entrance of the Marquis of Bishton brightened a number of female eyes, and caused wistfulness in certain young gentlemen, who had been thinking themselves all the crack until they glimpsed his lordship's simple elegance.

A country dance with his niece, a waltz with a wallflower who possessed more brains than looks, an agreeable few minutes of flirtation with Lady Jersey, and Giles departed. He was next driven to a discreet gambling hall on Curzon Street, where he played a few rounds of macao (with indifferent success) and struck up an apparently aimless conversation with another gentleman over the buffet table. Once again the marquis gracefully departed, to be finally seen at White's. Here he joined a group for basset, removed indolently to a table of baccarat, and ended playing piquet with General Sir Richard Pocklington, which drew approval from all members.

"Demmed good-natured," said the elders to each other. "Never forgets old friends of his father, always the soul of courtesy. Well, I ask you: nobody'd endure Pocklington in the general way . . . terrible bore, always prosing on about his days in India!"

But by the time his lordship was returned to Bishton House, he'd gained a lot of information. This was reinforced by his secretary, whose evening had led in other directions that produced the definite fact of Lord Robert's financial distress. "Thus far he has not failed to pay," George Graham reported meticulously, "but it is thought he is in low water. There have been occasional delays in retrieving his vowels—not undue, but enough to cause remark. Not much is known of Sir Francis. He is an excellent swordsman, holds a high record at Manton's, patronizes Schultz rather than Weston for his coats . . . too cow-handed for the Four Horse Club, belongs to Boodle's and the Cocoa Tree but doesn't play high. He has a private income from his mother." As an afterthought, George added, "It's not substantiated, but thought that he has an arrangement with Mrs. Illington—whoever she is."

Giles's eyes flickered slightly. "Well, you have done

THE WICKED GUARDIAN

your usual thorough job. I do not know how I should go on without you, George."

"Nor I without you, milord," the secretary returned pensively. "You constantly create interest in my days. I do not ask, I know better, but this concern over the Eddystones—it is intriguing. I hope eventually I may be admitted to your confidence in the matter."

His employer grinned unrepentantly. "Perhaps, George, perhaps . . . but first I must put it all together."

By evening it *was* all together, and Giles had no idea what to do with it. On the one hand, by the apparently strange man in Curzon Street, Giles was instructed to make one more trip to France in an effort to unmask Boney's most valued English spy. On the other hand, the presence of Araminta Surtaine in Black Jack's circus camp was bound to draw the attention of the law, with Bow Street Runners at the very moment Giles would need Jack for cover. He could not bring himself to direct Jack to surrender the girl to the Eddystones; she must be concealed until she was eighteen, when she would be out of his power, whether or not her memory returned. Where to hide her?

Throughout his preparation for the evening, Giles pondered deeply. He had four different houses, but all were bachelor establishments not suited for an un-chaperoned young female. True that no harm would come to Araminta, for the servants would care for her faithfully, but the mere fact that she had been in an establishment of the Marquis of Bishton—even if he were not present—would ruin her forever if it were known. Yet who could he get to provide propriety?

Fogg had given him the London address of Araminta, and the name of her duenna, but to persuade Mrs. Hobson to steal away and join her charge at the residence of a totally unknown young man would take more time than Giles could spare. In any case, the mysterious vanishing of Mrs. Hobson would only set the Runners more firmly on the trail. There would certainly be a slip somewhere. Experience had taught Giles that the fewer people involved in any enterprise, the better. No, leave Mrs. Hobson bewildered in London—genuinely unable to say more than that Miss Surtaine had left town in the care of her guardian.

At this point, Giles thought of the dowager Marchioness of Bishton—not his mother, but his grandmother. Technically, both ladies enjoyed the title, but to the fury of Giles's mother, only the older was known as the dowager. "At your age, I should think you'd be glad to be styled 'your ladyship' rather than considered a has-been," said the dowager innocently.

"Yes," Giles said to himself with relief, "Grandie's the one to ask." Submerged in his bath, the marquis instructed Noakes to send word to ask if his grandmother could receive him before her evening engagements. Certain of her acquiescence, he leisurely arrayed himself in full Court dress, for the dowager set store on such niceties, and roundly condemned modern fashions. "Call 'em 'Inexpressibles,' " she sniffed, "and it is exactly what they *are,* clingin' to the male rump, leavin' nothing to the imagination! Disgraceful!"

"Can it be that grandfather's manly form was a disappointment when stripped?"

"Nonsense! He was the *perfect* figure of a man, a tragedy that none of his descendants equaled him!"

"You were fortunate, ma'am. Today's young females are more cautious, and wish some general idea of what they are getting," Giles returned irrepressibly; but because he was genuinely fond of the old lady, he took pains to meet her standards.

Tonight it was doubly important to put her in good humor. By the time the footman returned to say the

dowager marchioness would be at home to her grandson anytime in the next few hours, Giles was a sym-
phony of correct black and white, with a single pearl
securing the lace at his throat. Topped by his coppery
curls arranged à la Brutus, he was quite infamously
handsome, as the dowager told him with asperity.
"Oh, there you are—devil-may-care as usual," she remarked when he was shown into her drawing room.
"And what young female are you bemusing this season?
Have a care! They'll sigh for you now, but very soon
you'll be too old for 'em—another Prinny." She wrinkled her nose, extending her hand for his bow and
kiss.

"Good God, ma'am, not *that!*" he protested.

"Oh, he was beautiful in youth," she assured him.
"Florizel, they called him, and he'd have had his pick
of any female in the world. Threw it all away, and
look at him now! I don't say you'll go the same road,"
she added with great fairness. "The Ormeraux don't
run to fat, but I wish you would set up your nursery
while anyone will still have you, Giles. I've a fancy to
see my great-grandson before I die."

"In that case, I've a number of years yet," Giles remarked, seating himself at her wave of the hand. "Don't
tell me you've any plan for turning up the toes a minute
before need be. It is one of my most consoling reflections, ma'am, for I cannot imagine a world without
you."

"Lud, how gracefully you slide away," the dowager
returned, preening herself slightly. "I still tell you to
make your choice while you have one. With all the
girls of England gathered into London for the season,
there must be one pretty-behaved young female you
could bear to take to bed. Find her!"

"Perhaps I have," Giles said carefully, "although not
quite as you put it, ma'am. In fact, at the moment she

is a deuced inconvenience. It is why I have come to consult you."

The dowager marchioness sat up alertly, and stared piercingly at her grandson. "Who is she? What's her lineage, where'd you encounter?" she demanded.

"In a traveling circus . . ."

"WHAT?"

". . . where she is being sheltered from a wicked guardian," Giles went on imperturbably. "Her lineage is excellent, she is an extremely rich orphan—and due to a blow on the head while jumping from her abductor's carriage, she has not the least idea who she is."

"Good God!"

"Exactly," Giles agreed. "For various reasons, it is essential to remove her from the camp at once. In less than two weeks she will be eighteen, and whether or not she regains her memory, by the terms of her father's will, the guardian loses all control of her money. He may refuse his consent for her marriage until she is twenty-five, but it is the money he wants. From my information, I believe it was his intention to force marriage upon her—either to himself or his son. Could he discover her, there remain still ten days in which he might accomplish his design, for she is totally alone in the world. There are no relatives to protect her, ma'am."

"Good God," the dowager said again. Sinking back in her chair, she stared blankly into space. "Who is she? No, no, don't tell me—better I don't know, but" —her fingers pleated and unpleated the thick silk of her old-fashioned wide skirt—"should I like her?"

Giles considered. "Very much," he decided. "It's a beautiful child—silky black hair, immense gray eyes, a figure most daintily formed, every attribute of breeding in voice and manner. Yes, you would like her, ma'am, but do not be building a romance." He grinned impishly. "I wish her well, and would save her from her guardian's plots, but principally I wish her out of my path. At the moment it does not suit me for the law to be interested in that circus, yet where to send her? She would be safe at Rushley or Desmond, but mine are bachelor establishments; the most respectable of housekeepers will not suffice for her good reputation.

"It occurred to me . . . you are acquainted with so many respectable but impecunious old ladies, ma'am; is there one who might be glad to undertake a few weeks of paid chaperonage at short notice and without undue curiosity?"

"Lud, yes. I could name a dozen, but in the end it will come out," his grandmother said absently, "and will look no better, if you do not mean to marry her. I had better take her myself, keep it in the family."

"Nothing could be better, ma'am," Giles exclaimed, startled, "but I've no wish to interrupt your enjoyment of the season. I had in mind someone withdrawn from active society; I'd not ask you to abandon engagements and renewal of old friendships."

"Pish, tush," she returned impatiently. "At my age, all seasons are alike, and demmed boring they are. I've seen as much as I want of old friends, and they're demmed boring, too. It's no hardship for me to go home to Transome with a pretty child to keep me company . . . but you had better tell me the rest. No, no, I don't wish to know *why* this circus is important, although I never thought to find my grandson connected with free-traders."

"I'm not," Giles said without thinking, and shuffled his feet uncomfortably beneath the dowager's steady gaze.

"Hmph, so that's what you're about on these mysterious absences. No, don't tell me." She raised a warning hand and snorted. "I don't know that I'm surprised," she remarked after a moment. "Your uncles were hand in glove with that Blakeney during the Revolution. We never knew how many there'd be for breakfast. A feckless bunch, the French, but one didn't like to think of their being killed . . . well"—she drew a long breath—"best to keep it between us. Who is she, who is this guardian?"

The dowager marchioness had never heard of Oliver Surtaine, but Lord Robert Eddystone produced a small nugget. "Hmph, I can believe anything of the Eddystones," she remarked. "The title's old, but ill-bestowed. They were always fortune hunters with a taste for gambling. One sees the father and son here or there, they are not déclassé, although one wonders how they afford certain of their more expensive friendships . . . for there was never any money, you know, unless"— she narrowed her eyes thoughtfully—"they have somehow induced Bonaparte to return the mother's estates. I believe a few of the emigrés have been reinstated in return for their support of his ambitions.

"Never mind." She shook herself briskly. "Do you send a night express to this circus, apprising them I shall take the girl morning after tomorrow. It cannot be sooner, no matter how we contrive, Giles. At my age, one travels slowly. I shall lie at Cambridge for the night. Once I have Araminta, there will still be country roads, but with luck, we can reach Transome by evening."

She spoke calmly, but it was a fearfully long journey for an elderly woman. "You are the best of good sports, ma'am." Giles leaned to kiss her hand gently. "But I feel it will be more than you should undertake. Should I not instead send a carriage to get her and transfer her to meet you at Transome?"

The dowager pursed her lips. "No," she decided,

"for whoever may be observing will see only that a carriage has turned in to the encampment, and later drives away. You'd better be thinking how to explain 'Meg's' disappearance, because Lord Robert will be there next."

"For sure he will," Giles agreed, "but he'll not have heard of 'Meg.' "

"Don't depend on it," his grandmother advised. "He'll speer about, or send a servant who'll discover there's a new girl in the camp. What's become of her? Somebody'll leak, never fear!"

"You're right, of course—what d'you suggest?"

"The owner says the gel's run away to a gypsy caravan, using as many oaths as possible," the dowager replied promptly. "You'd better know where the gypsy caravans are, and perhaps pay a bit to someone to remove himself as far north as possible. I expect you'll know how to do it."

"Why should you suppose I'm acquainted with gypsies, ma'am?"

"Well, somebody'll know in that group of yours," she retorted. "Don't tell me anything—I don't want to know—but I wasn't born yesterday, lad! What's wanted is red herrings, lots of 'em, in all different directions. Keep the constabulary chasin' about, while you're doing whatever you're doing. I'll take care of your gel. Transome's big enough to hide her forever, or until you get back from . . . wherever."

Giles arose with a laugh and bent formally over her hand. "You," he murmured, "are a wicked old woman."

"Of course," the dowager said, astonished. "Why else would your grandfather have married me?"

CHAPTER 5

In point of fact, Francis Eddystone had reached London not many hours after the marquis. On his father's instructions, he first presented himself at Araminta's house, saying he understood Lord Robert was visiting his ward. Mrs. Hobson was all astonishment. "There is some mistake, Sir Francis. Lord Robert and Minta left London yesterday for Surtaine Manor; there was a matter of business."

"Ah?" Francis raised his eyebrows languidly. "His servants garbled the affair, but it's not important."

Having ascertained that Araminta had not somehow reached home, Francis dispatched his valet next morning with a purported express from the North, containing the news to Mrs. Hobson that the business proved more complicated than anticipated. It would be necessary to stay several days; she should not look for Lord Robert and his ward until they arrived. "No need to agitate the woman; she's the sort to make a commotion that would impress the matter on the servants' memories," said Lord Robert. "I must always have written some such letter, even had the scheme gone smoothly."

His duties discharged, Francis returned to his usual pursuits, of which the first was a visit to Mrs. Illington. Her name might not be known to George Graham, but meant much to his employer—none of it favorable, although it fitted the picture he was beginning to build of Francis Eddystone.

Clara Illington was one of those rich widows with vague claims to gentility who perennially skirmished about the edges of the *haut ton*. She was distantly related to a Scottish earl, which she emphasized heavily while setting up a luxurious London residence with her husband's money—of which she said as little as possible. There was plenty of it, and it all smelled of the shop. However, her dinners were good; one could be sure of high play following the food, and a certain number of lesser titles found her excellent company; among them was Sir Francis Eddystone.

Clara was exactly to his taste: a blonde of uncertain age, always beautifully dressed, completely presentable for an evening at theater, Ranelagh, or Vauxhall Gardens. She might be unacquainted with the foremost ladies of the *ton,* and be unacceptable at Almack's, but was able to exchange bows with various titles at the hour of Promenade. Two or three times a season, she received an invitation to one of the bigger, less important squeezes. She could not be entirely overlooked by her distant relatives; she had never been involved in scandal or rated déclassé.

Best of all in Sir Francis' eyes, unlike the usual rapacious ladybirds, Cyprians, opera dancers of his earlier days, Clara required no expenditures. In fact, it was quite the reverse: Clara was immensely and cleverly open-handed. Aside from her excellent dinners, it was most often she who devised, and paid for, the evening's scheme. At suitable moments she gave him presents: a cloisonné jar filled with his Own Sort, accompanied by a superbly enameled snuff box; a gold-mounted walking stick; a dozen handkerchiefs of finest lawn lavishly monogrammed by Irish nuns; a diamond sunburst to secure his neckcloth. Nothing ostentatious, but all chosen to enhance the standing of a beau with more heritage than money.

In return, Clara was delighted by flowers or a modest box of sweetmeats.

Francis was under no delusions. He was quite aware that Clara meant to marry him if she could contrive it, and equally certain that despite the lure of her money, he would never sink so low. In fact, if all went well, he rather fancied he might shortly be in a position to dust off his cuffs, make a full return to society, and end with a well-dowered titled miss. Had it succeeded, his father's plot would have had the advantage of speed together with no need for change in his way of life. Francis admitted to himself that he did not relish hewing to the straight and narrow for long enough to convince the *ton* of his reformation, but the inadvertent mislaying of Araminta did not affect his basic plan.

On her side, Clara Illington was equally clear-headed. She was perfectly aware that she could not aspire to any major title, yet a title she meant to have, and Sir Francis Eddystone would do. She was not past bearing a child—hopefully it would be a boy—to inherit the baronage. Joe Illington's money would pay for Eton and Oxford, and whatever Francis thought, he'd not get his hands on a penny Clara didn't give him; Joe's will took care of that, bless him!

But to make matters doubly sure, she had put Sir Francis Eddystone in a position where he would either marry her or go to prison for treason!

There were times when Clara was impatient that it should have been so easy. "Are all the town beaux so stupid, or just Francis?" she wondered, but his was the best title she had acquired in several years of London life, and undeniably he pleased her in the bedchamber. Nevertheless, she wondered. Did he really suppose Clara did not know of his business dealings with Louis de Saumont? Was he really so naïve as to believe Louis either could or would aid Francis to retrieve his mother's French estates?

Very carefully and unobtrusively, Mrs. Clara had woven her spider web. After more than a year of patient observation, she felt it was time to entrap her fly.

As matters stood, any accusation could only be substantiated by her testimony, which would be inadmissible if she were Lady Francis Eddystone. However, this latest unexplained absence from town made her uneasy. Francis had certainly not gone to France, for Louis de Saumont had been looking for him. Where, then, had Clara's prey been?

When he was shown into her breakfast parlor, she cooed at him delightedly. "Sir Francis! One thought you gone from town—there was a famous scheme for Monday evening, and the word was that you were rusticating. Yet here you are back already; where did you go, to be bored so quickly?"

"To Crossthwaite with my father on a matter of business." He kissed her hand. "Your servant, ma'am."

"Crossthwaite and Lord Robert? Oh, what a whisker," she thought, even more uneasy. Where the devil had he really been? Let it pass for the moment; in time Francis would let fall something from which she'd deduce the truth. Clara swiftly changed the subject to the present. "You are returned in good time, for you must know we think of making a theater party for this evening, with a snug little supper to follow." She smiled. "Louis was for commanding a table at the Plaza, but I think more enjoyable to be private here, with a game or two after. Would it amuse you?"

"Exactly right! How well you know my taste," he approved flatteringly, his eyes drifting down to the plump breasts thrusting against the blue silk peignoir.

"It is decided, then." Clara was perfectly aware of his gaze, and deliberately allowed a glimpse of rounded white flesh by reaching for the cream pitcher. "Tonight," she thought exultantly. "We'll have it out tonight. Wherever he's been, he found nothing so good." "Louis was looking for you, by the by," she said casually. "He was surprised you were gone without a word."

"Louis?" Francis frowned. "What the devil could he want?"

"I thought," Clara murmured, "he might have news for you." As Francis stared at her, she smiled affectionately. "About your French property—you never thought I wouldn't know your hope of gaining your rightful inheritance? My love, why else would Sir Francis Eddystone waste time on an emigré?" By the glaze of his eyes, Clara felt she had successfully inserted the opening wedge, and once again she smoothly changed the subject. "Oh, the latest *on dit:* Monty Buford's trying to fix an interest! Yes, I thought that would amaze you—but there can be no doubt. It is Maria Harford— one had thought her an antidote, it is her third season, and there is a younger sister making her curtsy, but however, Miss Harford is back, and Monty is *aux anges!* Even, he has procured the vouchers for Almack, and can scarce spare the curtest of nods for his old friends, if one encounters in the Promenade." Clara chatted along lightly, allowing Francis time to regain his control.

Finally, she dismissed him coyly. "There is a fitting at Fanchon's; I shall be very late. Until tonight?"

"Until tonight," he repeated automatically, bending over her hand. "How shall I fill these lonely hours?"

"With anticipation," she murmured seductively, swaying against him as she rose from the table.

"Oh, sad stuff! Reality is always better." Francis threw a strong arm about her, and bent to her lips.

As always when Francis made love to her, Clara was both totally undermined and doubly determined. The feel of this particular body; the mingled odors of shaving soap, snuff, good wine, and hair pomade; the urgent hands holding her immovable—all were uncombatable, but Clara meant to be *sure* of them.

Breaking away from him, "What if a servant should come in! No—no more until tonight . . ."

"Why can't I come up while you dress?" he muttered huskily. "Send the servant away. . . ."

"No, I can't—I won't—I'll not ruin all for a tuppence of tar," Clara panted, fending him off, and protecting herself by a dash to the other side of the table. "Be off with you—until tonight . . ."

"It'll be twice as hard on you," he promised, picking up hat and cane as the footman entered to remove breakfast dishes. "Your servant, ma'am. . . ."

Clara's barb was more deeply disturbing than she knew. Francis went directly from her house to Louis de Saumont's lodgings, where he found the slim little Frenchman languidly toying with an omelet. A scarf saturated with lavender water was swathed rakishly about his head, attesting a merry evening past. "Francis! You are returned." Louis smiled. "Where have you been?"

"To Crossthwaite with my father. What the devil have you told Clara?" Francis demanded wrathfully.

Louis winced. "Nothing . . . and please to lower the voice," he begged. "I am not in good frame this morning."

"You must have said something." Francis sank into a chair, eyeing Louis suspiciously. "Or where did she get the idea you were aiding me to recover my French property?"

"*What?*" Louis struggled to sit erect, thrusting the bandage away from his forehead. "But I have said *nothing!*" he protested, alarmed. "*Mon dieu,* would I risk so much as a glance, a breath? That would be to ruin all. Tell me of this, if you please: what did she say?"

"That you had inquired for me"—Francis shrugged

—"and she thought perhaps you had some news." He repeated Clara's words, fixing Louis with a grim stare. "You *must* have said something, which puts all at an end, Louis. I'll not risk another trip. Do it yourself."

De Saumont fingered his chin nervously. *"Sacrébleu, les femmes!"* he muttered. "How they deduce from nothing—but you are right that we must take care. *Voyez-vous,* there is a vital paper that will shortly come into my hands. It must be gotten across somehow, yet I cannot go. That is to tempt fate too hard. My position here is far from secure; you must know that all emigrés are kept under surveillance of some sort—not merely the English authorities, but the Bourbon court—and at the same time there are those in France who would not hesitate to kill me for aiding Napoleon.

"But how else are we to regain our properties?" He shrugged. "And the money is useful besides, while we are waiting. It should not be much longer. I told you, already I have learned our efforts have been brought to his attention and highly commended. This paper should be the very thing to turn the trick, Francis, but it must be taken personally. If it is merely sent by the ordinary couriers, our participation might go unrecognized."

"God, I had thought it would be settled by now," Francis burst out after a moment. "I begin to wonder if Napoleon means ever to give us anything, or is it all a delusion?"

"No, no," Louis said quickly. "I told you, the Vauclairs have been reaffirmed. Naturally, it is not to be mentioned; they would deny vehemently, but I know it for fact. They wait only for the emperor's return from the Russian campaign before leaving for France. I confess I had hoped we might have been confirmed by now, but one supposes affairs of state—alliances with

Prussia, Austria, and formation of his army—would precede reimbursement claims in France."

Francis nodded gloomily. "I mislike it, Louis. Clara is far too shrewd. She would not have given so broad a hint unless she had something up her sleeve. Another absence may serve to confirm her suspicions. If only it were possible to deliver the paper to someone near the coast, I could slip over and back in the space of two nights, but the drive to Paris and return will take a full three days. How is she to be put off the track?"

Louis debated, finishing the omelet in silence. "This Crossthwaite," he said suddenly. "Where is it, what is it? Your father resides there?"

"No more than he can help." Francis grimaced. "It is his estate, on the coast of Norfolk—fiendishly uncomfortable."

"But you have recently been there with him, and it is near the coast," Louis murmured. "Hmmm, it is a possibility. There is perhaps some spot for a ship to shelter unremarked?"

"Lud, yes—the entire coast is a series of coves, well-known to free-traders. The whole area is alive with revenuers."

"Nevertheless, it is our best bet. *Ecoutez:* when the paper is in my hands, we must work speedily. You will say you are summoned by your father's illness . . ."

"She'd not credit that for a moment. She well knows I'm not all that fond of him." Francis shook his head. "Besides, he's not like to stay so long from town. She'll see from the *Gazette* that so far from being ill, he's staying at Oatlands or gone to Newmarket with a racing party."

"*Alors,* you say that since he is from home, you take the opportunity to inspect for yourself," Louis countered. "What is more natural than a concern for property you must one day inherit? The reason for your last visit was to agree to a mortgage on the estate. You are gravely alarmed, you suspect the property to be seriously encumbered, and wish to learn the extent of your father's indebtedness, which naturally cannot be discovered in his presence. Et cetera, et cetera." Louis shrugged.

"It might work." Francis rubbed his nose thoughtfully. "Anything connected to money always gains her immediate interest, like a good shopkeeper's wife. Well, I will see what I can do. Have you no definite day when you will have the paper?"

"No, although it must be within the week. It is a matter of abstracting it unobserved and at such a moment when it will not be inquired for, you understand? There will be a copy, *naturellement,* which you will leave in Paris, but they have wished to see the original. When it has been examined, you will bring it back, to be returned as unobtrusively as it left." Louis tossed aside his napkin and stood up cautiously. *"Oh, ma tête! Alors,* do you join us tonight?"

"Yes, Clara has ordered supper at her house, with games to follow." Francis rose in his turn, picking up hat and stick. "Well, I'll be off—look in at Tatt's, see how the wagers stand. I may have made a lucky hit, waiting to be collected."

"I very much hope so, *mon ami,"* Louis murmured courteously. "Until tonight, then . . . *au revoir."* But when the door had closed behind Francis, the Frenchman continued to stand leaning lightly on the table and staring into space.

Even less than Sir Francis Eddystone did Louis de Saumont wish Mrs. Illington to know his activities. *"Nom d'un chien,"* he thought worriedly, "she cannot prove anything, she would never involve Francis—it is to involve herself as well. Who would believe his mistress innocent?" Nevertheless, in the present state of English nerves, a formal accusation would be un-necessary. The authorities were alert for any chance word, however vague. It did not suit Louis's schedule to be forced back to France before Napoleon's victo-rious return from Russia. Then Louis would quietly vanish, to claim the title and lands already promised him.

He might even say a word on Francis' behalf, al-though Louis had always wondered how he meant to explain acceptance of his mother's properties from En-gland's arch enemy. Still, he wasn't a bad fellow, and Louis had no objection to helping, if possible. Mrs. Illington was a dangerous complication. She must be kept quiet for these next months. Once Louis was safely away, Francis had only to be as shocked as every-one else that a man in his social circle had sold out to the emperor. There might be questions, an interroga-tion, but Louis felt sure nothing could be proved.

He was equally certain that so long as Clara hoped to become Lady Eddystone, she would take care not to cast a cloud on Francis. "He will have to handle it in the bedchamber," Louis decided, and went to dress.

Francis had already figured this out for himself, al-though he was unaware of Louis's projected timing. He went back to his lodgings and spent an hour in careful reflection, after which he concluded that Louis was right: Clara did not—could not—*know* anything. Her suspicion was damnably accurate, which was discon-certing, but unless she had employed someone to follow him constantly, it was only surmise.

"Find out what she has discovered," he decided coldly. "Set a seal on her lips by mentioning marriage, and hedge off after this trip. Hellish risky, she'll pounce on the least word and be twice as furious when it comes to naught, but she's aware my father doesn't fancy her for his in-law. If there's nothing in writing or before witnesses, she'll only lose what little standing she has by making a scandal. Yes, I fancy we'll brush through it satisfactorily—and God knows I need the money."

On that note, he put the matter aside and rambled toward the heart of London, where he found himself the richer by a hundred pounds due to a filly named Sweeter Than Ever. Francis took this as a good omen, and promptly spent some of it on a charming fan of stiffened lace, which he dispatched in company with a nosegay to Mrs. Illington. He then continued along St. James's Street to his club, where he was absorbed into a table of macao. Lady Luck was smiling today; it appeared Francis had hit a winning streak. He was half-minded to excuse himself from the theater in order to take full advantage of his chance, but he feared Clara's displeasure.

Regretfully, he departed at the last moment to dress for the evening, and succeeded in arriving just as Clara's chair was set down before the playhouse. She carried both fan and flowers, and in the flickering light of the flambeaux, she looked no more than twenty-five, although Francis felt certain she was well past thirty. She was in her most roguish mood, thanking him profusely for his gift and simultaneously taking him to task for extravagance, as they arranged themselves in the stall.

Thus it was that Giles saw them upon entering his own box on the opposite side. Upon leaving his grandmother, he had penned a letter to Black Jack and sent it express. He dined at home, debating the relative merits of two private balls, a musicale, and a reception versus one of his clubs, where he would find a whist game. His mind was still not fixed as he strolled away from his house, and on seeing the playbills, he turned impulsively into the theater.

The family box was already occupied by his sister Eleanor, with her husband and some friends. Giles was forced to stand in the shadows by the door. The play was well-advanced, and if there had ever been any sense to it, he had evidently missed the first installment. He found it incomprehensible, and determined to leave as soon as he had made his bow to the party. Meanwhile his attention wandered, and was finally caught by the sight of Mrs. Illington.

She was accompanied by two women he remembered to have seen but could not name. He rather thought they were dashers in keeping, and felt confirmed in his opinion when he glimpsed the flushed face of Sir John Apthorp, who was notorious for more money than gentility. He recognized Louis de Saumont, but the third man was a stranger. "Eddystone, for a guinea," he told himself, observing the bend forward to whisper in Mrs. Illington's ear, and her intimate glances. He got a clear view when the curtain lowered and the audience began to shift about. Francis stood up, and was revealed as a man of middle height with black hair and eyes. Raising an ornate quizzing glass, he peered languidly about, his expression one of arrogant boredom.

Black Jack had described him as a scented fop, but Giles rated Eddystone as a man well able to account for himself in a fight. His shoulders were muscular, he handled his body with coordination, but Giles's real interest was in his acquaintance with De Saumont. George had not included Louis among Eddystone's intimates, but there was no doubt they were close friends. The dowager's words flitted through Giles's mind. "I wonder," he said to himself, and after exchanging courtesies with his sister's guests, he quietly departed as the curtain rose.

Rambling from one club to another, Giles found

them nearly deserted. The *haut ton* was evidently at one of the private parties, leaving only elderly gentlemen quietly enjoying piquet or billiards. He finally found his objective immersed in periodicals at Boodles! "Good evening, milord—may I join you?"

Lord Denning eyed the marquis beneath beetling gray eyebrows, and waved a hand to the adjoining chair. "By all means," he said affably. "Care to look at the *Sportsman?* I'm finished with it."

For a space both men read in silence, ignoring the entrance and exit of other members. Then, "What is it?" the home secretary asked quietly.

"I believe a number of information leaks have recently been suspected." Giles continued to peruse his paper. "What is known of Louis de Saumont?"

"Nothing against him." Lord Denning looked startled. "An emigré, escaped with his parents—they're dead now—lives modestly, hasn't the money for society, I suppose, although he's accepted at Almack's. Why d'you ask?"

"He is a very good friend of Sir Francis Eddystone, whose father is part of the prince regent's set, and whose late mother was Vicomtesse de Bally. One supposes there may be confiscated property. Both Eddystones are thought to be in shallow water financially, and my grandmother mentioned only this evening that Bonaparte has returned estates to those who aid him."

The home secretary nodded somberly. "A number of the younger emigrés have given their allegiance to the emperor. One cannot blame them, in view of Louis Philippe, but Eddystone is English."

"Only half," Giles pointed out, "and his father has the freedom of the Horse Guards."

"Good God!" Lord Denning stared blankly into space. "I thank you for the hint, Giles."

"Don't mention it." Setting his paper aside, the marquis rose lazily. "Your servant, milord."

Avoiding General Pocklington, whom he had drained dry concerning nabobs the previous evening, Giles took his leave. All in all, he felt it had been a good day's work, and he might now go home to bed.

The dowager Marchioness of Bishton was also abed, having severely jolted her staff by the announcement of her remove to Transome on the morrow. "The fourgon, milady?" her butler murmured shakily. "Even did we pack the household goods tonight, it cannot reach Transome for three days."

"That will do nicely." The dowager smiled. "I mean to take up a young friend who will visit me."

"Y-yes, milady." The butler bowed himself away in bewilderment, but by superhuman efforts, the wagon was loaded and started at six, while the dowager slept dreamlessly.

So, too, did the residents of the caravan and Lord Robert, although he was simply not in shape for dreams. Having emptied the brandy decanter, to the accompaniment of nightmare visions of ruin, he was sufficiently castaway that it had taken the united efforts of Martin and his wife to heave their employer upstairs. They had managed to remove his top layer of clothing—discovering his corsets in the process, which widened Mrs. Martin's eyes. "Lawks, how come he be wearing women's clothes?"

"Regents wears 'em, they be fashionable no doubt," Martin said. "We can't get any more off him. Do you take one arm, and when I count *three,* maybe we can get him on the bed."

There Lord Robert now lay motionless, breathing stertorously. Martin had thoughtfully pulled on the nightcap, while his wife tucked a quilt securely in place. "Eh, he'll be long sleeping this off. Poor old gentleman, worrying about the girl. What can have become of her?"

In London, Francis had carefully drunk very little. He felt he was going to need a clear head for dealing with Clara, and found himself decidedly nervous. After taking correct leave with the other guests, it required two full turns around the block before he tapped on the side door, to be admitted by Mrs. Illington herself. She cast herself into his arms affectionately. "Francis, my love! Come in—the servants are abed, you'll have to play ladies' maid," she tittered archly.

"Your servant to command in all things, ma'am."

"What a Bunbury tale," she scoffed, "when you quit town without a word!"

"Have to do my duty when my father summons, m' dear. He's not been well of late. Age and Oatlands are catching up with him. Besides, Crossthwaite will be mine eventually. I hadn't been there in years, thought I might as well see what case it's in."

"And?"

"He's let everything go, I doubt not the place will be sold for the mortgages." Francis sighed artistically, while his accustomed fingers undid the fastenings of her gown. "It was never comfortable; the house is awkwardly placed, it sits too close to the road, without space for a proper carriage drive, and is too far removed from London. I must have sold in favor of an estate closer to town, but now I wonder if there will be anything to sell."

"Good God," she said, shocked, "is there nothing to be done?"

"I don't know. I mean to speak privately to his man in the City; I doubt he'll tell me anything; he's the soul of ethics." Francis pulled a long face. "And as soon as my father leaves, I believe I shall go up quietly to inspect for myself. I had no opportunity, you know, for I stayed but two nights."

To his relief, Clara fell in with this idea at once. "Of course, it involves property, which is money," he thought cynically.

"Oh, I would, certainly go, Francis! It may be found there is a want of competent management, which, once put straight, would produce income to clear the encumbrances."

"I doubt it would answer. He would merely spend the extra. Need we talk of problems at this moment?" Francis put his arms about Clara urgently, reaching beneath the dressing robe to stroke warm flesh. Instantly she acquiesced, melting against him murmurously and removing his scarf pin, neckcloth . . . opening waistcoat and shirt buttons while he fondled her.

But she had not forgotten Crossthwaite. It might be insignificant, poorly located, but it was *property* deeded by Charles II. It must descend to Francis, and in such condition as to be converted into a more suitable neighborhood. Lord Robert could not be allowed to make ducks and drakes of it. She was vastly disturbed by the prospect. Her money could staff and operate an estate, but if Francis proved not to have one, Clara had not sufficient to buy land as well. It was a development not envisioned, and she cursed herself roundly for failure to probe more deeply. Had she wasted three years on a man who had *nothing* but a title? Almost she could have pushed the somnolent body beside her to the floor!

"What are you thinking, my love?"

"Of Crossthwaite," Clara said truthfully. "My poor Francis, something must be done. It will be too cruel if that is lost, as well as your French inheritance, for I must tell you I place no reliance on any effort from Louis to regain them for you."

"Lud, no." Francis exhibited amazement. "Where had you such a notion? I recall you mentioned some such idea this morning, but it is quite impossible, Clara. Bonaparte would never return property to an Englishman! Now, if Wellington continues in the peninsula, and the Russian campaign does not fare well, there might be a Bourbon on the throne once more. In that case, one might *hope*." Out of the corner of his eyes, he noted that Clara was looking uncertain, and he thought exultantly, "She doesn't *know* anything!"

"Oh, if wishes were horses." She shrugged. "But all the more reason not to lose what's at hand. Why did he call you to Crossthwaite? He is not really sick, is he?"

"He is not at death's door, if that's what you mean. There's plenty of go left in him."

"And you stayed only two nights? What could he intend, to drag you away from town at this time of year?"

"He needed my signature for a mortgage. That is what put me onto the situation," Francis said grimly. By now, he was half-believing it was truth. "It has reached a point where they will give him no more without approval of his heir."

Clara stared at him. "Surely you refused?"

Lord Robert was not the only actor in the family. "No, how could I?" Francis groaned. "That were merely to stand by while my father is rolled up and tossed into the basket. The scandal would be frightful, Clara: for a son to be so callous and unfeeling. We have not always seen eye to eye, but I must do my possible for him."

Mrs. Illington sat bolt upright, clutching the covers to her chin and narrowing her eyes. "We'll see about that," she muttered. "You've every right to take steps to protect what is rightfully yours. Do you consult his business man tomorrow, while I see what my people can discover. If we learn the extent of encumbrage, it might be possible to pay off and hold in our own hands."

Clara's unconscious use of "we" struck cold to Francis' soul. "Dear heart, it's like you to think sensibly. I own I could wish to know how badly he's dipped, but almost worse, when tthere's nothing to be done." He sighed. "I've only my mother's income; he ceased making an heir's allowance some years ago."

Now was the moment for her to say, "I'll buy up the mortgages." Francis waited with bated breath, but he'd gambled correctly: much as she wanted to marry a title, Clara Illington would wait to see before she parted with so much money. He did not doubt she would have the figures to the last pence in twenty-four hours. Again, it was a calculated risk; Crossthwaite was heavily encumbered, he was certain. Else, why had Lord Robert plotted to acquire the Surtaine money?

His bleak picture of a penniless future was the right approach. Clara was frowning slightly. "My poor Francis," she said again mechanically, "I knew, of course, that you were not plump in the pocket, but this—it is beyond words disgraceful for your father to waste the substance that is your proper expectation. You do not wish to appear callous and unfeeling; I think it is quite the opposite. Indeed, he must be restrained, my love! What does he expect you to do with a ramshackle estate in the hinterlands, and no money?"

Francis gathered his nerve and cast himself on the metaphorical waters. "He expects me to marry a rich girl, whose portion will preserve Crossthwaite and provide an allowance for *him*," Francis snorted.

"What?" Clara's eyes widened incredulously.

"Oh, yes." He nodded. "He went on and on at me about it: I should make a push to settle suitably, be seen at Almack's, and take my place in the *ton*. According to him, it is the easiest thing in the world, and had I done it long ago, we would not now be in this pass."

"He must be mad!" Clara exclaimed with more honesty than tact.

"Exactly so," Francis agreed. "Did I find a female I could tolerate, what family would allow her to throw herself away on a penniless man of five-and-thirty? And to make a 'push,' as he calls it, is to turn myself into a gazetted fortune hunter, at which I draw the line."

"Unthinkable!"

"Yes, so I told him. We parted quite out of charity with each other, to a point that I left before he waked yesterday morning." Francis cast off the covers and slid from the bed, to put on his clothes. Clara continued to sit silently, with an expression of concentrated thought until he leaned to kiss her tenderly. "Do not worry for me, my love. In my salad days I'd no wish to marry," he murmured, "and when I lost my heart, it was too late. I had nothing to offer. Sleep well, sweeting, and tomorrow will be another day."

"Yes." She returned his kiss absently, but as Francis left the bedchamber, she was still sitting in a sort of suspended animation. He went down the stairs to the side door, softly let himself out, and shortly gained the street walk without observation. Then he allowed himself to chuckle with satisfaction. All the way to his lodgings he mentally rubbed his hands with glee.

It had been so easy!

CHAPTER 6

Giles's express reached the circus at seven the next morning, and greatly relieved Jack's mind. "Eh, he's settled all," he told Sally. "His grandma's coming to pick up Meg tomorrow and take her to visit for a fortnight. She'll be right away out, and I'm glad!"

"Let me see." Sally took the letter and read it with widening eyes. "Mercy on us, Jack—she's an heiress, and those men were trying to get her money! Now, aren't you satisfied I insisted on keeping her?"

"Yes, but have a care. There's still today and part of tomorrow to get through," Jack cautioned, "and his lordship is searching hard, Sal. His coach was back and forth yesterday, constable's been asked to inquire house to house, keeper's been asked to search the woods, and for all constable told him, the circus was searched, he'll be back. Keep the girl under your eye all the time, Sally, and hide her in another search, but did I not let him in, it'd look odd."

Sally nodded absently. "How'll I explain she's to go visiting? She thinks she belongs here."

"You'll think of something." He clapped her shoulder comfortably. "You're a grand one for ideas!"

While Sally appreciated his praise, she had not the faintest idea what to do. Minta made the decision for her. Throughout the day she helped Sally here or there; she was still quickly picking up from whatever Sally was doing. It was Minta who washed the dishes and made the beds. She took away Sally's broom and finished sweeping out the caravan. She took away the basket of fresh peas Alfie had brought from Mrs. Upson and finished shelling them. In between, she knitted and played with El Cid. Sally let her do whatever she chose. "Better for the child to be busy, and a little domesticity won't hurt her."

In the afternoon, Minta rambled around the midway with Alfie, who was making the most of the remaining hours with his goddess. He was strictly forbidden to mention the forthcoming separation—and strictly charged to stay right with Araminta. "Might as well," Jack chuckled indulgently to Sally. "He's too bemused to be any help elsewhere."

Joe was not much better, but he was also excused from work. A party of three, they visited the animals in turn, ending at the circus ring, where the trained horses were being exercised. "Oh," Araminta clapped her hands together delightedly, "it is so long since I have gone riding. Could I have a turn?"

"Of course you can." The trainer beamed, swinging her up to the steadiest mare; but once into the saddle, it was immediately obvious that Minta was an accomplished equestrienne. Twice she jogged around the ring. Then, by the lightest touch on the reins, she was turning and twisting the horse into a caracole. "Lumme," said the trainer admiringly when Minta slid from the saddle, "you do ride a treat, Meg."

"Of course," she returned in surprise. "I got the silver cup, don't you remember?"

The trainer gulped. "Now, if I hadn't forgotten that, Meg!"

She smiled sweetly. "It wouldn't mean as much to you—you must have so many awards—but it was my *first* competition. I keep it on the mantel in my bedroom, where I can see it every day!" Her smile faded into uncertainty. "At least, I think I do. I haven't seen it recently."

"Let's go fishing," Alfie inserted quickly. "It's not too far for you to walk, if we go slowly. Joe, bring the lines and bait."

Araminta winced at sight of the can of wrigglers. "Do they bite?"

"Naw, 'tis fish bites *'em*," Joe scoffed, threading the fish hook expertly. "Here you are, Meg. Just wiggle it a bit—not too fast—and when there's tug, draw it up quick."

Somewhat dubiously, Minta dropped her line into the shadows surrounding the outcrop on which they were established. Obediently she wiggled her finger as the boys did, staring dreamily at the water. The tug, when it came, so startled her that she squealed. "What do I do now?"

"Draw 'un in," Joe said sensibly. "Hand-over-hand, like."

It was a large gray sole, flapping wildly as it emerged from the water. Minta squealed again and recoiled while it gasped and flopped about. "How do I get it off? It doesn't lie still."

"I'll do it, hold my line." Alfie thrust it into her hand and swiftly removed the fish hook. He tossed the sole into the rush basket and baited her hook again, by which time Minta had another bite. She drew it in—a big plaice—and eagerly exchanged the lines to dangle hers once more. "Oh, what fun this is! We never fished in the sea before, did we? There was a stream, with trout"—she frowned slightly—"wasn't there?"

"Naw, we always fish the sea," Joe said. " 'Tis free. With streams, there's keepers."

"Are there? I don't remember, it was all so long ago."

Alfie scowled warningly at Joe. "Meg wasn't let to

come with us, you dudgeon! She was too little; Ma was afraid she'd fall in," he improvised.

"Oh, aye, that was the way of it," Joe muttered feebly. "I'd forgot."

It seemed a satisfactory explanation. Minta's face cleared, and she fished along with growing excitement. She was even unable to wait for one of the boys to take a fish from her line, but ruthlessly hauled it off for herself and rebaited the hook. They had apparently hit a good run, and shortly the basket was full. " 'Tis enough," Alfie said. "Never take more nor can be used; 'tis wasteful of the Lord's bounty."

Minta sighed regretfully. "I suppose so, but"—brightening—"we can come again tomorrow, can't we?" She folded up her line neatly, in imitation of the boys, and surveyed the full basket with pride. "What do we do next?"

"We take 'em down to shore and clean 'em in sea," said Joe, tossing scaler and knives atop the gasping fish.

"Can I go wading?" Minta asked eagerly.

The boys consulted each other silently. "Think she can make it?"

"Take fish down first, and come back for Meg," Alfie decided, holding out his hand to help Minta to her feet and up to the top of the outcrop. "You wait here while we move basket," he ordered. " 'Tis heavier nor you'd think, but we've got enough for whole camp."

"Oh, good!" Docilely, Araminta stayed where she was, while Joe and Alfie slowly got the basket down the rude cliff path. They came back, panting, and eyed her dubiously.

"I dunno, should we chance it? Do she slip, it'd be bad for her bandages."

"No!" Araminta wailed. "I'm sure I'll be all right, and I want to go wading. I know," she exclaimed, "I'll go down backwards, like a ladder. Alfie, go first to set my foot on the next spot, and Joe can be above to direct me."

Alfie surrendered at once to her pleading face. "Well—we can try it," he agreed weakly, but it worked out satisfactorily, although involving a display of feminine limbs that would have horrified Mrs. Hobson. However, neither of the boys made anything of it; they were too accustomed to legs in tights on the midway or standing on the prancing horses. Once safely down to the sandy beach, Araminta breathed deep of the sea air, rambling about happily while the boys scaled and gutted the catch. The tide was fully out, leaving a long sloping expanse of wet sand.

"Clams," said Joe, "and maybe mussels."

"What'll we put 'em in? Basket's full."

"Leave 'em up on dry sand, and come back with basket." Joe eyed the exposed clumps of mussels clinging to rocks with a greedy eye. "Make us a feast, like." He was already prospecting for air holes in the damp stretch, and stamping his heel to identify a clam by its frightened spurt of water. "Eh, there's lots today! Come on!"

"What are you doing?" Minta asked curiously. When it was explained, she insisted on helping. "Well, if you think it might be bad for my legs, couldn't I gather the mussels?"

For nearly an hour the youngsters worked vigorously. More resourceful than the boys, Araminta removed her petticoat in the lee of an outcrop and made a sling to carry the clumps of mussels. "We could put the clams in my sunbonnet," she suggested when she came back.

"Aye—we've only to wash 'em first," Joe agreed. "Bonnet'll dry."

Eventually they got everything washed free of mud, including the petticoat, and found they could put all the shellfish into it without needing the sunbonnet. They rinsed their feet, sat in a row for the sun to dry before putting on hose and shoes, and regaled themselves on the fresh cold clams that Joe opened with the scaling knife. "What a heavenly day!" Minta murmured dreamily. "It is so long since we had a picnic by the sea. I was quite a little girl, and Papa held me in his arms to splash in the shallow water. Was it here?"

"No, it was another cove farther to the north," Alfie mumbled, scrambling to his feet. "We better get back, 'tis near suppertime. Joe, take basket up first." With Minta's petticoat load of shellfish atop, it was a formidable load. When they'd reached the top of the path, they stood panting for a moment. "Watch what you say, Joe," Alfie warned. "She's beginning to remember. Doctor said she would, but 'tis best not to confuse her until all comes back normal, like."

"Arr, she's a proper right 'un, pluck down to her toes," Joe agreed. "Not afeared of anything, once she see *how*—taking off fish and baiting hook, pulling down mussels! I wish she hadn't to go."

"So do I, but this here ain't right for gentry-morts, Joe. Do she get back where she belongs, she'll remember all . . . nor she won't forget us," Alfie returned valiantly. "The gentry don't . . . real ones, that is. Come on, if you're ready. We got to get her up again."

The ascent was much easier; with Joe's hand holding Minta's and Alfie bracing from the rear, she was up in two-twoes, where they took a breather. "Now for the last lap," said Alfie, "but 'tis mostly downhill. Meg, take my hand. Joe, take other end of basket and sling mussels over shoulder to balance load."

At a leisurely pace, they swung along down through the trees, until the camp lay before them. In its midst was a traveling coach, with a stocky figure in gleaming Hessians engaged in talk with Black Jack. Araminta's hand closed painfully on Alfie's. "No!" she said wildly. "I don't want to go any farther. Oh, please —let me hide until it's gone away."

Alfie abandoned his handle of the fish basket and swiftly pushed Araminta into the shadow of the scrub. "Stay here! Don't move until Joe or me comes back," he ordered. "You'll be safe, Pa won't let 'un fright you, Meg. Just stay here." He picked up his side of the fish again. "Come on, Joe . . . and say naught, just agree with me."

"Aye, but 'tis same coach," Joe muttered uneasily, "and he were looking this way. I saw 'un Alfie. He'll ask, where's the girl was with you? What to say?"

Alfie was not Jack and Sally Bickell's son for nothing. " 'Twas Gypsy Meg, who's gone cross fields for wild strawberries," he decided rapidly. "I'll talk, you just nod and take fish into square for everyone to share. Then go back as quick as may be to lead her t'other way along sea cliff to upper cave." Assessing Lord Robert's portly figure, Alfie snorted, "Hmph, he'll not walk a mile to see for himself. You'll see, he'll tell constable to do it." He eyed Joe's downcast eyes and craven expression with contempt. "Eh, buck up, Joe —throw up your chin, and look innocent-surprised, like. You'd not let yon fat flawn get his hands on Meg again, would you?"

Joe gulped, but after inspecting the cockerel figure of Lord Robert, he clenched his teeth. "No, I'll not. He'm worse than the one t'other day . . . but you do the talking, Alfie. I'm not clever enough, I'll make a mistake somewhere."

"All right. Here we go." The two boys staggered down the last small rise onto the encampment square, dropping basket and sling of shellfish. "Come get your fresh fish!" Alfie cried, ignoring the consultation between Jack and Lord Robert. "Enough for everybody —with mussels and clams, too. Come, parcel it out."

All the women hastened to surround the boys, tipping the basket onto a stretch of grass and efficiently spreading the haul, until they could separate what they wanted. Joe emptied the shellfish into another pile, and swiftly thrust the damp petticoat into his mother's hands. "Hide 'un!" He'd vanished before Black Jack and Lord Robert could reach the crowd.

"Where'd the other lad go—and the girl?" Lord Robert demanded testily. "I distinctly saw her at the edge of the camp, Bickell. Who was she?"

" 'Twas only Gypsy Meg," Alfie inserted. "She'm gone along to get wild strawberries."

"What about the boy?"

Alfie looked up innocently. "He'm gone to piss, sir."

His father took charge, keeping a very sober face. "This is my son Alfred—make your bow to Lord Robert Eddystone, son." To Lord Robert's surprise, it was a very creditable leg, accompanied by the conventional, "Your servant, sir!" Automatically, the baron bowed in return, while Jack continued, "Alfie, you'll remember we searched camp the other day for his lordship's ward? I'd no thought but she'd be found safely by now, but she has not. His lordship is begging our help in the search. He fears some tragic accident. Mayhap the young lady fell from coach where she was tucked up to sleep for the last part of the long journey, and half-dazed, she might have wandered into woods.

"He's asking everyone in the locality to look for her, and particularly all our youngsters. I'll put you in charge, Alfie: get everyone in a line, and walk straight through the woods, staying within sight and sound of each other, you understand? Then you'll reform and come back over a different section, until you've covered every inch. Keepers will help; they've already checked all traps for fear she'd stepped into one in the dark. They'll leave 'em sprung until you've finished working over the woods. Set about it right away, Alfie."

"Yes, sir. What about Minchampton Mere, and the stream?"

"The keepers have gone the length of the stream," Lord Robert inserted. "They doubt she could have walked so far in the woods at night, but tomorrow they'll drag." He sighed deeply. "You can understand my anxiety, Bickell: a gently bred young female . . . her clothing not suited for walking or exposure to the elements . . . four *days;* thank God, the weather has been mild, but without food?" He shook his head distractedly, nor was it any pretense. His lordship was not merely exhausted by driving here and there; he was frantic with worry.

Black Jack could sympathize, but steeled by Giles's letter, he maintained an impassive expression. "You'll leave it to Alfie," he stated. "They'll have time to make one pass of the woods before dark tonight. Tomorrow they'll do the rest. Keepers'll understand. They'm not keen for youngsters in the woods, nor you can't blame 'em. Ours is well-behaved," Jack added blandly, "but their voices and romping around—it frights the birds."

Lord Robert nodded. "The keepers have been instructed by the earl to lend every assistance. It goes without saying I'll make it up to the children for their time, and there'll be a handsome reward for finding Miss Surtaine . . . alive or dead." His voice shook slightly.

"Don't think on it, milord," Jack advised, as Lord Robert turned wearily to his coach, "nor worry about rewards. We'll be pleased to help. Do we find any clue, we'll send word to you at once."

"Thank you, thank you." The baron hauled himself to the driver's seat. "And my apologies again for subjecting you to the search, Bickell. Sir Francis knows little of coast country, he'd no realization he was giving revenuers a golden opportunity, was appalled when I explained."

"Eh, 'twas nothing, milord—mayhap did us a service," Jack returned with a smile. "'Tis natural to suspect our sort of free-trading, and I suspicion there's a many taking part—but here's my people cleared. That's good for us, Lord Robert. I should rather thank Sir Francis for making it possible."

The baron stared at him very hard but saw no indication of impertinence. "Hmph, I'll hope to hear good news from you shortly. Good day to you." And with a flick of his whip, Lord Robert was bowling away down the lane to the main road.

"Whew!" Jack exhaled with relief, while the circus people surged forward as soon as the carriage had disappeared.

"Well?" Sam demanded.

"'Tis all right for the moment," Jack said tersely. "By tomorrow she'll be gone; Mr. Giles has arranged all; I'll tell later. The less you know, the better, but 'tis very serious to protect the girl!"

"Arrr, yon's a fat rascal," Sam growled, "and do it not be for Meg, baby'd be eaten by tiger. You'll count on me, Jack."

"On all of us," Ted said firmly, supported by a general murmur from the others.

Jack grinned at them wickedly. "He wants all the youngsters to walk back and forth through woods, to cover every inch—says he'll pay for their time," he remarked. "We may know 'tis wasted, but 'tis best to do it, and no matter for money Mayhap young'uns will pick up something on the way."

A chuckle rippled through the crowd. "Aye, gives 'em a chance to see lay of the land," someone observed innocently. "Find new rabbit run, or best way to trout stream, eh?"

The chuckle exploded in laughter. " 'Tis an ill wind blows no good," Sam said. "Aye, send out the kids, and see what they get."

Straight-faced and authoritative, Alfie organized his search crew as soon as Joe brought Araminta back to the caravan. She was still trembling, only partially re-assured by the absence of the coach. "You'll not worry," Sally said. "We'll not let anything happen to you, Meg."

Minta nodded slowly, picking El Cid into her arms and sinking into a chair. "Is that really my name?" she asked suddenly, looking earnestly at Sally. "It . . . doesn't sound right, somehow."

Sally drew a long breath and plunged. "Nor it isn't, my dearie," she said gently, "but we didn't know when Alfie and Joe found you."

"Where was I?"

"You fell from the carriage and hit your head. The boys brought you home, and for a while we didn't know who you were, but doctor says it's all right. You'll remember in a while"—Sally smiled—"and tomorrow your grandma is coming to get you."

"Grandmother?" Minta looked confused. "Do I have

one? If only I could remember." She sighed, rubbing her forehead. "If I'm not Meg, who am I, please?"

"Your name is Araminta Surtaine."

"Araminta . . . Minta! Yes, that sounds right, but I still don't remember." Her voice trailed away unhappily. After a moment, "How did you learn?"

"Mr. Giles found out as soon as he reached London," Sally said carefully, "and sent us word."

"Giles!" Minta's face brightened. "Oh, then it's all right." She drew a long breath of relief and smiled at Sally. "You've been so kind, so *very* kind," she said earnestly. "I hope I've not been a trouble to you. If only I could remember . . ."

"You will; you're beginning already, but doctor says best to let it come naturally—and you'd never be a trouble to anyone, my dearie!" Sally put her arm about Minta and kissed her check warmly. "Eh, it's been a treat to have you staying with us!"

Araminta nodded absently, tickling El Cid's throat. "Who was that man, please?"

"Your guardian, Lord Robert Eddystone." Sally chose her words carefully. "He's main worried not to find you, but Mr. Giles charged us to keep you safe until Grandma comes. After that, they'll handle all. Don't fret you, my lovely."

After a moment Araminta said with decision, "Well, I won't, then. Giles will know best what to do. It *is* nice to have a man to tell one how to go on, isn't it?"

"That it is—not but what," Sally said dryly, "there's many a time they needs *us* to show *them* how to go on. Now I'll look at bandages, and you'll set table if you've a mind, while I start supper."

Robert Percival Charles, third Baron Eddystone, was in a mood of fatigued fury as he drove back to Crossthwaite. His head still ached dully from the excesses of the previous evening. The prospect of yet another bucolic meal without conversation was dreadful. Almost, he was sufficiently exasperated to hope Araminta was dead! There was still a week in which to pull around; all that was needed was to *find* the girl. Before he'd fuddled himself with brandy last night, Lord Robert had taken the bull by the horns and sent an express to Bow Street, asking assistance. Simultaneously, he had sent a preliminary final accounting to Araminta's financial man. It would be a pittance, if she were dead—but would at least stave the wolf from the door, giving him a breathing spell.

Swinging himself heavily down from the driver's seat and stomping into his house, Lord Robert felt himself in the middle of a nightmare. He paced back and forth in the study, cursing his son for parsimony in not being in a separate following carriage to see what became of the girl. He closed his eyes and suppressed a shiver at the memory of absence from London; this very night he was engaged to dine with two of the prince regent's close friends, before a game of whist at Carlton House. He had thought to send his excuses, along with the other expresses, but the contrast between Crossthwaite and a cozy dinner with the latest town gossip increased his exasperation.

Well, the matter was out of his hands. He could think of nothing more to do, no place he had not inquired. Let the Runners take charge. At least he would be relieved of the constant driving day after day. It was too much for a man of his age; he ached from head to foot. "Damme, I'm getting *old*," he thought gloomily, and was too discouraged to put on his corsets again when he had bathed before dinner.

In the private parlor of the Cock and Bull at Cambridge, the dowager Marchioness of Bishton would have agreed, although her weariness was alleviated by a sense of wicked adventure. "Ought to be a handsome hero riding to the rescue instead of a decrepit old lady," she chuckled to herself. Jiggling back and forth in her coach, well-sprung as it was, the dowager had amused herself by thoughts of her grandson's surrender to parson's mousetrap. She could not remember ever to have heard Giles describe a female in such glowing terms, nor had he ever bestirred himself to rise in order to wave farewell to his grandmother's traveling coach.

While reminding herself that one swallow did not make a summer, and Giles's primary purpose was to remove this circus from the notice of the law, the dowager's decision to retrieve Araminta was prompted by propinquity: if the girl were staying with his grandmother, Giles would of necessity see more of her. *"Anything* might happen!" she thought happily. She was further buoyed by a possible triumph over his mother and sisters, not that she disliked them, but what a feather in her cap if *she* managed to settle Giles after all the years they'd been trying!

Nor was she impervious to the subtle flattery in his seeking her help. For all she called him a graceless scoundrel, she owned to a particular fondness for the boy. He was far more like his grandfather than his father; Edward had been an excellent landholder, but there was a panache about Giles, a quickness of humor, a lightness of touch that was reminiscent of old Ludovic. The dowager sighed; the boy even looked like Ludo. Boy? She did some mental arithmetic and said aloud, "God bless me! Giles is *thirty!*"

It was the more troubling in that the dowager knew in her bones that the Marquis of Bishton was not happy. Like all old ladies of the *ton,* the dowager marchioness was abreast of even the best-concealed *on dits.* If she chose, she could tell you exactly who fathered every baby born in the last ten years. Equally, she knew who was keeping whom, who were the flats and which the legs, and was perfectly aware of her grandson's ladybirds . . . but—she frowned thoughtfully—they took care only of the natural requirements of a highly bred gentleman. Giles needed more; the proof was in whatever devilment was engaging him.

"It all comes of letting him inherit outright," she grumbled worriedly. "Not that one expected Edward to die when Giles was only eighteen—but there should have been guardians, some control. He should not have been allowed to dash off to the Continent the instant peace was declared, with no knowing where he was nor whom he met. Unsettled him! Made him too mature for his years, politic-minded when he should have been kicking up larks at Oxford and boxing the Watch in the hole—hmph, now we see the result. *Bored*, that's what it is."

After a moment the dowager added, "Well, so am I, if it comes to that. At least this girl is something out of the common, gives me something to do. Lord, what a story: wicked guardians, abductions, loss of memory." She chuckled. "It's better than Horry Walpole's silly old Otranto!"

Refreshed by a good night's rest, her ladyship arose betimes and enjoyed an excellent breakfast. She was in prime fettle and smiling to herself—"Bang up to the knocker!" as Giles would say. It had occurred to the dowager that the appearance of a crested traveling chariot, accompanied by postilions, outriders, and footmen, might occasion undue curiosity if noticed bowling into the circus encampment. Tchk, Giles should have thought of that! Preening herself on her perspicacity, she penned a note to Mr. Bickell and dispatched one of the outriders at once: have the girl waiting near the main road.

She then rang for her maid, and was assisted in dressing. Miss Crims was at a loss for such an early hour and preserved a silence of faint disapproval that much amused her mistress. By ten o'clock, they were ready to leave. "And a good thing," said Lady Bishton. "That's a hellish racket in the Ordinary!"

"Night mail's just come in, milady," the landlord apologized, harassed, "nor you'd not likely be disturbed, being as we put you in the farthest chamber. I trust all was to your ladyship's satisfaction?"

"Entirely," the dowager assured him graciously, "and a good day to you, my man."

Head erect, bonnet plumes waving, she swept along the hall and out to her carriage without a glance for the crowd in the barroom.

She was not unobserved, however. Messrs. Pigott and Stibling, inconspicuously clad as befitted men from Bow Street, stood by the door with pints of ale. It was their business to notice things; they had already noticed the coroneted crest on the coach door, the luggage (equally crested) tied securely in place, the superb glossy horses and spry young liveried footmen, the coachman's grizzled beard, the postilions' horns, the outrider. When her ladyship was assisted into her seat, followed by a prim elderly dresser, Pigott said to the passing maid, " 'Oo's yer titled guest?"

"Dowager Marchioness of Bishton," the girl threw over her shoulder, planking plates of ham and eggs before other travelers. "Allus stays here—on her way to Transome, belike . . . and what'll *you* fancy?"

"Two plates o' the same, with bread and cheese." Stibling turned away as the coach drove off. "Table over there . . ."

Meanwhile, the dowager was borne along the highway at a good pace. Following Giles's instructions, she

halted at Mr. Reddy's tavern to change horses and refresh herself with a pot of tea. The outrider returned
with a note exactly as she finished; all was going excellently. "First oak tree after fork beyond third hamlet . . ."

"Desire the coachman to step in to me, please . . ."
When the man arrived, "Oh, Thomas, we will take this
side road, and turn across here to rejoin the turnpike."
The dowager handed over Giles's rough map. "And
stand ready to pull up when I give you word."

"Very good, your ladyship, but 'tis a main bad
road." Thomas frowned. "You'll not be comfortable—
saving your pardon."

"No matter," the dowager returned regally. "I am
picking up a young visitor. Once we have her, make
what speed you can back to the highway."

Mr. Reddy bowed her out personally, with his wife
beaming in the background. "Always a pleasure to
serve your ladyship—and such fine weather! You'll
be for Transome, of course—no doubt of your reaching
it in good time."

"Yes, thank you." She nodded suavely; but once
around the curve, Thomas was turning off, and he was
right: the road was *abominable!* "Good God, do they
never drag it?" Her ladyship clung to the hand strap
while they jolted back and forth from potholes to
more potholes, interspersed with rocks. All that supported her was the inner excitement of shortly seeing
this child that had stirred Giles's compassion. Peering
curiously from the coach, she found the countryside
neat, yet bleak from the sea winds. Thrifty farms, well-
tended fields, and small flocks—a few farm wains on
the road, an occasional pond or thick stand of trees,
and at last they were through the third cluster of houses.
The dowager's eyes sharpened . . . *there!*

A boy, sitting on a grass tussock, obviously waiting.

. . . Her ladyship raised her cane and battered on the coachman's panel. "Stop!" As the carriage slowed to a halt, another boy appeared from the other side of the hill, leading a girl. Together they helped her carefully down the incline, lifted her bodily over the ditch, and came up to the door as the footman opened it.

Looking down, the Dowager Marchioness of Bishton caught her breath. Heart-shaped face, porcelain skin, silky black hair caught loosely by a ribbon, and huge gray eyes staring up anxiously. The dowager leaned forward with a smile, extending her hand. "Good morning, Araminta. . . ."

CHAPTER 7

The combined efforts of Beth and Sally had contrived to wash and repair Minta's original clothing into a semblance of wearability, although the fashionable high-poke bonnet was crushed beyond help. Nothing served to straighten the bent wire frame into smooth curves. "Throw it away," Bess said finally. "It'd not look right anyway, without a proper hair style."

Aware this was her last night in the caravan, Araminta was torn between relief at getting away from that man Sally said was her guardian, and distress at the unfinished socks. "Should I take them with me, or leave them to finish when I come back?" she asked.

"Leave them for me to finish, they're so nearly done."

A more pressing problem was El Cid, and here Sally was at a loss. "I'd like to have him. Alfie gave him to me, you know, but"—Minta's forehead wrinkled—"I can't remember if Grandmother likes cats. Mrs. Hobson didn't. . . ."

"Take the kit with you to coach," Black Jack said resourcefully, "and ask. If she don't want Sid, Alfie'll bring him back and take care of him for you."

That seemed all there was to making Araminta ready to visit. When the dowager's messenger had come and gone next morning, there was still time to say good-bye to her new friends, including all the animals, before Joe and Alfie led her circuitously across to the meeting place by the road.

At the final moment, Minta rather clung to Sally, "I . . . I hate to leave," she said tremulously. "You're been so kind, and . . . and I don't know where I'm going, or who will be there."

"Your grandmother will be there, and probably Mr. Giles," Sally reminded her gently. "I don't know who else, but I expect you'll recognize them. 'Tis better for you to be with your own people, my dearie."

Araminta brightened slightly. "That's so. Giles arranged it, didn't he—so I'm sure to be perfectly safe." She released Sally, went from one to another, hugging Jack, Alfie, even Joe (who went scarlet and nearly fainted). "Thank you so much for taking care of me," she said earnestly. "I'll come home as soon as I'm well again."

"We'll be looking forward," Jack assured her heartily, but when her little figure had disappeared with the boys around the hill and into the stand of trees, he sighed with relief. "Well, that's that, and I'm glad on't for all she was a sweet child. The gentry's what you don't want to tangle wtih in our line of work, Sal!"

"Aye, she'll be best among her own kind," Sally agreed, "and do the youngsters take their time about this searching, it'll quiet the guardian until she's well away." Sally lifted her chin gallantly. "It weren't to be, and Alfie's a grand lad. Did you see his bow to Lord Robert yesterday?"

Jack nodded. "He'll make his way out, God willing and do I give him some help. We'll expect Mr. Giles shortly, best to make bed ready for whenever," Jack added casually. "I'll go along to tent. . . ."

Arrived at the appointed spot, Joe was posted as lookout, while Araminta sat on an outcrop well dusted by Alfie's bandanna. It was a lovely fair day, but the wait seemed long, and Minta began to look anxious. "Is she really coming?"

"She sent messenger to say so," Alfie said sturdily. Casting about for entertainment, he spied some wild strawberries. They were not full ripe, but served to while away some time. Then Minta discovered violets; they had gathered an appreciable bunch when Joe's piercing whistle brought them back to the road, where a coach was drawn up. In spite of herself, Araminta shivered and drew back. " 'Tis not yesterday's," Alfie told her, " 'tis much finer, with coachman and all. This'll be right. Come on."

A footman had sprung down to open the door. Timidly, Minta went forward and looked up—to one of the kindest, merriest smiles! An elderly lady with white hair beneath a fashionable plumed bonnet, and sparkling hazel eyes. She leaned forward, stretching out her hand. "Good morning, Araminta!"

Instinctively, Minta smiled in return. "Good morning, ma'am."

"Come up quickly, child. This road is slow traveling; we must be on our way."

"Yes, ma'am. Oh, please, can I bring El Cid, or must I leave him here?" she asked anxiously. "Alfie gave him to me—but if you should dislike cats, ma'am, he'll take care of El Cid for me." Silently Alfie exhibited the white kitten tucked into his pocket with its head and forepaws hanging over the edge.

"What a love! Bring him, of course. I am very fond of cats," the dowager said firmly, "and you have found violets, too! Robert, lift Miss Surtaine into the carriage, please, and give her the kitten. Crims, be so good as to move your feet until Miss Surtaine is settled. Sit here, my dear. Mmmmm, how sweet the scent of violets!"

"Please, ma'am, won't you have them?" Araminta thrust them at her rescuer earnestly. "I shall have El Cid to hold, you know."

"Why, thank you, my love." Without a qualm, Lady Bishton accepted the untidy bunch of flowers, to the instant ruination of her pale lavender kid gloves.

"Robert, hand this to Master Alfred, if you please."
She extended an envelope with a smile for the woebe-
gone faces of the two boys looking up at Araminta.
"And then you may close the door, and tell Thomas to
go on."

Araminta leaned to the coach window impulsively.
"Good-bye, Alfie, Joe—don't be sad! I'll soon be back,
and we'll go fishing again!" As the wheels began to turn
and pick up speed, she eyed her hostess shyly. "It was
so good in you to come for me, ma'am."

"Not at all." The dowager shrugged, steadying herself on the hand strap. "It is a fine day for a drive, and
a long while since I have been within smell of the sea.
A pleasant change, eh, Crims?"

"Yes, your ladyship."

"Araminta, this is Crims, my dresser—Miss Surtaine
will be visiting indefinitely, Crims."

"How do you do, Crims?" Araminta's voice was
gentle, and she smiled at the maid. She was feeling
more and more comfortable, sitting beside this friendly
old lady who talked so calmly, and appeared to know
her very well. Araminta Surtaine . . . it *did* sound right.
Now that she was safely away from that man, she
was sure she would begin to remember very soon—
Sally had said so.

El Cid was already bridging all social gaps, while
the carriage lumbered along the rutted road. With the
aplomb of innocence, he picked his way daintily from
Minta's hands across to clamber into the dowager's
lap, where he first opened his small mouth in a gigantic
yawn, and then began purring bigger than himself.
Automatically the dowager's gnarled fingers reached
to tickle his throat and ears.

"Oh, pray, do not let him be a bother to you,
ma'am!"

"No, no, he's an impudent little rascal, like all cats. Alfie gave him to you?"

"Yes, the farmer's wife was going to have the litter drowned, you know, but it would be a shame," Minta said earnestly, "for he is really a very good cat, and the greatest company, ma'am."

"I can see that he is—only look how he is reaching to play with my locket! There, then." The dowager dangled the jeweled oval until it glinted in the sunlight, while El Cid reared unsteadily to bat it back and forth. By the time he'd tired of the game and curled into a sleepy ball, the ice was completely broken, and Minta was eagerly relating all the delights of the circus.

The coach lurched along rather slowly, and finally turned off, to return to the highway. "Only a matter of ten miles," Thomas said thankfully to the footman beside him, "nor we ain't broke nothing, nor lamed a horse, *and* we're in good time."

"Thank Gord, I'm fair shook to pieces this road," the man muttered. "What we're doing here along, picking up little miss with no luggage—who's she?"

Thomas flicked his whip austerely. "Arr, you'll learn, my lad: there's no accounting for the aristocracy. . . ."

Messrs. Pigott and Stibling had long since concluded this. Leaving Cambridge on the Northern Mail, a full hour after the marchioness, they had been set down at the Dog and Duck at about the same time her Grace was pulling away from Mr. Reddy's inn. Consulting their instructions, they first arranged to be driven to the crossroads for the back-country stage, and finding there was considerable time to spare, filled it by a sustaining portion of rabbit pasty washed down by a pint of the best.

Thus, they were nearly two hours behind the dowager, but since Thomas was driving slowly on the pitted road and there had been the delay while Araminta joined them, the stage finally overtook the coach shortly after it started off with its new passenger. The stagecoach driver was not so considerate as Thomas. "Bloody gurt chariot in t' way," he spat contemptuously. "Blow up, and we'll pass 'un on next downhill." With a fine and fancy disregard for his freight, he pulled his team out at the top of the rise, and with a crack of his whip sent them thundering down full-tilt.

The inside of the coach resounded with cries of fright and indignation; the vehicle swayed dangerously; and with one accord, the far-side passengers plunged forward to create balance . . . whereby Pigott found himself breathlessly involved with an immense-bosomed female in a magenta cloak. Stibling was more fortunate; despite being thrust away from a small man clutching a clerk's case and uttering squeaks of outrage, he had a clear view of the carriage as they swept past.

"Beg pardon, sir—no offense meant—couldn't 'elp meself," he muttered, straining for a last look, but there was no doubt: that was the traveling chariot of the dowager Marchioness of Bishton. Sinking into his seat, he collected his thoughts. By the time Pigott had disentangled himself from the magenta lady—whose arch giggles and fluttered eyelashes indicated she was inclined to make something of the encounter—Stibling poked his companion in the ribs. "Did you see coach?"

" 'Ow could I?" Pigott snarled, avoiding the magenta lady's eyes.

"It were that marchioness we saw in Cambridge," Stibling said portentously.

"Well, and if it were?"

"Wot's it doing on a back road?"

"And a demmed bad one, too," Pigott muttered. "Why arsk me? *I* don't know."

"Nor I," Stibling agreed, "but in that coach, *in that coach*"—he eyed Pigott commandingly, "there was not two, but *three* females."

"Oooo-er!"

"*And,*" Mr. Stibling continued, " 'ow many outriders did we see in Cambridge?"

"One," said Mr. Pigott after some reflection, "with two postilions, coachman, and three footmen."

"Arrr—but now there's a second outrider. What d'you think on that?"

"Sent ahead to arrange for horses"—Pigott shrugged—"and third woman's another maid, probably already inside. We didn't see the coach pulled forward until the old lady came out. Gord"—as they hurtled around another curve—" 'ow much farther is it? I'm black and blue into me guts."

But shortly the horses were being pulled slower, the coachman was leaning back to yell raucously, "Crossthwaite—get yer traps and be ready!" From long experience, Pigott and Stibling grasped their bags and stumbled to the door. The coach would not, they knew, come to a full halt; the secondary would merely unlatch the door, and the passengers would get off as best they could in return for an unscheduled stop.

Breathlessly, they leaped one after another, and pulling themselves erect, watched the stagecoach disappearing over the hill. In silence they turned to the estate entrance, unconsciously lingering, but there was no sign of the dowager's carriage coming into view. "Paying 'er respects to the Earl of Minchampton." Pigott shrugged at length. "Come on."

Lord Robert received them with ill-concealed distaste, but while all Runners were aware that Bow Street was held in low esteem (no aristocrat ever asked

their aid except as the last resort), in the present instance, Messrs. Pigott and Stibling concluded their in-
terview with Baron Eddystone with equal distaste,
though better concealed. Succinctly, he illustrated his
own course as marked on local section maps, and dismissed them to plan their future action.

"Don't seem as your lordship has left much for us to
do," Stibling observed politely. "You say the girl *has* to
be in this locality, but all's been searched and everyone alerted. Were you wishful we should do it again?"

"How the devil should I know?" Lord Robert returned irritably. "I say my ward is missing—find her.
Do whatever you normally do, and be quick about it."

"Yes, milord." Pigott looked dubious. "But five
days? If you'd called on us sooner . . ."

Lord Robert clenched his jaws. "I wouldn't call on
you now if I'd any choice," he remarked, "and if this
is all you have to say, it appears a waste of time." He
waved his hand toward the study door. "You can use
the servants' hall for consultation."

Silently the Runners bobbed their heads and retired.
"I say it's fishy, *vairy* fishy," Pigott muttered when
they'd spread the maps on the long table for a thorough study. "In London, the servants said the girl was
gone to Surtaine Manor with her guardian; why did he
bring her this road? *He* says he sent back her travel
men because South stage stops at Reddy's, but seems
more like he didn't want 'em to *know* he were taking a
side trip."

"Arrr," Stibling agreed heavily, "and this son, now:
in London, they didn't know *he* was along. If you
want to know what *I* think—*I* think it's more nor
fishy, Pigott. *I* think it's hanky-panky!"

"Exactly my sentiments! Point is: we have to find
the girl." Pigott pursed his lips. "If there's hanky-

panky, it'll be stopped when magistrate gets our report; he'll sort it out. We just find her."

"Where?" Stibling inquired simply. "Baron's been all over, asking. Who'd hide her, and why? That circus sounds the first place, of course—but it was gone over by the constables *and* the revenuers; Lord Robert admits the owner has a clean reputation, offered every help when he asked."

"He still thinks she might be there."

"Why? He mentioned a reward, alive or dead," Stibling countered.

"All the same, start there. Ask about the gypsy Lord Robert says he only saw at a distance, and if the youngsters found any clue in the woods. Talk to Minchampton's keepers, see about dragging ponds," Pigott decided. "Get it out of the way today and tomorrow. She may turn up dead, but if you want to know what *I* think . . ."

Stibling raised his eyebrows. "Arrr?"

"She ran away. Lookee"—Pigott lowered his voice and leaned forward—"he says she didn't feel well, might have slipped out of the coach before they left Reddy's Inn. I think she suspected the hanky-panky! Wot does she do?" dramatically. "She 'ides till they've gone, that's wot, and then she lopes off. But the last place she'd go is this manor, nor she wouldn't go back to London; 'e'd be looking those roads first. No, 'e thinks she'd no money, but 'e don't *know*." Pigott's aitches were scattered to the wind in his intensity. "She might have had plenty o' blunt, and did she not, she'd have jewelry, Stibling."

"Who'd take it for paying a post chaise?" Stibling objected. "Young female with no luggage . . . nobody'd chance her earbobs wasn't stolen."

"I dunno. But," Pigott said out of long and bitter

experience, "young females 'as a way of doing things. They make up tales you wouldn't believe—and find someone to believe 'em! And by his lordship's description, this girl's uncommonly well-favored. You'll see," Pigott prophesied with a sign, "we'll wear out our shoes walking around, and get hoarse from talking to everyone in the vicinity, and all the time, she'll be 'iding in some farmhouse or gone off to stay with an old servant somewheres. I know the gentry, Stibling: very artful they are when pushed. They look at you, feeble-minded and witless, but some of 'em are smart behind it.

"Not all," Pigott added fairly, "but you can't tell which is and which ain't—they all look the same stupid."

Stibling sighed in his turn and stood up. "Well, we better start. . . ."

At about the time the Runners were reaching Crossthwaite, Mrs. Illington's business man was being shown into her morning room. "I trust I see you well?" Mr. Stukes said ingratiatingly, rubbing his hands together and sitting in the chair she indicated. "Yes, yes—well, I have brought some information in answer to your request. There may be more, but I think this will serve to go on with." He extended a sheaf of papers and settled himself comfortably while she rapidly went through them. Mr. Stukes knew better than to offer any assitance to Mrs. Illington, who had a most unfeminine competence in business matters.

She saw now that Lord Robert's affairs, while somewhat tangled, were not nearly so bad as she had feared. The estate was heavily mortgaged, and appeared to produce no more than would satisfy interest payments. Further, the Crossthwaite income seemed only rentals. Clara frowned; did Lord Robert have no crops or stock? She went over the reports again, but found no mention of produce, although the property was (hearteningly) far more extensive than she'd imagined. In addition, his lordship had a small but respectable London residence, and something in the Funds—amount unknown. There was a mortgage on the house; it was not large, and of long standing.

Mrs. Illington frowned again and studied the Crossthwaite mortgages: both were almost equally old. Where was the one Francis had gone north to countersign? Or so he *said;* all her suspicions were revived, plus an extra measure of contempt for such a stupid lie. *If* there were a new mortgage, she conceded it might not yet have been recorded, but Francis had said the baron could not raise more money without his heir's approval. At a glance, that was absurd! Nowhere was any note of interest arrears, Lord Robert could easily refund his obligations by putting any one of the mortgages back to its original figure.

"Well, that is very satisfactory, Mr. Stukes," she said finally. "If you learn anything more, about Sir Francis as well as his father, please let me know."

"Certainly, ma'am." Mr. Stukes smiled to himself, not in the least deceived by her interest in the Eddystones. In fact, he considered Clara his most enjoyable client. Mr. Stukes could recall when Joe Illington had married her, in high fettle at getting his toe in the door. A pity he couldn't have had the son he hoped for, but Clara made him happy. She'd truly loved old Joe, mourned him sincerely, and never forgotten or snubbed his trade friends. At the same time, Mr. Stukes watched her establishment of herself on the edge of the *ton* with admiration. By the way she went about it, he began to feel it was carrying out some private plan between her and Joe.

These Eddystones—a pity she couldn't buy something better, but the title was sound, nothing really *wrong* with either of 'em aside from Lord Robert's intimacy with York and Prinny. Mr. Stukes cleared his throat gently. "Were you considering an investment in mortgages, ma'am? I am not certain any of these would be for sale—would you wish me to inquire?"

Mrs. Illington looked up quickly. "I hadn't thought of that," she murmured, tapping her finger absently on the desk. "Hmmm, yes," she decided. "At least, find out the figure remaining to be paid . . . and do your best to ascertain the Funds?"

"Yes, indeed." Mr. Stukes rose. "I'll bid you good day, Mrs. Illington."

Clara got up too, and extended her hand with a friendly smile. "Thank you so much for coming, you are always the *greatest* help . . . and how is Mrs. Stukes? Pray give her my compliments."

Mr. Stukes was shown out by a very correct footman, and tilting his hat at a jaunty angle, he walked away in search of a hackney. "That Clara," he chuckled silently, "smart as a steel trap—old Joe'd be proud of her!"

Left behind in the morning room, Mrs. Illington was not too proud of herself. "I should have inquired long since, I should have thought of acquiring those mortgages. Now what's to be done?"

Francis' clumsy fabrication worried her more than a bit. If he had not gone to Crossthwaite about a mortgage, why had he gone? There was a ring of truth about that part of it; Francis *had* been at Crossthwaite. It was not connected to Louis de Saumont—Louis hadn't known where Francis was. Could Lord Robert actually have arranged a suitable marriage contract for his son? The baron's affairs seemed not nearly so black as Francis painted them; he might have a tidy fortune in the Funds, which would be nearly impossible to evaluate. For that matter, Francis himself might be far more solvent than he appeared.

The longer she pondered, the more anxious Mrs. Illington grew. "It was a mistake to hint about Louis; he denied everything, of course, but it put him on his guard," she fretted. "I should have gathered something more; now it is only suspicion. Francis won't fear that. He knows that I'll say nothing so long as there's a chance of marriage." Equally, Mrs. Illington had no positive evidence to force that issue, and with a shiver she recalled his reference to Lord Robert's desire for a suitable marriage.

In retrospect, it sounded very sinister. Suppose the baron had managed to find a squint-eyed, pocked, titled heiress, whose family would be willing to settle for Sir Francis Eddystone? Why should they not? If not a grand match, what more could be expected for a girl who must be rated an instant antidote did they try to put her in the marriage market?

"And Francis would agree, if there were enough money," Clara thought gloomily. "I have played the hand entirely wrong."

Later she cheered up slightly. If marriage were in the wind, it must still be in the discussion period. Had a contract been signed, it would have been announced in the *Gazette* by now. Clara had carefully refrained from any word to Francis these past days, until Stukes should inform her of the Eddystone fortunes. It now struck her with a cold chill that Francis had sent no word to *her,* since his dawnlight departure. Did that mean something, or nothing? *Better find out. . . .*

"When there's puzzle, always step up and come to grips," old Joe used to say. "What's t' worst? Find yer been diddled, yer cut yer losses—but come to grips, t' maybe too soon fer other chap. E'll be thrown out in 'is reckoning, gives yer a charnce to mend yer own fences, eh?"

Accordingly, Mrs. Clara wrote a number of notes, declaring herself moped to death and in a mood for a snug dinner with friends. These she dispatched by the footman, and then sent for her chef. In early days, Jean-Baptiste had been shocked by such summonses from the mistress; almost, he had departed this bourgeois establishment, but by a combination of Mrs. Illington's excellent French and her charming smiles, he had been brought to believe these consultations were the highest flattery. The fact that the eventual menu contained few, if any, of his suggestions escaped his notice—but he was French, after all.

By chance, Mrs. Illington's footman encountered Sir Francis Eddystone exactly as Francis was descending the steps from his lodgings. "From Mrs. Illington, sir." The footman presented the envelope, and congratulated himself on being able to report that it was personally delivered, "for he's the acceptance she wants," John told himself knowingly, "and if he comes, we'll be dismissed early to bed. Good-o!"

Francis was not so satisfied. Damnit, why had the man to catch him on the steps? Five minutes earlier, or later, and Clara's invitation would have waited for his return—could have been ignored, or politely declined for "a previous engagement." Now the footman would tell her Sir Francis had received it at half after eleven. Perforce an answer must be sent shortly; it could go from his club, though. "Give me time to think," he told himself. Clara was correct that he had deliberately avoided her, nor had he expected her summons so soon. He had wagered himself he'd hear nothing until she had fully probed the Eddystone finances, and never imagined she could do it so quickly.

That was disturbing in itself, although encouraging that she was not dropping him. By implication, Lord Robert was not yet rolled up. Francis was frankly curious for details his father was too secretive to reveal. Undoubtedly Clara would tell him tonight in the bedchamber; but might this not create a dangerous idea of *alliance* in her mind? Perhaps better not to go —thus delicately emphasizing his allegiance to family, of which Mrs. Illington was not and never would be a member.

On the other hand, it provided an opportunity to see Louis, whom he was equally avoiding, although by pre-arrangement. "You have given her the magnificent red herring, *mon ami,*" Louis chuckled approvingly to Francis' report over the breakfast table, "but I think wiser now to be separate for a while, until the matter arranges itself. Gaston will go to inform the captain of the new meeting place, while I am waiting for the paper. You will go here, I shall go there; we will not be observed together."

But after three days, Louis might have some report of progress which could be innocently imparted tonight. That was dangerous, too; Clara would certainly be watching sharply. Still, there was always that interim when the party took its leave: Francis to walk around the block while she dismissed the servants and waited at the side door for his return. Yes, it was decided: he would go.

Louis' plan of avoiding each other was purely a precaution to confuse Clara in these next critical days. "Someone is sure to remark that Francis and I were in company together, and a woman's imagination will do the rest," he thought irritably. *"Nom de Dieu,* why must the man be so *stupide* as to choose a mistress with claims to respectability!" Had Louis known, he was entirely right to worry about feminine flights of fancy, although it was the dowager Marchioness of Bishton's that posed the real threat.

When Giles had gracefully kissed his grandmother's hand, stepped back for the footman to close the carriage door, and given a final wave as the entourage turned the corner, he felt at a loss. Only ten in the morning, quite too early for any of the *ton* to be abroad . . . even too early for them to have reached the breakfast table. He could go home, and gladden George's heart by doing some work. Giles chuckled wickedly, "More likely to give him a heart attack!" But since he was up and about and wide awake, Giles thought he would be virtuous.

His secretary certainly blinked speechlessly when he discovered the marquis leisurely perusing the *Gazette* behind the study desk. "G-good morning, my lord," he gulped.

"Good morning, George. I trust I see you well? Ah, the mail . . . is there anything of importance?" Giles extended a lazy hand, with a twinkle that made the secretary's lips twitch.

"Not *this* morning," George returned blandly, "which would perhaps permit time for your lordship to glance at certain previous correspondence of more urgency?"

"Exactly what I had in mind! You may bring *everything* to my attention, George—I've nothing better to do for a few hours," and Giles burst out laughing, until the secretary was chuckling helplessly.

Nevertheless, George was lost in admiration for the decisive speed with which his employer went through the accumulation. At a few minutes short of noon, the desk was swept clean, leaving him with enough work to require two weeks of concentration—nor would the marquis expect it completed until it *could* be completed. "Well"—Giles smiled across the bare mahogany —"What more?"

"Nothing," George admitted, "but if your lordship feels at *point non plus,* there is notice of a question to be raised in the House that might be of interest."

"Trevithick's letter to the Board of Agriculture?" Giles nodded, glancing idly at the *Gazette.* "Yes, I see he predicts the use of the steam engine will double the population of the kingdom—and Alversey is objecting to a grant for further development. One sees his point, of course." Giles narrowed his eyes thoughtfully. "With—what is it . . . twelve or fourteen children of his own?—there seems no need for Trevithick's engine, Lord Alversey has the population expansion well in hand . . . or do you suppose his lordship means to suggest a grant might be better employed to develop *him,* on the score of proven results?"

His secretary could no longer restrain his gasps of mirth. "Oh, I wish you would *not,* sir! My sides are aching!"

Giles stood up with a laugh. "All the same, it is an excellent suggestion, George. I've not taken my seat for some time; today bids fair to afford more amusement than usual. I thank you for bringing it to my notice," Giles murmured. "I might even be moved to speak."

"Good God." George controlled himself with a gulp. "You *wouldn't!*"

"Wouldn't I? Well, perhaps not. Alversey's a decent old prose-body," the marquis reflected. "We must see how it strikes me, and you will read the result in tomorrow's *Gazette.* That is all for the moment, George."

"Uh, yes, Lord Bishton." The secretary retired with his armload of papers and stood uneasily for a full two minutes before dropping everything on his own desk. "No, he *won't*—he'd never be so unkind," George said to himself finally, and drew a long breath of relief.

"Not but what it was devilish apt! Damme, but he's a quick wit. . . ."

No, of course the Marquis of Bishton would never cause needless embarrassment to anyone; but as Giles sauntered from his study to be assisted into coat and curly-brimmed beaver, he wistfully savored his irrepressible quip. A pity not to share it; his secretary, he knew, would never repeat a word; for all his enjoyment, George was the soul of discretion. Leisurely descending to the pavement and waving away the sedan chair and hackney competing for his patronage, he strolled toward St. James's Street, enjoying the soft May breeze. A light repast at White's, Giles decided, and demmed if he wouldn't go to Parliament, not merely to hear Alversey, but on the chance of seeing the home secretary. If Giles knew Lord Denning, he'd have set the mills in action early this morning—might already have turned up something. If he hadn't—well, there'd be a certain amusement in observing the faces of his peers when the Marquis of Bishton took his seat!

And so there was, partcularly when he glimpsed the placid countenance of Lord Alversey on the facing benches. How any man could look so much like a sheep! "Demonstrably he's a ram." Giles suppressed a chuckle. "Damme, the person who'd really enjoy it is m' grandmother." She'd be tooling along through Luton, reaching Cambridge for tea. What a game old biddy she was, pluck to the backbone, alive on any suit; but she'd like Araminta.

Then he composed himself to listen to the debates, which were as dull as always. Lord Alversey raised his question, but it developed that his opposition was based on a desire for more explicit information. When this was (rather passionately) produced by a staunch Trevithick supporter, his lordship arose to withdraw his objection and formally endorse "this worthy project that will carry forward all the efforts of myself and my distinguished colleagues for the increased growth and sound future of our nation."

By now the marquis was silently commenting, "Ah, thinks *he's* done enough for the increase—feeling tired —can't expect *one* man to do it all, let youth take the torch from failing hands and continue the race. Hmmm, I wager Lady Alversey will be happy to learn that!" He felt slightly ashamed of his irreverence, however enjoyable, and to everyone's intense astonishment, found himself rising to his feet with a graceful bow to Alversey.

"I must applaud my noble colleague, both for requesting a more precise explanation on the use of the funds and for his foresight in grasping the potential advantages to our land through development of Mr. Trevithick's engines." ("Hear, hear!" from the staunch supporter.) "In this time of total confusion engendered by the French emperor on the Continent . . . complicated by the economic loss of the colonies . . . it is inspiring—I repeat, milords: *inspiring*—that among us are still those capable of leadership to the future!

"Picture, if you will"—Giles was sternly controlling inner laughter at the effect of his oratory; even the Duke of Ramsay was awake—"the benefits to be gained if *England* achieves superiority in a new method of transport that will send our goods more quickly to the harbors. We shall be a century in advance of all Europe!" (A chorus of "Hear, hear!" from the facing benches, where Lord Alversey sat openmouthed.) "It is *our* ships, *our* produce, *our* manufactories that will be needed to repair the ravages of war, milords—think on the financial gains, can we be enabled to speed that supply!"

While his Majesty's Loyal Opposition was nodding and shouting "Hear, hear!" Giles's Tory neighbors were begging him "For God's sake, be *quiet!* You're all about in your head, Bishton—the damned thing doesn't work!"

"That's not to say it *wouldn't* if Trevithick has enough money to tinker with it," Glies said perversely. "I put it to you, milords: *all* these inventions are the work of *Englishmen,* or Scots or Welsh, but *our* countrymen." Giles threw out his hand dramatically and declaimed, "Shall *we* overlook their contribution, *their* efforts for their country?" ("Hear, hear, hear!") "I say *no,* milords! Ours is the sacred responsibility to guide, to preserve, to oversee our lands, but always to exercise wise encouragement of those among the lesser orders who provide our trade—without which we cannot live, milords. It ought to be—it *must* be—our deep concern to aid those who will give us, through their inventions, increased opportunity to achieve that solid, that undoubted superiority England has always enjoyed!" (General pandemonium of "Hear, hear!")

"And I wish you would stop pulling my coattails, Evelyn," the marquis added serverly. "Damme, you've all wasted far more money on far less promising ventures. Why, you even voted for that Home for Indigent Females, and six months later it proved to be a flourishing bordello!" When the roar of laughter subsided, "I say: give Trevithick his grant. Whether or not he can get the thing to work, it won't spread the pox about London."

The motion was carried almost unanimously.

Before Giles could make his way from his seat, Lord Alversey had scrambled across to seize his hand warmly. "Thankee, thankee, Bishton! Couldn't have put it better meself. Well, it's heartening to find a youngster ready to take up the standard, damme!" The old man beamed, clapping Giles on the shoulder. "Take a glass of wine with me in the 'tiring room?"

"May I claim it another time, sir?" Giles had caught the flicker of an eyelid from the home secretary as Lord Denning left his place. "I've pressing duties; I'm already behind the time."

"Of course, of course." Alversey nodded. "Sometime when we can sit down together for a serious talk. Yes, yes! I must say, Bishton, I'd no notion you were so informed, so earnest in promoting the new inventions—for they'll save the country, y'know! *Vital* to forge ahead! Make hay while the sun shines and Boney's back is turned, eh?"

"Exactly so, sir." Giles extricated himself with a bow and a smile, feeling decidedly ashamed of himself. By the time he'd run a gamut of congratulations on "Demmed good speech!" and "Must say, I never thought you had it in you, boy, but demmed if you didn't swing the entire House!" the Marquis of Bishton wore a rueful face when he encountered the home secretary.

"What the devil possessed you?" Lord Denning demanded.

"I was apologizing, mentally."

"For *what,* in heaven's name?" But when Giles had told him, the home secretary laughed even more heartily than George Graham. "Oh, by Jove—famous, famous! No, I'll not repeat it—you know better."

"I wondered if anything had come to light?"

"Nothing definite—it's to be fully investigated, of course. They'll put out a couple of men to observe." Denning shrugged. "I'll keep you informed, Bishton."

Since the home secretary was a man of his word, this was how the marquis learned two days later that although Francis and Louis de Saumont had neither met nor communicated, Lord Robert Eddystone was still at Crossthwaite and had requested the aid of Bow Street in the matter of a missing person.

CHAPTER 8

While Pigott and Stibling were beginning their investigations, the dowager's coach was traveling swiftly across country and reached Transome in time for late tea. If her ladyship's staff wondered at a beautiful young lady without luggage, they were far too well trained to raise the question. The dowager marchioness herself, however, had been giving the matter some thought, and as soon as Araminta had been taken away to her chamber, her ladyship rang for her dresser.

"You may sit down, Crims," she stated regally. "I shall need your help."

"Yes, milady." Perched genteelly on the edge of a chair, Miss Crims exhibited none of her quivering excitement or preening satisfaction in being chosen for confidante.

"Miss Surtaine is the daughter of a family long our friends. She has not previously come in my way; it was her grandparents I knew, of course. They are now dead, as also her parents. By chance, I learned that she had suffered a carriage accident, from which she was saved and faithfully cared for by local people. I made haste, as you know"—the dowager smiled—"to come to her aid . . . for you must know, Crims, there is a certain loss of memory."

"Oh, milady!" Miss Crims's eyes widened with pleasurable shock. "Such a sweet pretty little thing!"

"Exactly. The doctors believe it to be temporary, but meanwhile it is best for her to be in proper surroundings. While Transome itself is unfamiliar, the ordering of the household must aid in reminding her of similarity with the past, which the circus people—

good and true as they were—could not do." Her lady-ship looked solemnly at the maid, lowering her voice confidentially. "I believe them to be of unusually high reputation, Crims. Certainly they have behaved throughout with the utmost kindness, and the boys, you know—for all their rough clothing—you noticed they were clean? There was even a certain *manner* in the one named Alfie."

"Oh, yes, milady—quite a good bow he made—and by what she was saying in the carriage . . . for I couldn't help overhearing, milady . . . she was quite enjoying her stay. But of course, she'll be better here."

"Exactly," the dowager approved. "Now, I shall need your help in two matters, Crims. First, we must contrive some clothing, for all her luggage was de-stroyed in the accident, you know. I believe any *per-sonal* visits to tradesmen might be too great a strain for her, so I shall charge you to drive alone to Peter-borough and select enough to go on with. Who could better be trusted?" Her ladyship smiled warmly. "You have always displayed a nicety of taste that has been the greatest comfort to me, Crims!"

"Oh, milady—I'm sure!" Miss Crims went scarlet, beaming and bridling at the compliment, the while she modestly disclaimed.

"Nonsense! After thirty years together, you and I know each other very well," the dowager remarked with a chuckle. "Now, the second thing is to prevent any undue curiosity or chatter. I fancy it will suffice merely to repeat the gist of what I have told you. Some curiosity there must be, naturally, but your demeanor will do much to satisfy the staff that there is no reason to gossip."

"Indeed there is not, milady, nor we don't permit it in our hall," Miss Crims returned firmly. "Mr. Royle is very strict on it . . . and it comes to me: there's the frocks and undergarments outgrown by Miss Adela last summer. Lady Eleanor bade me discard, but I'd not give such fine things to the *tweeny,* milady, who's the only one could wear 'em. I'll warrant we'll find something for Miss Surtaine, until I can visit the shops."

"An excellent suggestion! I knew I might rely upon you, Crims!"

Thus easily did Araminta slip into the life of Transome. Clad in a hastily pressed schoolgirl frock of sprigged muslin, with her silky black hair nicely brushed on the curling stick and caught into a fashionable topknot, she enjoyed an excellent dinner. Observing Minta's perfect manners, the dowager thought herself more clever than she knew. What had been a smooth fiction to Crims was proving true: Araminta *was* regaining snippets of memory in a well-appointed dining salon with the usual complement of servants.

"I fancy food never tastes so good as when one has been traveling," she observed. "Do not you think the squabs particularly delicious tonight, ma'am? Pierre has a special way with squabs, as well as the trifle of cock's combs. I must send him my compliments." She looked innocently at her hostess. "As Mrs. Hobson says, it is such a *little* thing, but it means so much to Pierre that I have *noticed.*"

"You are quite right, my dear. A word of appreciation often means more than a salary."

Throughout the meal, the dowager found herself acquiring a number of such fleeting memories, from which she constructed a very satisfactory picture of Araminta's background. The child was still confused between past and present. At one moment she spoke of what was obviously her London establishment, and at the next she talked of the circus caravan. The baked river eel in parsley sauce reminded her of fishing with Alfie and Joe . . . but brought a shiver at its end.

"Sally said it was my guardian, but I cannot like him, ma'am."

"You need not worry, Lord Eddystone's trusteeship will end very shortly."

Araminta accepted a single glass of white wine, refused replenishment of her glass. "Delicious!" She sipped dreamily. "Giles gave me a glass of Madeira—it was the night he found me, you know. I expect he told you, ma'am?"

"Yes, he told me everything." The dowager nodded calmly. "We were so relieved to learn your safety. I came at once to get you, but at my age"—she smiled ruefully—"it was still several days. However, we knew you to be well cared for."

"Oh, no people could be kinder, ma'am—for I did not know who I was, nor where, nor what had occurred." Minta's lip quivered.

"Don't think on it, my dear," the dowager said authoritatively. "It will come back naturally; no need to press yourself."

The beautifully glazed strawberry tarts were another memory. "I don't know," Minta said, "they are very good—but d'you know, ma'am, I fancy the fresh fruit has a different savor. Alfie brought a great basket full, with fresh cream—it was the morning he got El Cid—and I think nothing was ever more delicious."

"El Cid—it seems an unusual name for a kitten."

"I expect he will have to grow up to it, ma'am." Araminta dimpled. "But I wanted a name for a knight in shining armor, you know. I did think of 'Giles,' for he was there that night, and it was all so comfortable, but I thought perhaps he might not quite like to be a godfather to a *cat*." Minta chuckled infectiously. "Although it might have passed off, for you must know he has the greatest sense of humor, ma'am! But, however, it was not truly apt in any case, for he has red hair."

"Do you dislike it?"

"No, indeed, ma'am!" Araminta stared into space, holding her fork suspended. "It is not really *red*—it is more the color of a lovely autumn sunset, is it not? For I collect you are well acquainted. Sally told me Giles had arranged all."

"He did so." The dowager laid aside her napkin as Minta finished the final bite of strawberry tart. "Let us remove to the salon. Bring the tea tray as soon as may be, Royle. I fancy we shall seek our beds early, after the journey."

"Oh"—Minta halted—"the compliments for Pierre, ma'am?"

"Very true—I had forgot." Her ladyship turned to the butler. "You will deliver our appreciation to the chef, if you please."

"Certainly, milady." By not so much as a hair did the butler indicate that Lady Bishton's chef was not Pierre, but Jean-Louis.

When they were settled in the salon before a cozy fire, conversation dwindled. The dowager Marchioness of Bishton was overtaken by drowsiness, a natural result of swaying about in a coach for some hours combined with innocent prattle to which she must attend, followed by a warm repast. Her eyelids drooped, her head nodded and moved sideways to rest against the wing of her chair. She did not snore.

Araminta sat still; she had a vague sense that she ought to be doing something, and yet here—in this great house full of servants—it seemed quite normal to sit idle. Lady Bishton was right that similar, if unfamiliar, surroundings would be helpful. Minta was beginning to remember. At first it was principally by contrast. Black Jack's entire caravan would have fitted comfortably in the center of this salon, but while Minta felt perfectly at home among the elegant furnishings, she had a growing sense that the salon to which she had been accustomed was far smaller.

After a while she got up and moved quietly about to look at the ornaments and pictures. Surely she should recognize *something* in her grandmother's home? Intently examining the French mantel clock, the branched silver candlesticks, even the arrangement of furniture and the deep green brocade draperies, Araminta was increasingly troubled. All that seemed in any way familiar was a fawn leatherbound book, *Sense and Sensibility*. Yes! She picked it up eagerly, she distinctly recalled reading this. The heroines were Marianne and Elinor, but when she opened the volume, there was a book plate. It bore a coat of arms surmounted by a coronet, and the lettering was "Elizabeth Marchioness of Bishton."

Araminta softly laid it down, and continued her tour with deep discouragement. Everyone *said* she would remember in time, but when? It seemed most shocking of all that she should not recognize her own grandmother. Minta was trembling inside, on the verge of tears, by the time she'd reached the farther end of the salon; and there, hanging on the wall above a delicate escritoire, was a miniature. Unmistakably, it was Giles! With a gasp of relief, she removed it from the hook and stood looking at it, struggling for memory.

Here, within the gold frame studded with brilliants, his expression was more serious than on the night she'd waked in the caravan. Strange—she could recall his deep voice, the merry twinkle, the long slender steel-strong fingers pouring her wine and cutting the bread; he had seemed to know her, called her "Meg." Sally'd said he'd arranged for her to visit her grandmother. . . .

What was his miniature doing here, then? Could he be a cousin? If so, why would he not call her "Minta"?

Perhaps they had feared it harmful to say too much before she was well; and yet, and yet . . . She could feel herself beginning to shake inside, beginning to be positive she had never seen any of these people before. Then where was she, who were they?

Behind her was the clink of china, a sputter of embers as the fire was mended, the dowager's voice. "Eh? Oh, thank you, Royle. Araminta? Tea, my love."

Slowly Minta returned to her seat; she *did* feel safe, but if this dear old lady was not her grandmother, *who was she?*

"Will you pour, my dear? I'm still half-asleep." Her ladyship smothered a yawn and shook herself erect in the wing chair, to smile at Araminta.

"Yes, ma'am. Please, ma'am"—Minta was still clutching the miniature, her gray eyes fixed anxiously on the dowager—"th-they said you were my grandmother, but . . . but I think it cannot be true. I could not have forgotten you—*could* I?"

Lady Bishton was fully, warily awake in an instant. Her sharp glance took in the miniature pressed to Araminta's bosom, and knew it for Giles's without needing to see it. Truth would be best, she decided. "No, no, I am *Giles's* grandmother," she said calmly. "What a stupid mistake! Did it worry you, child? I am sorry for it." *Giles* was evidently the "Open Sesame" for Araminta. She laid aside the miniature with a sigh of relief, and filled the cups quite naturally. "No, no," the dowager continued smoothly, "you must know I used to be a friend to *your* grandmother, my dear, and upon finding you at the circus, Giles recalled the fact. We thought it best to bring you to stay here quietly with me for a time, for you have no relatives, my love."

"Yes," Araminta said unexpectedly, "I *do* remember that now. It is why I have been living with Mrs.

Hobson, who is very nice, but she is paid, you know
. . . and there was Miss Benbridge, who taught me
things. She was the greatest fun, not at all like a governess. We used to run away together and do all sorts of
things that would have sent Hobby into the vapors!"
She chuckled. "We went to a zoo, and the tigers were
all asleep—it is how I knew it would be safe to get
Johnny out of Sinbad's cage at the circus, although
everyone thought I was so brave!" Araminta chuckled
again. "And once Benny took me and Jane to a
country circus—it was when we were staying with
Lady Urbaugh, and I think she was not best pleased,
but Benny talked her around." Araminta's face grew
pensive. "I was almost sorry to grow out of the school-
room, ma'am, for they said Miss Benbridge must go,
I'd no more need of her—but it wasn't true!

"I should have liked her to be with me when I make
my season, for she could have told me exactly how to
go on, you know. She had had a season of her own, or
at least *part,* but from some reason or other, her father
was in financial difficulties and all had to be abandoned," Minta said regretfully. "It was the greatest
pity, for then he died, and it proved necessary for her
to earn her living."

Lady Bishton was digging in the recesses of her
mind: Benbridge? Good God, was he not the one who'd
rolled up and shot himself on the steps when his lady-
bird's butler refused to admit him? And his daughter
reduced to *penury?* "How *very* sad," she said to Araminta, and extended her cup. "May I have more
tea, my dear? I can understand your sorrow at losing
her, but certainly Miss Benbridge must have gone to an
excellent position."

Araminta frowned while she refilled the cups. "I
wrote a glowing recommendation, and so did Hobby,
but could any position compensate for the loss of her

chance to be suitably established?" she asked simply. "I should have liked to keep her with me, where she could be certain of kind treatment—and you know, ma'am, it might have been possible for her to find a husband, for she was not above thirty, and looked far less. I could have given her a few thousand pounds' dowry; I should not miss it, I am very rich; at least"— her face was uncertain—"I *think* I am."

"Yes, you are." Lady Bishton nodded calmly, accepting her teacup and sitting very quietly in her chair. She'd have liked to go to bed, but if Araminta were beginning to remember, it was better to encourage it. "I collect you lived in London?"

"Number 14, Mount Street," Araminta murmured automatically, sitting down once more. "It is in no way so fine as this, ma'am, but as Mrs. Hobson said, it will not be necessary to have larger accommodations, for Lady Urbaugh is to present me with her own daughter Jane. I shall need only suitable reception chambers for formal calls, or tea. Without a relative to play host or hostess, I cannot *entertain* but in the simplest fashion." She sighed. "Which is a pity, for Pierre is quite an exceptional chef."

"But once your acquaintance is enlarged, I fancy there will often be impromptu supper parties, or refreshments needed for an informal gathering. Pierre will find himself busy enough," said the dowager. "And when do you make your curtsy?"

"It could have been this year, but"—Minta's voice slowed, her eyes wandered—"but . . . there was some objection, I forget what it was. However, it was as well, for Jane is younger, you know, and it will be all the better for us to share our season next year."

"Yes, it is twice the fun when one has a particular friend. And now"—Lady Bishton drained her cup and set it aside—"I think we shall dismiss ourselves to bed,

Araminta. It has been a long, exhausting day for both of us, and we will be the better for a good night's sleep."

A number of other people involved in the drama of Araminta felt the same way—notably Pigott and Stibling, although Lord Robert and his son were not far behind in their separate ways. The Bow Street Runners had divided responsibility quite simply, on the basis of Pigott's seniority: he would have the farm gig and cart horse; Stibling would walk the ditches and speak with the Earl of Minchampton's keepers. "Tomorrow you can have horse and cart," Pigott offered handsomely, to which Stibling nodded gloomily; but after a half-mile, it became obvious that the horse was no Derby entrant.

Striding along the edge of the road, Stibling was easily able to keep pace with Pigott in the wagon. "If you're going that slow, I might as well come up with you and rest me backside," he pointed out finally. "You'll set me down at the earl's entrance gates." When they parted company, Pigott ambled along until he turned into the circus approach. He had painstakingly figured out a story, which he gave to Black Jack when he'd got up to the center of the caravans.

"Afternoon," Pigott said politely. "I'm looking for a young female named Meg, or it might be Peg, who was in stagecoach accident awhile back. Owners are hoping she might be able to give us some information on exactly what happened."

Jack shook his head. "We've no one here of that name," he began, and Sally smoothly added, "who's been in any accident, that is. I suppose you've heard of our famous equestrienne, Gypsy Meg?"

"Arrr," Pigott agreed eagerly. He could hardly believe the luck! "that'd be the name. Could I have a word with her?"

"Of course," Sally said cordially. "She'll be resting for the performance. Bess, step around to the equestrienne's caravan and ask Gypsy Meg if she'll be so good as to come out to us?" With a nod, Bess disappeared, to return shortly with one of the riders.

"Yer want me? Wotever for?" she inquired stridently.

Pigott gulped. The baron had described his ward as a beauty, with black hair and gray eyes; this girl was as coarse in features as in voice; her hair was light brown, her eyes were pale blue, and she was at least thirty. "You are Gypsy Meg?" Lamely he repeated his story of a coach accident, and upon her denial of being the passenger, instantly climbed back into the wagon and departed. He was too downcast to observe the glee he left behind him.

"Oooo-er! Thanks, Polly—you were grand!"

"Better to be rid of 'un for good. I doubt he'll be back, but for a few days Tam'll introduce me as Gypsy Meg. That's a Runner, for sure," Polly returned wisely, "and they'd work a pair on this."

"Aye," Jack agreed, "and we ain't seen t'other one. He might come to a performance, innocent-like, and wonder what's become of that famous equestrienne, Gypsy Meg," at which they all laughed heartily, but when Polly had lounged away to her caravan, he sighed. "Thank the Lord we got the little miss safely away! Did you see envelope Alfie brought? 'Tis fifty pounds! 'To divide as you think best among those who saved and cared for Miss Surtaine.' What d'you think on *that!*"

"Generous!" Bess approved. "Not that she was a trouble, and Sam would have give *her* as much for saving his baby. What'll you do with money, Jack?"

"Put it by safely, half for Alfie and half for Joe—but

say nothing," Jack said slowly. "Do Joe's pa learn, he'll take t' money, go off to a boozing ken, Joe'll have no good of it."

"Money!" Sally's eyes widened; horror-stricken, she turned to Bess, who clapped a hand to her mouth in sudden memory. "What became on't?"

" 'Tis still under tiger, I forgot . . ." Bess whirled and darted toward Sinbad's cage, to feel in the costume bunk beneath.

"What's this?" Jack asked, bewildered, when she came back with Araminta's reticule.

The women were busily counting and comparing notes. " 'Tis all here, thank heavens!" Sally sighed. "Saving only the gold piece we took for clothes."

"What are you saying?" Jack frowned.

" 'Tis hers, Jack. We found it when we undressed her: a hundred and fifty pounds . . . and all her jewelry. 'Tis simple, for a *young* lady, but 'tis good of its kind."

"We counted together," Bess inserted, "but best to say nothing. Nobody'd take, but 'tis a large sum—enough to cause gossip—and when constable came, we put reticule with the girl in costume bunk, and forgot it when we brought her out to doctor. Oh, me, what's to do?"

Silently they contemplated Araminta's assets. "We could write to say it's safe, did we have a direction," Bess offered. Sally shook her head. "We've none but this Surtaine Manor. Should we send there?"

"Scare 'em into fits, do they get her reticule anonymous-like," Jack said briefly. "No, I'll put away, and ask Mr. Giles. 'Tis no matter when it's returned, so long as it *is*."

Upon leaving Pigott, Mr. Stibling presented himself to the Earl of Minchampton's gate keeper, saying he'd been sent to assist in the search for the little girl. The gate keeper's wife was an affable chatty soul, pleasurably titillated by the loss of Araminta. "You'll find children's walking back and forth across woods in home forest. Keepers are up t' mire, making ready to drag 'un. Eh, it's a good thing his lordship's from home," she remarked, rolling her eyes dramatically skyward, "for what he'd say I *don't* like to think!

"Not that he'd refuse permission to look on his land when 'tis question of a person lost—a grand old gentleman, he is," she said affectionately. "But to say truth, he's no opinion of Baron Eddystone."

Out of this, Stibling picked the earl's absence. "Arrr, he'd dislike to be stravaged for *that* one?" he deduced with a knowing wink. "Well, perhaps he'll know naught of it. Least said, soonest mended, eh?"

"Oh, keeper'll tell him in the report, but he'll not be back for several months," she said comfortably. "He always removes to Harrowgate on the first of May—for the waters—and goes on to his daughter in Scotland for the grouse shooting. Makes it easy on us. Why, aside from this start over the little girl—the baron and constables and I don't know who all—there's been nobody ringing bell for near three weeks."

As Stibling followed the path she indicated, he filed away the fact that the dowager Marchioness of Bishton had *not* paid her respects to the Earl of Minchampton. "Where'd she go?" he inquired, when Pigott returned from his fruitless tour. "She weren't on the road behind us; we waited long enough to see."

"There's a turn-off to the turnpike, about a mile beyond the circus." Pigott shrugged wearily. "She'd go that way."

"Arr—but why'd she take *this* road, if she were meaning to go back to the highway?" Stibling insisted. "Miles out of the way, and God knows it ain't surfaced fit for man nor beast!"

"Coo-er, it ain't!" Pigott muttered feelingly. "You're thinking the old lady come along and picked up the girl—but where'd she been all these days?"

"In the circus, of course! Never mind it was searched, I got enough at Minchampton that says there ain't no one in this here vicinity'd tell Eddystone the time o' day." Stibling lowered his voice earnestly. "I say the circus owner took her in, and sent word to London that'd be about right, Pigott: allow two days to get a letter down, and another two days for the old lady to get up here."

"It could be, but why?"

" 'Ow should I know? Maybe she 'ates the baron, too."

Pigott growled, but when Lord Robert disavowed all acquaintance with the dowager Marchioness of Bishton, he returned from his report session in discouragement. "Proper starched up, he was, cursing me up and down, but damned if I see where to go next," he said glumly.

"Didn't you get *nothing?*"

"Nah, this Gypsy Meg's a horse rider—and seen better days, if you arsk me. What abaht you?"

"Gord, I walked me legs off with them young varmints, and don't tell me they didn't hand-scoop enough trout for dinner! Polite as yer please," Stibling snorted, "but they was all over the place—a hundred of 'em, or seemed like. All looking as like as two peas, you couldn't tell which was who. They did a thorough job, though, and she ain't anywhere in Minchampton's woods. The biggest lad, name of Alfie, says there's another stretch, other side of the road; they'll do that tomorrow morning, and then they'll go along the sea coast.

"Acted like it was a holiday outing." Stibling massaged his aching calves with a groan. "Howsomever, the keepers said them young 'uns won't miss an inch, nor no one won't refuse 'em for miles around; and if they pick up a rabbit or a cock pheasant on the way, call it pay for the work. Eddystone should have got 'em out first day, say the keepers, but I'm thinking them children knows well enough she'll not be found.

"Keepers dragged the mire, and a demmed hard job it was," Stibling finished, "wot with his High-and-Mightiness standing there, giving orders—went stamping off in a filthy temper, with not so much as the price of a pint all round for the work. I'll tell yer wot, Pigott: I don't like this case!"

"Nor me neither," Pigott grunted. "They're none of 'em so to speak *savory,* or we wouldn't be called, but this here's downright smelly. Listen"—he leaned forward, lowering his voice—"we ain't seen aught but the study—the Martins say house is closed, he don't come here above once in a year—*but* seems Peculiar there ain't more'n one old horse and farm cart in the stable. That coach—that's the *girl's* carriage; he ain't got one, just a curricle for London."

Stibling rubbed his nose thoughtfully. "Well, of course, he'd not need more—at his age and with no family females."

"He did have one, though," Pigott returned, "and laid it up two years ago, according to the stableman. Nor he ain't got a groom now in London, only a valet. *You* say he didn't give the keepers nothing, and *I* tell you I'd the devil's work to get five guineas out o' him for expenses—what does that say to you?"

"He's rolled up," Stibling said promptly. "This ward's his meal ticket. Of course," he added fairly, "he could just be one o' these misers."

Pigott hitched himself even farther forward. "And if I was to tell you," he muttered portentously, "there was someone else 'ere that night—a Mr. Hankins, wot arrived by stage in the afternoon, same like us—then wot'd you say?"

"Ooo-er! The hanky-panky! How'd you find that?"

"Mrs. Martin—she and her husband don't suspicion nothing; honest, they are, and not given to gossip, but 'appening to learn she's from Thetford and my wife's cousin the same, of course," Mr. Pigott said innocently, "it made a difference."

"But you ain't got a wife. . . ."

"If I did 'ave, she might 'ave a cousin in Thetford," Pigott returned with dignity. "Anyways, Mrs. Martin says his lordship sent word the week before. She was to open *four* chambers, and provision for three days."

"A *week's* notice? Blimey, it were hanky-panky, right enough," Stibling murmured worriedly. "He's saying it were last minute, he meets the son by chance, and decides to detour this road for a personal look—no need to bring her servants, when all's so close—and now we find it's always planned. Queers me why he'd tell such a tale; he should have known Mrs. Martin'd give it the lie."

"She wouldn't, except for me wife's cousin." Pigott grinned. "Makes all different, see? She don't personally *know* the woman; I ain't sure of the marriage name, but she feels more comfortable with me, see? So she tells me this Hankins is a seedy gentleman who's well-spoken, knows his fork from his knife, enjoys his wine and likes the brandy bottle even better . . . to a point they've to bring a fresh bottle when the Eddystones arrived.

"And when it's discovered the girl's missing, she ain't found all next day, Lord Robert rings a peal over his son for stupidity, and packs him back to London *with* this Hankins the morning after," Pigott finished. "Now wot d'yer say?"

Stibling looked about cautiously and leaned to his

partner. "I say it's money," he whispered. "She's got it, he needs it, and this Hankins is a lawyer or notary or something; and wot's more, I say I don't like it!"

Lord Robert wasn't liking it, either. He'd expected to stay no more than three days; it was almost a week, for which he was unprepared with funds. Added to his anxiety over Araminta was a furious resentment to be forced to expand money on rented horses, on a kitchen helper for Mrs. Martin, on food and reimbursement for the Runners. He was worn to the bone, aching in every joint from constant driving, and bored with solitude, but after so many years' absence from the locality, he had no more than formal acquaintances. It was not a *ton* neighborhood, in any case; hereabouts were only squires and a few petty knights, preoccupied with the management of their trifling estates. It was why he had gradually removed to London, particularly when the need for corsets had made hunting inadvisable.

Now there was no one to say "Come and eat your mutton with us." Expressions of honest concern for his predicament there certainly were, as well as immediate orders for search and reports delivered by grooms or stableboys: "Please to tell his lordship we'm gone all over and found nothing." Their masters bowed civilly if passing Lord Robert in his carriage, but did not halt for converse. The nearest market town was ten miles, and while he was politely made free of the country club, it contained no gaming room, and the single copy of the *Gazette* was twenty-four hours old.

Tonight he was more than commonly irritated— from the morning's drive to arrange for a draft on his London bankers, the afternoon's atteandance while Minchampton's keepers dragged the mire. He had, for some reason, become convinced that Araminta's lifeless body would be recovered, and the discovery of nothing more than an ancient hunting boot was frustration. Stibling's description of his lordship's filthy temper was only the half of it. The carriage road on the earl's estate did not pass the mire; its nearest approach left a full two miles of walking over woodland paths.

To Lord Robert, who never walked more than the length of St. James's Street, such an extent of rusticity was endurable only in the expectation that it was the final effort required of him. His expression was already composed for melancholy, his handkerchief ready for application to the eyes, and the realization—after two hours of standing about—that he must retrace two miles to the carriage *without* a corpse to show for it. . . . Good God!

If Araminta were not dead, it followed she must be alive—somewhere. Could someone have done away with her and secretly buried the body? Lord Robert thought not; after the intensive search in this locality, any freshly turned earth would have been discovered. Had she been kidnapped? Might there already be a ransom demand waiting for him in London? He was tempted to go back at once, but if there were no such word, he would only encounter awkward questions. Finally, he sent an express to Francis, requesting him to investigate whatever messages had arrived in the past few days.

After which, his lordship went to bed. So much *thinking* had made him tired. . . .

By the time Lord Robert's letter reached his son next morning, Sir Francis was equally tired. Clara's snug little dinner had been delicious, as always, but there was a certain archness in her manner that made him uneasy. Louis' eyes were sharp with caution, and he took care to exchange no word with Francis that could not be overheard by Mrs. Illington. Altogether the evening was a decided strain, with more to come, if her sidelong glances were any gauge. The only relief was her faint surprise that Louis took his leave a full quarter-hour in advance of Francis. Hah, they had diddled her! Francis even dared to protest the window-dressing of departure and secret return, feeling confident Clara would not permit him to remain while she dismissed the servants—nor did she, "as if they didn't *know*," he thought cynically, the while he was kissing her hand formally and murmuring, "Later!"

At the corner, a shadow parted from other shadows and stepped alongside him. *"Alors, mon copain,"* Louis said softly, "I will give myself the pleasure of a saunter with you. A breath of fresh air to clear the head for the bedchamber, eh?"

"Nothing is better for sending you to sleep quickly after a social evening," Francis agreed with a straight face that drew an appreciative chuckle from his companion. He had never yet admitted in so many words that there was any intimacy with Mrs. Illington, a discretion that deeply amused Louis.

"Oh, you English!" he said now. "Always so correct, so silent on what everyone knows."

"But cannot swear," Francis returned blandly. "I cannot be responsible for your romantic French imagination, after all, but in a court of law—let us say, for breach of promise?—what could you testify?"

"Sapristi!" said Louis after a moment. "You are right, *mon vieux:* I know, but I do *not* know, there is nothing I could say. You have been more clever than I realized; but there is not this possibility of a suing, is there?"

"Lord, no—for what d'you take me, Louis? I'm no lamb for the fleecing!"

"Du vrai, you are no lamb!" Louis chuckled, and went serious. "I have the paper, Gaston has arranged in Portsmouth: the ship is already under weigh, should reach your stretch of coast in two—at most three—days. *C'est convenable pour vous?"*

"Yes." Francis clenched his teeth. "Must I go to Paris, or is there any chance of meeting someone sooner? Have you had any news?"

"Yes, and all goes well, but it must be Paris. *Je* regrette . . ."

"All right, it's the last time. Give me the paper."

"I have not brought it." Louis sounded shocked. "One does not walk about with such things, *mon ami.* Besides, you will be . . . occupied, and when you are *disrobé,* who knows what might occur? As you say, I know nothing, but my imagination tells me it will be better that you come to pick up this paper in the early dawn, eh?"

"D'accord," Francis said mechanically. "I'll go north tomorrow night, or the next day. I suppose Dubois will send word when he's at anchor? It's a good four miles from Crossthwaite to our cove; I can't be trotting that way every day without being noted; night's best, in any case."

"Have no fear, Dubois will arrange. *Alors, à toute à l'heure* . . ." Louis shook hands heartily and turned away at the next corner while Francis continued around the block.

Two inconspicuous black shadows sped forward. "Well, 'ere's where I leave yer," said one cheerfully. The other sighed. "Yer lucky. Mine ain't bound for home this road. Gord, don't these people never rest? 'E's been on the toddle since noon, except to put on his dinner clothes."

"Arrr, by the looks of it, 'e'll be resting snug somewhere," his fellow rejoined with a vulgar wink, "and don't yer wish yer with 'im?"

"Depends . . . by the looks of 'im, we ain't got the same taste in females. Anyways, I think I'm too tired."

Unaware of his unobtrusive companion, Sir Francis continued. "Ooo-er, so she *is* the one," the shadow said to itself when Francis had silently disappeared. "Now, is 'e quick, or is 'e fancy?" With a sigh, the man settled himself to wait behind a luxuriant syringa bush, his eyes on the infinitesimal but telltale lightness behind the upper-right-corner draperies. No sound broke the darkness, dim-lit by the low-hanging, overripe moon. The observer suppressed a gigantic yawn, shook his eyes open with determination, yawned again . . . and was shortly asleep.

Thereby he missed the quiet departure of Sir Francis Eddystone, neither observed nor observing the unfamiliar dark hump under the shrubbery.

Francis walked away briskly in the dawn, feeling the most tremendous relief—not merely physical, but mental. God, Clara had played directly into his hands! She'd not admitted any knowledge of Lord Robert's affairs, but "I have been thinking, Francis, and I believe you should go back to Crossthwaite as soon as may be. There is certainly some lack of management —perhaps a change of bailiff would set all straight."

He'd made a show of reluctance. "How can I interfere?" And shortly, she was *urging* him to make a proper inspection, at least. Slowly he allowed himself to be half-convinced the journey was necessary, "but the time must be chosen carefully—when I am certain he is not there. It will be a matter of seizing the moment."

"Yes, of course," but her final reminder was (with a lingering kiss) not to forget Crossthwaite.

"Hah, it'd serve her right if she had to live there!"

Francis chuckled sardonically as he quietly knocked on the rear door of Louis de Saumont's lodgings. Admitted by a sleep-bleared Gaston, he went upstairs to shake Louis awake. "Give me the paper and the directions."

"Nom d'un nom," the Frenchman groaned, "at five of the morning? One supposed nine, or at the least eight o'clock—who is abroad at such hours? This discretion is excessive!"

"Never mind! She is urging me, *commanding* me, to visit Crossthwaite as soon as possible! I must see for myself, and perhaps a new bailiff is all that is needed —hah," Francis snorted. "My father doesn't *have* a bailiff, he's leased his land for years . . . but your part is to tell her casually that I've gone north." He wrinkled his forehead. "Perhaps in a day or so . . . and you might raise an eyebrow, wondering if there is some difficulty? I'll leave it to you, but the longer before she knows I'm gone from town, the better."

Louis nodded thoughtfully. "Pen a billet-doux to accompany flowers, which I will send in your name."

And since it was more direct, Francis also left by the rear door, while the watcher at the front was unaware of any visitor. In fact, Francis reached his lodgings exactly as the daytime man arrived, with no suspicion anywhere of his detour, which was why, when Lord Denning learned next day of a single vital sheet of missing paper, it seemed impossible that either Francis or Louis should have it.

CHAPTER 9

His Majesty's Postal Service was the gainer by numerous sixpences through the disappearance of Miss Araminta Surtaine. In addition to Lord Robert's express to his son, containing the awkward news that he was not merely still at Crossthwaite, but also entertaining two Bow Street Runners, the dowager Marchioness of Bishton had sent an express to her grandson, reassuring him of Minta's safety. This crossed Giles's missive, informing her that Bow Street had been summoned. Lady Bishton was glad to be abreast of the news, but felt comfortably unworried.

Unluckily, Pigott and Stibling were grasping at straws. When Lord Robert had gone to bed, they hunted out his copy of *Burke's Peerage* and shortly realized that Transome was some twenty-five miles directly inland. "See?" Stibling pointed out jubilantly. "Wot did I tell yer? She'd go straight up the highway, and be no more nor ten miles from the place; whyfor did she come this road, wot adds another fifteen?"

"Arrr," Pigott conceded, "it's worth a try, I suppose —we ain't got any other lead."

Accordingly, they were already embarked early next morning. The route was circuitous, involving two country stages, a stretch on the highway mail, and a final walk of four miles—all of which took a number of hours, but success awaited them. At first glance, Transome was overawing. "Ooo-er, now wot?" Stibling muttered. "Do we walk up to the gate and say we're calling on Miss Surtaine?"

"Of course not," Pigott said. "We goes along the

side until we finds a place to get through, or over, the hedge. Then we gets up in sight of the house, and lurk abaht."

It was noon before they reached a suitable vantage point, and having thoughtfully provided themselves with thick slabs of bread and meat, courtesy of Mrs. Martin, the two men took a rest for lunch. "Gord, it's a bliddy palace," Stibling said. "Take a day just to walk around it!"

Even Pigott, for all his superior experience, admitted to discouragement. If the girl were anywhere in that huge mansion—and that was uncertain, to begin with—it might be days before they could determine her presence. He didn't fancy sleeping in a hedgerow on such slim chance, but the nearest inn was a walk of eight miles, which Pigott fancied even less. Anyway, they hadn't the blunt for it. "Give it a try, long as we're here," he decided. "See how it's laid out—there'll be another road from the stables to the outside, for the servants and tradesmen. If there ain't another gatehouse, we could maybe wander in, and get into conversation. Come on."

Fortune smiled on them. When they had moved cautiously from one shrubbery clump to another and gained the opposite end of the entrance pleasance, *there was a girl!* They were too distant to see the color of her eyes, but she had black hair, and as she turned to speak to someone within the house, there was no doubt of her beauty. The clincher was her dress of rose pink. "That's 'er!" For a few minutes they watched breathless with triumph, while she wandered about and played with a white kitten. At length she disappeared through the open French windows, and with one accord the Runners swiftly retreated for consultation.

"Get out before we're seen . . . stables'll be back

there, slip to the left for the servants' exit," Pigott whispered.

Luck was still on their side. There was a rear gate-house—its gates were open, and drawn up was a large farm wain. The driver was evidently a friend; he jumped down, clapped the gate keeper's shoulder, and vanished into the house in a spate of jovial chaffer. Silently Pigott and Stibling stole past the wain, to draw a deep breath in the outer road. Once out of sight, they sat down gratefully on the verge. "Now wot?"

"We tell 'im where she is—it goes against me, she's a proper highbred 'un," Pigott said, "but it's our dooty. Then we goes back to London as fast as may be, and tells magistrate the whole—it's all we can do."

"Wot I'm thinking," Stibling said after a minute, "could we write a 'nonymous letter, like—to tip the old lady?"

Pigott considered. "No point to it—she could send the girl somewhere else, but in the end she'd have to say where. We know the girl *was* here; the baron's her legal guardian." He shook his head. "Marchioness or not, she can't 'ide the girl from a legal guardian."

"Delay it a bit, though, until we can tell magistrate?"

" 'Ow can we get away without telling Eddystone the case is finished?" Pigott countered sensibly. "No, we goes to Crossthwaite—getting the times for the stages, and if we do it right, we'll be down to magistrate tomorrow morning. Once the baron knows where she is, he'll rest easy. It'll be tomorrow before he comes to get her."

With the further luck of a friendly farmer, the Runners were spared the trudge to the cross-country stage halt. "We'll take the main highway coach down to the inn for the one back to Crossthwaite, and hire a chaise," Pigott said suddenly. "He'll be glad enough of the news to pay for it, and that way we'll get back for the south mail without any waiting."

When they reached Reddy's Inn, Stibling ordered two pints of mild, while Pigott inquired for a carriage. "Crossthwaite?" A man at the next table pricked up his ears, and after a practiced glance, said, "You'll be from Bow Street—I'm Constable Hasty. Is there any news of the young lady?"

"Visiting the dowager Marchioness of Bishton at Transome, near Peterborough," Pigott returned thoughtfully. "Constable Hasty? You'll be the one searching for her—you might spread the word all's well? No need to look further, she's found, nor I don't know how she got where she is, but I expect Lord Robert'll learn the story tomorrow. We'll be on the way to tell him, soon's the chaise is poled up."

Constable Hasty was innocently delighted. "Aye, he'd not set forth until daylight. Well, well, 'twas a demmed set-out, surely, but all will be glad she's safe."

Driving away in the chaise, Stibling inquired, "Are we supposed to tell constables anything?"

"No," Pigott said succinctly, "but in this here instance, the more people as know the girl's found, the better. Wotever the hanky-panky, he'll find it hard to carry on, with everyone driving up to congratulate him."

In fact, the word of Araminta's safety had spread like wildfire before the Runners ever reached Crossthwaite, and caused Dr. Alling to continue past his home for a visit to the circus. "Heaven knows how you got her to the dowager Marchioness of Bishton," he told Black Jack, "but the Runners have located her."

"S'truth!" Jack's face went black as his name. " 'Tis her grandmother came for her in a great carriage yesterday. Alfie said there was crest on coach door, with postilions and all, but weren't nobody on t' road while the girl were getting in. Runner was here, asking for Gypsy Meg; Bess fobbed 'un off with Polly; we figured they'd be a pair. Alfie saw t'other one when mire was dragged. How i' God's name did they get on the trail?"

Dr. Alling shrugged. "If it's her grandmother, I'm surprised Eddystone didn't look there to begin with. Anyway, the Runners told Hasty she's at Transome, near Peterborough. They're on their way to tell the baron."

"Well, thankee, doctor," Jack said heavily, turning into his caravan. "Girl's found," he told Sally. "What's to do now?"

"Send Alfie, of course."

"How? 'Tis miles and miles, near Peterborough."

"Ask Tam for a horse he can spare," she said after a moment. "We've the blunt in the girl's reticule—it'd be right to use it for this, Jack. We need the roads— doctor'll show Alfie on his maps, if we don't have 'em— and Alfie'll either change horses at a posting inn or wait an hour until Tam's is fit to go again. He's only to reach this place, Jack. They'll care for him and horse, after."

Jack smiled at her slowly, sliding an arm about her waist. "Eh, lass, what would I do without you?" He kissed her affectionately. "I'll be off to Tam. . . ."

Lord Robert indeed made no complaint for the cost of a chaise! He even, in his excess of relief that he would not have to account for the dead body of his ward, bestowed five pounds on each of his saviors. "No, no, it's little enough for setting my mind and heart at ease," he exclaimed. "I would it were more, but it happens to be all I have about me at this moment. In the

country, you know, one does not carry much money—
it cannot be needed, where one is known everywhere."

Neither did he object to their immediate departure
in the waiting chaise. "Yes, yes, of course you will
have fresh duties in London. The sooner this matter is
cleared from your books, the sooner you will be free to
aid other people in distress—but you must have some
slight rest and refreshment before you leave. I insist!
Martin, be so good as to ask Mrs. Martin to prepare
some sustenance before their journey, and open a bottle of claret for accompaniment."

It had occurred to Lord Robert that all was not entirely lost; there were still four days before the termi-
nation of his trusteeship. Equally, it had occurred to
Pigott and Stibling that Mrs. Martin's provender would
certainly surpass anything in an inn, plus being gratis.
"We've time enough—mail coach don't reach Reddy's
afore midnight. Do we leave 'ere at seven, we'll make
it, and to spare."

Lord Robert also had time enough for two letters
summoning Francis and Mr. Hankins to return as fast
as possible. In addition, he penned a letter of com-
mendation for Messrs. Pigott and Stibling, directed to
the magistrate, and jovially requested them to carry
the missives with them, "since you are already going
that way." There was a further guinea to pay for immediate delivery. "Hire a chairman, but the good news
must reach London as quickly as possible."

"Arrr," Stibling agreed, looking at the letters. "And
the hanky-panky's still going on. He's wrote to his
son, *and* to that Hankins, but where's a letter to the
girl's home?" They looked at each other. "Throw 'em
away?"

"Nah—but deliver 'em after we've seen magistrate."

"Hell and damnation take it," said Giles wrath-fully. "No offense, Lytell, and it's a tribute to your men, but I could wish they hadn't traced her so speed-ily, devil take it!"

The magistrate cleared his throat. "They wished the same, milord," he remarked, "and I may say that had you thought to tell me the circumstances at once, I could have instructed them *not* to be so assiduous."

"Damme, say you so? I thought you incorruptible, Lytell!"

"Why, so we are, milord—but when there are diver-gent views of a situation, it is obvious that those of a marquis must precede those of a baron," Mr. Lytell returned mildly, "and this is nowhere more evident than in the present instance, judging by Pigott's report. No"—as Giles extended imperious fingers—"the *unof-ficial* report."

His lordship listened in silence while the magistrate relayed the deductions, reactions, opinions of Stibling and Pigott. At the end, he nodded thoughtfully. "Well, it's not too desperate, I fancy, but I'd best go north at once. If Eddystone drove to Transome today, he'd be refused admittance—I'd already told m' grandmother what I knew, she'd not receive him—but from the circumstance of these letters . . .

"I fancy he'll not move until he's got his force mar-shaled—although, who the devil is this Hankins?"

Mr. Lytell looked squarely at the marquis and said evenly, "He is an ordained minister, currently without a living due to a fondness for the bottle, Lord Bishton."

"Good God!" said Lord Denning.

"So that's his devil's brew," Giles said under his breath. "I'll see him in hell first! A thousand thanks, Lytell." He pulled out his case, extracted two ten-pound notes. "One for each of those men, please? Anonymous, but it'll encourage 'em to report to you the next time they encounter 'hanky-panky'!"

The magistrate nodded, neatly tucking the notes into his pocket. "It'll encourage them in any case," he remarked. "Your lordships know the Runners are rated scum, but they're *needed,* to prevent just such dirty work as is apparently afoot. If there's any more help we can give, you've merely to send word, Lord Bishton." Mr. Lytell stood up with a faint smile. "And I have every hope this incident may raise your opinion of us. I bid you good day, milords."

When the door had closed, "There's more," Lord Denning said. "Lytell said his men deliberately delayed delivery of the baron's letters until late afternoon—but Francis Eddystone did not receive his. He had already left London by post chaise."

"Bound for?"

"The driver didn't know, except that it'd be a long trip." The home secretary shrugged. "By the grace of God, our watcher had time to send me word he'd follow to note the direction—but I'll confess to confusion, Bishton. It would seem *Eddystone* must have the paper, but if so, how the devil did he get it? We've had observers for both De Saumont and Eddystone at all times for the past days. Here are the reports."

Giles skimmed through the sheets with a frown. "Hmmm, well, I think we've got it the wrong way around, milord. It is not Eddystone, but De Saumont, with a friend at the Horse Guards. On the surface, it would appear they passed the paper at Mrs. Illington's party, but if it had gone from Eddystone to De Saumont, why should De Saumont linger for that walk around the block? To give instructions, of course. The observers are certain nothing was exchanged but conversation;

the men were not arm in arm. No, the paper came later."

"Unless Eddystone already had it?"

Giles shook his head authoritatively. "If you were a French spy, would you entrust a paper to a man about to engage in dalliance?" he remarked, with a wicked side glance at the home secretary. "It is well known that women sleep like cats, and quietly arise to inspect the contents of pockets." Lord Denning snorted appreciatively, and Giles finished, "No, De Saumont would take no such chance."

"But aside from Mrs. Illington's party and the street encounter, there has been no meeting between the two men; nor has anything been sent from one to the other by messengers," Denning fretted.

Giles scanned the reports again. "Well, the man attached to Eddystone admits he fell asleep, and the man for De Saumont saw no visitors, but," said the Marquis of Bishton, "is there no rear door?" He squinted reflectively. "If it were I—yes, I'd go to the rear door at such an hour: it'd be easier to rouse a servant; and when I'd finished"—Giles pondered briefly—"if I lived in Eddystone's lodgings, I think I'd find it more direct to leave by the same door. Walk up the mews, turn to the right—cuts off a good half-block."

There was a slight silence. "Well, thank God *you* aren't a French spy," Lord Denning observed. "You really think that's the way of it? De Saumont's had no visitors who might have given him the document; one can't help wondering if it's a mare's nest."

"No, I don't think so," Giles said slowly. "Here we have a man who *ought* to be in London to receive an express from his father, but he's already left town *before* the gladsome tidings of Miss Surtaine's safety have reached him. Why, milord, *why?* Let us be practical:

had Miss Surtaine been of the slightest concern personally to Sir Francis Eddystone—in fact, had the baron
been of the slightest concern to his son—Sir Francis
must have been assisting vigorously in the search about
Crossthwaite. Instead, he returns to London and re-
sumes his usual pursuits, until, on a sudden, he de-
parts exactly as a document has disappeared? Sug-
gestive, is it not? Incidentally, what *is* this paper—or
are you not at liberty to say?"

"I am not, but I grow old, Bishton." Lord Denning
put his fingertips together and looked witless. "And occasionally I talk to myself aloud—and if someone over-
hears me saying that I am disturbed to learn that the
War Office has somehow mislaid Lord Wellington's
handwritten list of supplies needed for the peninsula,
together with ports of embarkation and debarkation
. . . well, it is the absent-mindedness of age."

"Good God!" Giles murmured, appalled. "Good
God, what Soult would give for that!"

"Exactly," Lord Denning agreed dryly, "nor is there
any definite knowledge of the date of its disappearance, Bishton. It may have been long gone, long
known, and we are the day after the fair."

"I don't think it," Giles said at once. "They'd not
chance more than a swift in and out, hoping to go
unnoticed until it could be replaced. No, it'll be replaced tomorrow, but Eddystone's carrying a copy."

"I doubt *that,*" Denning returned grimly. "It
wouldn't need to be missing for more than an hour to
copy; and there already are two copies in other files.
No, what's wanted is the original in old Douro's own
hand! One glimpse of that, and the price will triple!"

There was a tap on the door. "Enter," said Lord
Denning.

"Beg pardon, milord, but Simpkins says he's on the

North Road, following a suspect. He thinks he has enough money to last out, and he'll try to leave word of the direction at the posting houses."

"Thank you." The home secretary nodded dismissal, as Giles got to his feet, reaching for curly-brimmed beaver and walking stick.

"That does it, I think," he said. "Never mind *how* he got the paper—he's *got* it and heading for Crossthwaite, which certainly has a cove on the sea; and" —Giles went into convulsive silent chuckles—"I'd give a monkey to see Sir Francis Eddystone's face when he finds his father expects him to marry the little heiress! Good God!" He threw back his head with an infectious full-throated laugh. "Of all the absurdities: here's Francis trying to slip off to France, and his father wanting him to wait long enough for a wedding? I would I could be there, and"—his jaw tightened—"do I start at once, I shall!"

At the door he paused to look back with a grin. "Do you get word to the revenue men to be watching for a ship in a cove—and be sure to tell them to leave the *Saucy Sukey* alone! I'll have need of her."

In the security of Transome, with a good night's sleep and a cup of chocolate in the morning, Araminta's memory continued to return. Encouraged gently by Lady Bishton, she remembered more and more every hour, until the only remaining gap was the period just before the circus; she still had no idea how she had got there, aside from a vague notion that it was connected to her guardian.

"He is Baron Eddystone, who was used to be a dear friend of my papa, which I have always wondered at, ma'am, for he is quite odiously pompous, with a detestable son." Araminta wrinkled her nose in distaste.

"We were used to see him no more than once or twice a year, but lately he has been very frequent. I *think* it has to do with ending the guardianship, but that is what I cannot quite recall."

"It will end next week, when you are eighteen."

"May 28—is it so *soon?* Well, I shall be glad to be rid of him, for it was he sent away Miss Benbridge, you know." Her eyes flashed militantly. "And he was forever having me order out my carriage to drive with him in the Promenade. He would not even bring Mrs. Hobson for an airing, saying I had no need of a maid or chaperon when I was with my guardian. It was a dead bore! Well"—Araminta's face brightened—"as soon as I'm free, I shall ask Benny to come back as a . . . a sort of companion. It may be unfashionable for young females to be educated, but for my part, ma'am, I do not understand it. I should like to know a great deal more than I do, and . . . and go traveling and . . . and *comprehend* the parliamentary debates reported in the *Gazette*."

"So should I," the dowager remarked, vastly amused by her guest's earnestness. "I often wonder if the speakers themselves know what they are talking about."

"Is it wrong to wish to know things, ma'am? Mrs. Hobson says it is *fatal* to become known as a bluestocking—gentlemen do not like it."

"Gentlemen do not like a woman to know more than they do," Lady Bishton said dryly, "and a great many gentlemen appear to know very little. However, some gentlemen—such as Giles—are extremely well informed and find themselves bored by the fashionable simpering goosecaps."

As always, the mention of Giles brightened Araminta's eyes. A good part of their conversation revolved about him, and Lady Bishton was satisfied that

Minta was well on the road to loving hero worship. "Good!" she said to herself, planning busily as a bee. On May 29 Araminta would be quit of her guardian— eighteen years of age, a beautiful heiress, *and* still a month remaining of the season. "The devil with Lady Urbaugh, whoever she may be," said Lady Bishton. "I'll take the girl back to London, and present her myself!"

She said only that she had an express from Giles, with no mention of Bow Street Runners, but early the following morning Miss Crims brought word of Alfie's arrival. "It's that boy, milady—says he's Alfred Bickell, with a very important message about Miss Surtaine, nor he won't give it to no one but yourself, milady."

"Good gracious!" Lady Bishton thrust aside the tray with her chocolate cup. "A dressing robe, Crims, and tell them to show the boy to the morning room."

The boy was sitting on the edge of a chair when she swept into the room. He got up at once, and made a rather nice bow before plunging into speech. "They'm found her, milady! Pa sent me to warn you," Alfie said anxiously. "Tam lent me one of the trained horses, and we'd the money in Meg's—Miss Surtaine's—reticule." He held it out to Lady Bishton. " 'Tis all there but a bit—Ma's wrote to explain how it was forgot when we took her out of the bunk underneath tiger's cage."

The dowager blinked faintly. "Good heavens! Sit down while I read your mother's letter, Alfred."

"Yes'm."

Sally's calligraphy was not elegantly formed, but was perfectly clear and well phrased. The dowager found herself impressed as well as intrigued by the Bickells. "Of course you should have used the money," she said cordially, refolding the note. "Your parents should have taken more, for there was all the food, as well as lodging, until I could come to fetch Araminta."

" 'Twas naught, we've always plenty," Alfie returned, "but what will we do now, ma'am?"

"We will have breakfast." Lady Bishton arose and pulled the bell, which produced a footman. "Show Master Alfred to a chamber, and bring hot water for him to remove travel dust. Tell Royle to lay a cover for Master Alfred in the breakfast room, and instruct the chef accordingly." She smiled at Alfie's awe-stricken expression. "Don't worry," she murmured, "you'll do!"

He looked at her, and suddenly grinned impishly. "Yes, ma'am—Ma's taught me how."

It was a merry breakfast, for all Lady Bishton's inner concern, and at a glance she realized the boy's mother *had* taught him well. He made no gaucheries at table more than expectable of a schoolboy, and Araminta was enchanted to see him. Her ladyship said little, listening with amusement to their eager chatter. It was good to have a young friend for the girl, and Sally Bickell's letter had said Alfie was to stay as long as he could be useful—or sent to carry messages, even to London if need be. "He is a very responsible boy, milady."

Yes, by all means let the boy stay, the dowager decided swiftly. He'd stick close to Araminta, keep her entertained and occupied for these next critical days. Let them wander in the woods, fish for trout, go riding . . . or would it be wiser to send the girl somewhere else entirely? After some consideration, she decided against that. It would be far easier to protect Araminta here, behind the closed gates of Transome. When Lord Robert arrived, he could be delayed long enough to get her out of sight, and Lady Bishton would deny all knowledge of her. As for the Runners' report, whatever it was—and the dowager only wished she knew, for it seemed *impossible* they could have seen the girl—but in any case, Lady Bishton would firmly say her young companion had been a granddaughter, who had already left.

How the devil *had* Araminta been traced? It must have been pure mischance; they had stopped only once for fresh horses at a highway inn well known to the dowager. No matter; when the baron arrived, Lady Bishton would send him to the rightabout; but by evening—when Lord Robert had *not* arrived—she was more worried than she liked. While her ladyship was unacquainted with the word "hanky-panky," her grandson's original story had left no doubt that the baron was up to mischief. At the outset, she had written Giles of the Runners' discovery and dispatched it by one of the grooms direct to London. At least the marquis would know the situation and could take whatever action seemed best.

The dowager's letter reached Giles on his return from Lord Denning. Hastily scanning the sheets, he exclaimed, "Alfie's there—good! Ringleby, send word I want the curricle in half an hour poled up with the chestnuts; give Lady Bishton's groom refreshment, and I'll take him with me; tell Noakes to ready my travel clothes . . ." He strode toward the study. "George?"

"Yes, milord?"

"Money," said Giles tersely. "As much as there is— or make out a draft for me to sign, and send to Boodle's." He sat down at the desk and swiftly drew out paper, while the secretary said, "We've nearly three hundred pounds—will you need more?"

"No, but I'll need it all. Make a draft to replace it tomorrow." The marquis was scribbling rapidly; he'd just finished when George returned with the cash box. "Sand and seal for me, write my grandmother's name on it, will you? Is that the bank draft?" Giles signed and pushed it toward the secretary. "Everything else must wait."

"There is nothing vital. Will you wish me to make your excuses for your engagements in the next days, milord?"

"Have I any? Good God, Louisa's ball!"

"Exactly so, milord, and I fear no excuse will suffice, for your niece was determined to open the dancing with you for her partner," George said pensively.

"What a hum!" Giles snorted. "She'd far rather have you—and you'd far rather deputize for me!" He chuckled at George's sheepish grin. "Think I don't know where the wind blows?"

"I'm very sure you do, milord."

The marquis halted in his progress to the door and eyed his secretary's sternly controlled face with faint surprise. "Oho, sits it serious?" he said quietly. "You were ever childhood playmates, but it's grown more? Then, go get her, George! Are you thinking of money? Our family marries where the heart is given. Can you make—what the devil's her name? . . . Elinor!—can you make her choose you, money won't matter. You've the birth and breeding, and my approval, for what it's worth."

"It's worth *everything,* you well know it," George muttered, and drew a short breath. "But what shall I tell Lady Louisa?"

Giles cast his eyes toward the ceiling and dictated, "Dear Louisa, I am summoned to Transome; there is some difficulty that disturbs our grandmother. Pray make my apologies to Elinor, and beg her to accept George Graham as my deputy." He smiled at George.

"Have it ready for me to sign when I descend in half an hour?"

While the occupants of Transome dined luxuriously, a number of conveyances were sweeping northward. Sir Francis Eddystone was the vanguard, in a post chaise, and not pushing the driver unduly; midnight would be time enough; unlikely Dubois could bring his ship to anchor before then. Mr. Hankins was on the Scotland stagecoach, whose driver prided himself on making fourteen miles an hour. Thus, when decanted at Mr. Reddy's Inn, the minister discovered his patron's son just finishing a substantial sirloin.

"What the devil brings you back here?" Sir Francis demanded, when Mr. Hankins recognized him with joviality.

"A request from your esteemed parent. I suppose we are bound on the same errand." Hankins disposed himself on an adjoining chair. "I regret I did not reach you in time to share your carriage; I was from home when Lord Robert's letter arrived, and by the time I had waited upon you, they told me at your lodgings that you had already left; but, however"—he sighed comfortably—"we can continue together, eh? I may say I was dreading the country stage to Crossthwaite; it is an extremely bad road, with a coachman who drives as though he were riding to hounds!"

Francis stared at him blankly, as he ordered "a bird and a bottle," and went on conversationally, "Well, well, so the little lady is found, eh? All continues as before? How relieved you must be, Sir Francis!"

On the contrary, it was the worst jolt yet, and Francis was thoroughly unstrung. It was bad enough to encounter Lord Robert alone, and be forced to invent a reason for returning to Crossthwaite; to have Araminta on his hands simultaneously was disastrous. Had the original scheme gone smoothly, it would have caught Mrs. Illington amidships, with nothing but a vague suspicion. To wed Minta now, in the course of the trickiest mission, would certainly infuriate Clara to the danger point. Already sharply on the *qui vive,* the instant she learned she was not destined to be Baroness Eddystone, Clara would make as much trouble as possible.

"Devil take Araminta Surtaine!" he thought viciously, but after two double brandies, he felt more calm. It began to look almost a bit of good luck: he would need no explanation for Lord Robert on his arrival, for one thing. For another, he could say Dubois was arranged as a honeymoon voyage, and in view of the circumstances, the baron would probably applaud his son's perspicacity! Francis laughed to himself sardonically; it was working out rather well, after all. He would marry the girl, take her to France, away from inconvenient questions, and leave her only long enough to deliver his paper. Dubois could then bring them back to Portsmouth, quite openly returning from a wedding trip.

"Damme, it covers everything," he exclaimed with satisfaction. "Let's be off and about it!"

The final northbound vehicle was the Marquis of Bishton's curricle, in which Lady Bishton's groom was enjoying the ride of his life, while his lordship was driving to the inch with the shortest stops for fresh horses. "There's no time for food, I'm sorry for it"— Giles smiled apologetically—"but you'll rest to draw breath at the inn, and take a more comfortable pace in the post chaise."

"Your pace suits me grand, milord—'tis a treat to

sit beside you," the groom returned with youthful admiration, while the marquis swept sweetly past the very stagecoach containing Mr. Hankins. In fact, at sixteen miles an hour, they reached Reddy's Inn not five minutes after Sir Francis. There Giles had the good luck of an empty chaise for the groom, who said, "I'll go straight on, milord, if you've no objection? I'll feed when I reach Transome, and her ladyship will be wishful to have your letter as soon as may be."

"Good lad!" said Giles cordially, thrusting a folded note into the groom's hand, and turning to swing himself back into the curricle. "Stand away, please. . . ."

He was, by now, a full hour ahead of everyone, with a discreet traveling coach trundling along at twelve miles an hour in the rear. It contained five expressionless agents of his Majesty's government, well armed and furnished with all necessary writs and warrants for search and/or seizure of anything, from people to houses to carriages to ships. . . .

CHAPTER 10

Guiding the curricle up the gradient toward the circus, Giles felt pensive. His cover was unmasked; there'd be no more jolly trips on the *Saucy Sukey,* with the spice of danger in collecting information and laying false trails to unsettle Bonaparte. It was all over, and never more clearly than in Black Jack's formality.

"Good evening, milord."

With a rueful sigh for finished deviltry, Giles tossed him the reins and climbed down. "Ask someone to care for the team, will you, Jack—and come inside, for there's work to do." Some part of the stiff respect vanished when the matter was explained. "We're depending on you and your people, Jack," Giles finished quietly. "It's no time for games or a bit of free-trading at the moment. Should that paper be delivered in France, it would mean eventual death for hundreds of Englishmen in the peninsula. The French would know Wellington's strategy, and be waiting for him. Do you tell your men that, and I miss my guess if they don't agree it's more important than a cargo of brandy."

"In course they will—but revenuers . . ." Jack shook his head.

"They've been told to leave the *Saucy Sukey* alone, but you'll send someone out the headland—don't tell me there isn't a signal arrangement." Giles grinned. "Let her keep off shore until we've got the ship we want . . . and if Eddystone slips past us, I'll need her myself for pursuit. Will you aid us?"

"For certain sure!" Sally thrust aside the rear curtains and added defiantly, "Yes, I've been listening,

187

but that you've been telling—that there is *treason* to be helping Frenchies, and there ain't no one in this circus as would stand for it. Jack, you'll get all together and let his lordship tell the tale—he'll tell it better nor you."

"Please!" Giles held up his hand. "I am still 'Mr. Giles' until all's finished," he said soberly. "Sally, Jack" —he looked from one to the other—"you'll forgive the small deceit? You'll not know how much you've done for England, neither did any man have truer friends, but"—he chuckled merrily—"do you all turn *respectful . . .* good God, we'll be at *point non plus!*"

"Whole circus knows you're the Marquis of Bishton," Jack began, but Sally interrupted.

" 'Tis no matter what they know, Jack Bickell. I'll slip along to Bess to say his lordship's incognito for the moment—and send Joe over to watch at Crossthwaite," she said firmly. "Tam'll spare another horse, Joe'll let us know what's afoot, and when this minister arrives."

"He might be there already." Jack frowned. "Along with that son, and Lord Robert's got little miss . . ."

"No, he has not." Sally shook her head. "Alfie'd be here to tell us, he's got Tam's horse—and did he not, her ladyship would have give him a mount."

"Yes, she would, and sent a groom with him," Giles murmured, "but I fancy all's planned for tomorrow. They've no least idea we've rumbled the lay, you see. The baron will expect to drive up to the gates of Transome, send word that he has come for his ward, and after an exchange of courtesies, drive off with her. It would be interesting to hear what tale he gives my grandmother—he is not a man of ingenuity, but I understand the son has considerable address. However" —he smiled sweetly at Sally—"my grandmother has even more. I believe she plans to exhibit total astonishment at his request, maintain that any young girl observed by the Runners was her granddaughter, who has now been called for by her mother." Giles's shoulders shook silently. "And I may say that although Grandy is the dearest person in nature, when she chooses to be the dowager Marchioness of Bishton, I know of no one more frightening!

"I fancy Lord Robert Eddystone will rapidly be at a stand," Giles finished, "and before he can marshal any legal backing, his guardianship will have ended."

On this point, however, the Marquis of Bishton had underestimated. The baron had no intention of approaching Lady Bishton. "God knows how she comes to be involved; I was unaware of any acquaintance," he told Francis, "but it would appear she came deliberately to get Araminta, who was all the time concealed at that demmed circus. I'll have a word or two to say about *that* to the local magistrates, but first we must get the girl back. Do we go to ask for her at the front entrance, we'll be denied—or the old beldame'll give us a Bunbury Tale, claiming the person seen by the Runners was a servant or a granddaughter or some such."

"But, good God, sir," Francis objected uneasily, "by the description in that Frogeater book of English homes, Transome is a full ten miles around. The house alone contains a hundred chambers. Araminta could be *anywhere,* and if the marchioness don't choose to surrender her, how the devil shall we go on?"

"We've still three days; it's worth the try," Lord Robert said grimly. "Drive over and reconnoiter; ten to one she'll be out riding with a groom somewhere in the home forest, if I know Minta. We'll take Hankins to help; he can hold the horses while we're getting the girl into the carriage—the groom won't be armed for riding on a private estate—we say Miss Surtaine's my ward, being kept under restraint . . . you point your pistol, and there we are." The baron rubbed his hands together cheerfully and refilled the brandy glasses. "I must say it was a clever thought to bring a schooner! Makes everything easier; you'll be married, go aboard, sail around for a week or two, and no questions asked, whatever she says later!" He warmed his brandy, took a sip. *"And,* we'll have the money."

"Yes," said Francis thoughtfully. "How much is there?"

"A good fifty thousand pounds, as well as the manor, which is a handsome residence—moderate in size, but well maintained, a very pretty gentleman's estate," Lord Robert mused, "quite unexceptionable in locality. Surtaine was used to hunt with the Quorn; I believe they were used to dine with the Earls of Lincoln and Huntingdon. Yes, we could be well placed there, and lease Crossthwaite for what it would fetch. It is not much," he sniffed, "but worth keeping as a property for your heir."

"Yes," Francis said again, but his mind was swimming in the glory of "fifty thousand pounds." "My God, I never knew it was so much," he thought exultantly. He was in a mood to be generous. "If only I can be reinstated in the French estates, I'll buy up the Crossthwaite mortgages—that'd keep the old man quiet, with an occasional thousand on the side."

Going up the stairs to bed, Lord Robert was saying to himself, "Forty thousand pounds—or I'll not give him the signed certificate of marriage."

Mr. Hankins alone had no ulterior thoughts, except from the hope that a decanter had been left in his chamber.

From his lurking spot in the shrubbery, Joe observed one . . . two . . . three darkened chambers. The stable was closed, the servants' quarters had long since been shut. Sleepily, Joe stumbled out to the covert where his horse was tethered, and trotted back to the circus. "They'm all asleep," he reported, keeping his eyes open by main force. " 'Twas only three chambers were lit."

"Come down," said Giles, lifting the boy from the saddle, "and find your doss. We'll need you tomorrow, sleep sound!" He clapped the boy heartily on the shoulder. "You've told us what we need to know, good lad! There's only the three men in the house—tomorrow it is."

"Aye, but what o'clock? I'd best ride over at dawn to watch for when they leave. It may be sooner nor you think, milor . . . uh, Mr. Giles, and did aught happen to little miss, I'd not forgive myself," said Sam tersely. "Ted, you'll watch out for the ship, and for t' rest— why not let young'uns swarm along cliffs and coves?"

"Women, too," said Sally, looking around the group. "We'll go berrying tomorrow—yes, we'll find little . . . but we'll be *in the way!*"

Giles burst out laughing. "Oh, wonderful, wonderful! Just don't get in the way of any government men —you understand, everyone? I doubt they'll challenge any of you; they'll have been told by their superiors that there'll be local assistance, they know who they're looking for. If you see anything, don't hesitate to tell it to the next man you see hiding behind a rock or tree!"

He stood up from his perch on the caravan steps and stretched luxuriously. "I think that does it." He looked around the circle with a smile. "To bed, and a good night's sleep; and"—quite suddenly his face was serious, he was the Marquis of Bishton—"tomorrow we will catch this spy—you and I together. Never doubt it, my friends!"

The carriage of government agents ran out on various side roads to the sea, leaving one after another of the passengers to take up a position. There was a tactful omission of the cove beyond the circus; the man stationed above the Minchampton cove certainly observed a series of faint lantern flashes from that headland, and what might have been fireflies offshore, but obedient to instructions, he looked the other way. Otherwise, in the deep golden light of the overripe moon, every cove was silent and untenanted.

Ted came back from the headland and said, " 'Tis all right—they'll hold until signals . . . and carriage went along cliff top. I reckon revenuers is in place."

"Good," said Giles with an immense yawn. "Sleep well!"

By midnight the arms of Morpheus had enfolded the countryside in peace, broken here and there by the night music of snores. From Transome, where the dowager Marchioness of Bishton's anxiety was allayed by her grandson's letter—to Crossthwaite, where Lord Robert wallowed in uncorseted comfort and celestial dreams of a winning whist evening at ten-pound points—to Black Jack's Traveling Circus and Sinbad rolled on his back, four paws in the air—all hearts and minds were at ease . . . which only goes to show that Lady Luck is unreliable.

Sam duly arose at dawn and stationed himself to observe Crossthwaite driveway. Shortly before ten, he came posting back on Tam's horse. "They'm gone, about half hour ago," he announced. "Sir Francis were driving, the baron and another gent sitting inside. Now what?"

"We wait for their return," Giles said calmly, "which —if I know my grandmother's strategy—will not be before dinnertime. By then, someone will have sighted the boat we want, making into a cove at twilight. Sir Francis will be neatly caught between the devil and the sea. He dares to accompany his father to Transome because the ship is not yet here, but when it arrives, he cannot delay in making his run for France, for every extra minute that paper is absent from its file increases the danger of discovery. Remember"—the marquis smiled with a diabolical sweetness that caused a shiver among the group—"he has no idea it is already discovered. I fancy it may be a shock."

"A demmed nightmare!" Sam muttered. "And serve 'un bliddy well right."

"Arrr, to be dangering lives of countrymen," Ted growled, " 'tis foul. Think old 'un is in it, too?"

"No." Giles shook his head. "He's a different scheme, to get hold of his ward's fortune. Well, I'll have a horse and amble along the coves for a chat with—whoever I meet." He pulled out his pocket watch. "Half after ten—they'll not reach Transome much before noon; my grandmother will send word that she has not completed her robing, which will keep them kicking their heels for an hour. When at last she descends, she will prove to be a witless old lady afflicted with deafness and requiring everything to be shouted at her twice." Giles grinned wickedly and drew an answering grin of comprehension.

"Aye," Jack chuckled, "there's naught like a woman for a quick turn!"

"And none better than my grandmother! When they have finally made her understand, there will be a further period before she can make *them* understand— and after that she will insist upon giving them refreshment."

"They'm needing it by then"—Ted guffawed—"particular the old 'un! Fat as a flawn, he be."

"So I fancy they'll not find it possible to leave until near four of the clock. There are not nearly so many advantages to rank as you may think, but in this instance," Giles finished blandly, "a baron will not wish to offend a marchioness by refusing her hospitality. Should all else fail"—he squinted thoughtfully into space—"she is quite capable of insisting on providing fresh horses, and privately directing the stable to pole up the one wheeler that may go lame." He laughed at Tam's involuntary snort of mirth. "Oh, she'll contrive, never fear."

And so Lady Bishton might have done had she had the chance, but capricious Fortune decreed that Minta and Alfie should go riding in a meadow within sight of the skirting road along which (having taken over the reins from Francis) Lord Robert was starting his reconnaissance. "By God, there she is!" he muttered, staying the horses. "Do you get down while I turn the carriage for a quick start."

It went smooth as Devonshire cream: Minta was dismounted, straying toward the fence for wildflowers; Alfie was half the field away; luxuriant oaks and chestnuts in all their glorious spring greenery shaded the carriage drawn still in the lane. Francis neatly displaced a section of the farm fence, and before Araminta could utter more than a single half-scream, he'd got her struggling form in a firm grip, dragging her toward the coach. Minta put up a game resistance, but she was no match for her adversary—particularly after she'd infuriated him by a long raking fingernail on his face, followed by a severe wallop to his ear. "You hellcat," he panted, "I'll teach you!" He picked her up bodily and literally threw her into the carriage, where Mr. Hankins said, "There, there, my dear— you're quite safe."

Minta stared at him blankly, pulling away from his soothing arms. She might be down, but she was not out. Breathlessly, she saw loathsome Francis Eddystone about to step into the carriage, and by an automatic reaction, her foot planted itself against his chest and shoved. Caught off his guard, Francis stumbled and fell flat on his back in the ditch. He was up in a flash, his face suffused with fury. "By God, you'll pay for this," he assured her softly, and was into the seat beside her with a ringing slap to her cheek that hurled her against Mr. Hankins with a moan.

Small as it was, though, Araminta's contrariness had been enough for Alfie to see her abduction—to ride at full speed toward the road, where he abandoned his horse and raced to pull himself onto the footman's step just as the carriage began to move. When he'd got his breath, he hauled up to fasten the leather strap about him; at least he was secure, and by leaning slightly to the side, he'd not be seen by the driver. It was some reassurance to recognize they were headed for home territory, but a jolting trip nevertheless. Without the footman's strap, Alfie must have fallen off a dozen times. "Ooo-er, he's springing 'em!" he said to himself. They'd not last this pace; nor did they, although the baron had been smart enough to procure fresh horses at the last possible inn before Transome, so they were only winded within sight of home.

As they came to the turn into the coaching road past Crossthwaite, the Baron slowed the horses to a walk. Alfie swiftly unbuckled the groom's strap and leaped to the offside, where he rolled down into the hedgerow until the carriage was moving away at a gentle trot.

Then he picked himself up and made for the circus. It was half after two when he came panting into the caravan circle. "They'm got her!"

"Oh, dear Lord, what's to do now?" Sally put her hand to her mouth, wild-eyed. "Jack?"

"Hush, lass, we'll figure it." Jack put a strong arm around his wife's trembling shoulders. "Joe, you'll take horse over to the house to see what occurs; Tam, you'll take horse after Mr. Giles; he'll be somewhere's along top of coves—probably to Minchampton by now. Ted, go out to headland and see if you can sight *Saucy Sukey;* call her in. Unload cargo quick as may be, and get her out to cruise along up shore. Do captain find another ship in an upper cove, tell him to heave to so's to block passage out to sea. The rest on you"—Black Jack's voice was deep and authoritative,—"prime your pistols, help to stash cargo, and stand ready for Mr. Giles. Right?"

"Right!"

"What can *I* do? Oh, Jack, that sweet little darling," Sally wailed. "I can't *bear* for anything to happen to her! Couldn't I go over with Joe, and try to get her away secretly? Bess, you'd come with me?"

"No, best to leave it for Mr. Giles," Jack said after a moment. "Do you try, and be discovered, it'd maybe ruin his catching the spy."

"Aye," Bess agreed. "It'd tip 'em the wink, and at this hour, I doubt they'll do anything that can't be undone in a trice when Mr. Giles learns of it."

The circus was very busy. When Alfie had regained his breath, he was dispatched to the entrance road to post a large sign: "NO PERFORMANCE TONIGHT." Every man aside from Black Jack was helping to unload the *Saucy Sukey*. "Spies, is it?" said the captain, and spat contemptuously onto the sand. "Well, we'll put 'paid' on *their* accounts, eh, lads?"

All of Tam's prancing horses were trotting here and there, delivering messages and getting in a few gallops which they greatly enjoyed. Unsettled by the commotion, the big cats paced restlessly in their cages, contributing an occasional deep-throated roar. When Alfie had described as much as he'd seen of the abduction, he was sent to join Joe. "One stays, t'other comes to say what's doing."

Meanwhile, completely ignorant of the preparations for their undoing. Lord Robert and his son had reached Crossthwaite, where they carried Araminta forcibly from carriage to the anteroom of the study and locked her in. "Whew!" Lord Robert wiped his perspiring face and shakily poured a glass of brandy all around.

Mr. Hankins was deeply distressed. "Dear, dear! The poor young lady! Ought we not to summon a doctor, milord? Such hysteria, such vapors—it cannot be good for her."

"There is no need for a country doctor," Lord Robert said smoothly, with a warning glance at Francis. "It is a nervous affliction to which she has ever been subject, but Sir Henry Halford assures us it will pass in time. I confess this has been more prolonged and severe than we have seen in some years—due, no doubt, to the incompetence and lack of comprehension of her condition by those who kidnapped her; but there is no need for alarm, Hankins. I have a measure of Sir Henry's soothing draft that will shortly restore her."

The mention of aristocracy's most favored physician set Mr. Hankins' mind at ease. "Oh, Sir Henry! In that case . . ." he murmured. "Dear, dear, how very sad, for she seemed not even to recognize her future husband in Sir Francis, you know. At one point she spoke quite wildly, denying all thought of marrying; we were forced to restrain her; she became almost violent."

"Indeed it is sad." Lord Robert nodded. "And is why the union was long agreed upon, for she is quite alone in the world, Hankins. There is no one to care for her, save my son and myself." The baron sighed lugubriously. "We had hoped she might recover sufficient stability to make her presentation to society possible, but it was not to be. My guardianship must shortly end. It goes without saying that I shall *ever* be at hand, out of my deep friendship for her father," impressively. "If only the dear man had thought to extend my term until she is twenty-five! But her nervous condition had not manifested itself at the time of his death, and now . . . consider my sentiments, Hankins!"

Lord Robert refilled the brandy glasses, and continued, "How best shall I protect this sweet child? There is some small property"—he shrugged—"but without legal standing, I cannot oversee her financial advisers—at least one of whom I mistrust, Hankins! No, Araminta must have a husband, and when she is herself, she is devoted to Francis . . . for you must know they were ever fond friends from her childhood. Is it not so, my boy?"

"Absolutely, Father," Francis agreed blandly. "I have watched her from nursery days, flowering into the beauty of today, and suffered when her indispositions overtook her, but I pray, I *believe,* this will prove a temporary setback. All will disappear, I am *certain,* when I can be with Araminta constantly, and to this I would devote my life," dramatically, "but we must be married, Hankins, and the sooner the better."

"Yes, yes, of course. I deeply commend your feelings of responsibility, but . . . dear, dear," the minister murmured worriedly, "how is it to be managed, if the young lady does not regain her senses?"

"Phoo, nonsense, Hankins," Lord Robert said authoritatively, refilling the brandy glasses once more. "You're aware it was long planned, should have occurred many days ago, but for this kidnapping that has unsettled her nerves. It's merely to hear her say 'I do,' and if she cannot repeat the vows, it's no matter. When she is recovered, she will be very grateful you did not heed any protests, I promise you.

"Let us allow some time for her to become calmer, eh? No doubt she will repose herself on the couch, and be the better for it." The baron turned jovially to the door. "And we will be the better for some food after the exhaustions of the journey."

Hankins got to his feet eagerly, if a bit unsteadily, and made his way to the wash room, leaving Lord Robert and his son to consult hastily. "I will send Mrs. Martin with tea and toast," the Baron said in an undertone, "and when we are finished at table, Minta should be drowsy enough to sign the papers, but it may be necessary to take her aboard with Hankins for the marriage. When does the ship arrive?"

"Momentarily." Francis shrugged, biting his lips nervously. "While we're eating, send Ben to see if she's reached the cove, and let us be off as quickly as possible, papers or no papers. Who knows but that interfering old woman will send after us? You may be able to convince a fuddled minister, but a constable or a marchioness will be a different matter, Father—particularly with Minta either screaming her head off or drugged."

"Leave it to me, she'll be more reasonable later," Lord Robert returned confidently. "Do you dispatch Ben, while I give the directions to Mrs. Martin."

However, Araminta was *not* more reasonable. So far

from reposing on the small settee, she had first investigated her jail, to find the doors locked and the window swelled immovably shut. In any case, it was set too high for safety; the ground sloped away sharply on that side of the house. With the aid of the poker, she cracked out one of the small panes to admit some air; the room was horridly stuffy.

Next she sat down and employed some time in careful thought. A number of encouraging points occurred to her, of which the best was Alfie: he must certainly have caught some glimpse of her abduction. Even if he had not, his quick wits would have deduced it when he came on her riderless horse and found no sign of her. "Foul Francis set aside some fencing, too," she remembered hopefully. "Alfie'll realize . . . he'd go straight back to tell Lady Bishton, and she'll come after me."

It would be several hours, though. Lord Robert had driven at breakneck speed; the dowager could not be expected to equal it. "She will give Alfie a horse, and send him ahead to tell Jack!" A good mount, carrying a boy's light weight, should cover twenty-five miles in little more than an hour. Alfie might already be nearing the circus, and even if Jack could not take her away from her guardian, he would do something. "Whatever Lord Robert plans, it will be thwarted when he learns people know I am here. No matter what he says, should anything happen to me, he would have to account for it," she thought, more hopefully still.

Lady Bishton, when she came, could not legally insist on removing Araminta from her legal guardian's residence, either. "But her presence must lend credence to whatever I say; it cannot be other than awkward for him. He might deny entrance to a constable, saying I was ill or something of the sort, but he cannot be so easily rid of a dowager marchioness!"

Araminta sat rigid at the sound of a key unlocking the door, but it proved to be a plump middle-aged woman, whose anxious expression cleared at sight of Minta. "There, now!" she exclaimed, bringing forward a tray. "His lordship would have it you were subject to bad spells and fits-like, but I said to myself, 'I'll be bound 'tis only jolting about in a carriage—fair turns the stomach, it do—little miss will be fine with some rest.' Well, I've brought you the tisane, as his lordship ordered." She was setting a small table and placing dishes. "And the toast . . . but I said to myself, 'Do little miss be recovered, she'll be more hungry nor *that!'*

"So here's cold chicken wings." She smiled conspiratorially, "and a saucer of fresh strawberries with a bit of cake. They'm all light on the stomach; you'll not regret to eat, miss."

"I'm sure I shan't—how good it looks! Thank you so much . . . I fear I don't know your name?"

"Mrs. Martin, miss. Martin and me cares for Crossthwaite permanent-like, but do his lordship come, I've me nieces to help."

In the face of this beaming woman, Araminta had no fears—aside from that tisane. His lordship had ordered it? His lordship had also drugged her wine at the inn. "Could I have a glass of plain water?"

"Of course you can—or there's fresh milk, if you'd prefer?"

Impossible to believe Mrs. Martin would doctor it, but Araminta was taking no chances; she might innocently be persuaded to add some "medicine" given her by Lord Robert. "Only water, please."

When it was brought and the door locked once more ("His lordship wants you to be undisturbed, miss, and I'm bound to admit that Mr. Hankins don't carry his wine like he should!"), Minta made a satisfactory meal of Mrs. Martin's contributions, washed down with cold well water. The tisane she delicately poured through the open windowpane.

When Lord Robert returned, he was dismayed to discover an extremely clear-eyed young lady. Nor could she be coaxed into taking the glass of wine he pressed upon her. "No, I thank you. I have no need of a restorative, and am not fond of Maderia in any case," she said sweetly, and poured it into the slop jar before he could stop her.

The baron gritted his teeth, silently longing to slap the chit—he had no more of the opiate. Fleetingly, he wondered if this game were worth the candle, but—fifty thousand pounds? He set himself to soothe and pacify. "My dear Minta, what is this?" he asked affectionately. "Surely you cannot distrust your beloved papa's dearest friend? I do not know what can have occurred in these terrible days since you were spirited away from me by total strangers . . ."

"They were *not*. Lady Bishton was used to be my grandmother's intimate, and as for saying I am to marry your odious son, it is the greatest nonsense," Araminta said hardily, "for I am betrothed to the Marquis of Bishton. It was arranged in our cradles between the families."

Lord Robert gulped at her calm voice. Good God, it was the first he had heard of this—could it be true? "My dear Minta," he protested, "where had you the idea that Francis . . . That is, I own that had you returned his tender passion, I should have been as delighted as he . . ."

"He would *not* be delighted for anything but to get his hands on my dowry," Araminta observed, "and rather than marry him, I would pay him a tithe to spend on his ladybirds."

"Araminta!" The baron gasped in honest shock.

"Your language! How wise I was to dismiss Miss Benbridge, if she allowed you to hear such vulgarisms. I assure you my son does not lead such a life; he is in the first stare of the *ton!*"

"Well, I am very sure he does have ladybirds, and opera dancers as well—and very probably you did, too, before you had to wear corsets," Minta returned stubbornly, "but he is not going to spend *my* money on them."

Lord Robert had never felt so completely at a loss. Once more he thought fleetingly of abandoning the fifty thousand pounds, but it would not hurt to make a push. "My dear, there is no question of it," he said gently. "It is entirely a mistaken notion, and I cannot refrain from saying I am astounded Lady Bishton would so agitate you! Now, shall we dismiss it from our minds and conclude the business that brought us here before this distressing mishap? There are still the papers to be signed; if you will sit here, Minta, and I will explain to you . . ."

"No," said Araminta.

"But . . . but, my dear child, they must be signed in order to end my responsibilities," he stuttered. "If all is not correct, I shall be gravely censured, involved in legal difficulties."

There ensued the most difficult half-hour of his life, but Araminta merely continued to say "No!" Lord Robert wondered why he had never before realized her striking similarity to her mother, who had been equally stubborn in the early months of his guardianship! After thirty minutes, the papers were still unsigned (including the marriage lines cunningly attached to a lease, as though only a second page). The baron was grown hoarse in expostulation, entreaty, and adult command. Minta was neither cowed nor impressed.

"Pray, do not distress yourself, my dear sir. I cannot believe anyone would call you to account for a technicality," she protested.

"On the contrary, I am the more vulnerable *because* of my rank."

"Well, I do not think I should sign anything now for exactly that reason," Minta returned limpidly. "Do but consider how it must *appear,* should Giles discover some flaw two days hence! The world must *wonder* that you could not wait so short a space to discuss with my future husband."

The baron felt a decided flinch in the stomach at her words; he had no desire to face the Marquis of Bishton—nor *any* marquis. "I feel sure he will have no question in my handling of your property, but I do not perfectly understand . . . that is, I have all this while been completely unaware of any betrothal," he said. "It was never mentioned by your dear mother; I have never encountered any member of that family in Mount Street. Such secrecy of the acquaintance seems very strange."

Araminta had not been a regular patron of Hookham's Lending Library for nothing. "Indeed, there is nothing strange, milord"—she widened her eyes innocently—"for you must know that it was agreed between our mothers that naught should be said until I had reached an age for thinking of marriage. Nor was there to be any constraint upon us. Had Giles found a wife to his taste, he knew himself free; but, however, he has not, and upon our meeting some weeks past," Minta said airily, "we instantly felt that decided partiality for each other that must make for a harmonious union."

"Why was I not informed of this?" Lord Robert asked suspiciously. "I understood you to be removing to Bath for the summer, as usual, and preparing for your presentation next season by Lady Urbaugh. I repeat: this secrecy is strange, indeed! My dear Araminta, his lordship must be an unexceptionable match —there can be no question—but I cannot refrain from saying that after the years in which I have watched over you, I am *wounded*—yes, hurt to the quick!—that you failed to confide such important news to me!"

"Oh, I had meant to have done so, but Giles was from town on his own affairs at the moment, and we thought it better to delay until he could wait upon you personally."

Lord Robert was becoming more and more suspicious; the sudden introduction of a premier marquis into the situation struck him as decidedly fishy. On the other hand, there was no denying that Araminta *had* been staying with the dowager Marchioness of Bishton. "I must honor such delicacy of mind," he said stiffly, "but I cannot see that it in any way affects the discharge of my duties. Let me remind you: I am still your legal guardian, and you will do as I bid you. Should Lord Bishton raise any later question, I will be answerable to him with perfect complaisance. Meanwhile, sign the papers."

"No," said Araminta, and broke the quill in half.

"Damnit," the baron roared irascibly, "it will not be I, but Bishton who will answer questions, my girl! I will know *why* he has set you against me. He knows me not, nor is there anyone to challenge my faithful handling of your affairs. I say you are to sign, and you shall do so, miss." He stamped to the door, and glowered at her. "I will leave you to reflect on your childish obstinacy."

Once more the door was locked, and Araminta

sank back in the chair tremulously. She could not repress a few tears of weariness and fright. If only it were true that Giles would save her! Remembering his merry face, the deep voice, and the gentle strength of his arms lifting her over to the caravan table, she wept with abandon. If only it were true that they were betrothed, and darling old Lady Bishton were to be her grandmother, too. . . .

That thought reduced her sobs to sniffles. "I have delayed Lord Robert successfully thus far, I must *not* give myself the headache, for there will be more to do before I can hope for her to rescue me," she said to herself, and blew her nose with decision on the hem of her petticoat. "Ugh! Oh, well, someone will wash it when I get away from here."

With a long sigh, she stood up and wandered over to the window, breathing deep of the fresh air and looking wistfully at unattainable freedom. The shadows of afternoon were lengthening, the branches of great trees swayed gently, and there was a sudden darting movement in the unkempt grounds below her. "Pssst!" Araminta caught her breath, half-faint with relief: *Alfie!*

CHAPTER 11

Cutting across the fields and deliberately trespassing through the Earl of Minchampton's woods, Joe reached the outskirts of Crossthwaite in time to see the coach being led off to the stable. Of Araminta there was no sign, nor anyone else aside from old Ben currying the horses. When he had made a stealthy circuit of the house, Joe settled patiently to his watch. He'd found a good clump of shrubbery from which he had a clear view of the entire driveway, extending to the stable-yard, and just as Alfie arrived, Joe had observed Martin summoning Ben to the house—not that he knew their names.

"House man's gone to get stable man," said Joe when Alfie was crouching beside him. "I went around house to see, but there's no way to get in—windows is all closed, looks shut for fair, except there's to-do in kitchen . . . two women a-running. I think they'm eating."

"Likely," Alfie agreed. "They didn't stop for *nothing* after they'd got her. Pa says we're to watch together, one on us stays and t'other goes back to report, do anything happen."

The first event that seemed worthy of notice was the sight of Ben mounted on the old farm horse and jogging slowly away along an overgrown track toward the coast. The boys looked at each other and debated. "He'm gone to see about boat," Alfie said finally. " 'Tis boat that's important, to get spy over to France. We wait till he comes back, and then you'll take same track to look for revenuer."

"Shouldn't I go back to circus to tell 'un if boat is there?"

"Maybe. We wait to see, but Mr. Giles is out along, with Tam after him to say they've got Minta. I think 'tis safe enough to wait; that way, do we see anything, we've fresh horses to follow."

In his turn, Alfie crawled around Crossthwaite, and after his short sojourn at Transome, he was better able to deduce its plan than Joe. Certain opened windows at the rear above the kitchen quarters betokened the dining salon, reinforced by the indistinct murmur of male voices. Darting from tree to tree across the rear, he could see great activity in the servants' area of kitchen and pantry. When he'd gained the far side of the house, more open windows indicated another room that was in use; it was either a study or a small salon, and above stairs was another room of open windows that must be a bedchamber. Otherwise, as Joe had said, all was closed, which only indicated there was no intention of staying here, "else, there'd be airing for chambers," Alfie said to himself.

When he'd rejoined Joe, he imparted his deductions. "There's plenty of trees; do you skin up for a look into upper rooms, Joe. It might be they've locked her in, and kept windows closed to prevent escape."

Obediently Joe scrambled up one after another of the great oaks, working his way around the house. He returned, breathing heavily, to say, "All's empty, save the one room with opened windows, but there's only t' three men at table. She ain't with 'em, nor she ain't in lower room with open windows .'Tis full of books."

"Where can they have put her?" Alfie frowned anxiously. "She'm *there*—we know it—but if all rooms is closed empty . . ."

"Cellars, maybe?"

"Shhhh, here comes the stable man. . . ." With one

accord, they scrambled silently through the underbrush, to hear Ben saying to Martin, "Tell Sir Francis the *Jolly Joan* is just beating in to anchor."

The boys looked at each other. "Now what?"

"When stableman's gone, you take horse and go out to coast," Alfie said. "Ride along this way and that, see if you can find the agent, Joe, and if you can't—go-be-damned for the circus to tell Pa. I'll stay here; do they try to take Minta away, I'll hang onto coach some-how."

When Joe had gone, Alfie made another cautious circuit of the house, but although he could see into the ground rooms, there was no Araminta. He found a half-opened wooden door with steps below leading to a root cellar, but when he whispered "Minta?" there was no answer. Common sense said she'd not have been put there, anyway, if the door was left open. He scrambled up several trees, to peer into upper cham-bers, but there was still no indication of occupancy. At one point he was caught in the branches, while Mrs. Martin was throwing trash onto the midden, and a demmed long time she took about it, while Alfie was clinging to a crotch!

Eventually he'd got back to the original spot, having seen nothing more than a broken pane in a window next the ones opened on the study, and shortly Joe came wriggling up beside him. " 'Tis all right," he panted in an undertone. "Mr. Giles is there, they've got all ready for catching spy, soon as he comes. We'm to keep watch, and try to let 'un know when horses is set to. We'm not to worry about girl, 'tis Sir Francis they want, and do they get him, girl will be safe."

While Alfie was relieved, he was still worried about Araminta. "She'm fair distraught, if only she could *know* all's right," he fretted. "I'm going around once more. You stay here, and if coach comes out—or anything else looking peculiar—you'll whistle."

"Arrr," Joe agreed as Alfie scurried away.

The best possibility was the open windows in Lord Robert's study. Alfie made a long detour through shrubbery and unscythed grass, across the front of Crossthwaite from one side to the drive to the other, and scuttled along the side of the house, assessing the trees. There was one that looked promising; Alfie darted across, and looking up to see how its branches extended, he saw Araminta leaning against the window with the broken pane! "Pssst"!

She'd heard him, her eyes widened with excitement, she leaned to the opening, with a finger to her lips cautioning silence, and mouthed, *"Alfie!"*

He grinned up at her cockily, and assessed the trees again. Finally he was scrambling up, and making his way carefully along a branch that approached her prison. "Can you hear?" When she nodded, "They've got ship, but Mr. Giles is there, and other people—all on us, we won't let nothing happen to you, Minta—so you needn't to worry, whatever they do."

Out of all this, Araminta picked only "Giles"; he was here, she would be perfectly safe! "Oh, *Alfie,*" she breathed, "bless you, bless you!" Behind her the door was being unlocked, and she made a warning gesture to the boy. There was just time for her to scud across to be seated primly on the settee before Lord Robert entered.

"Dear child," he said affectionately, "you have had a dull day of travel and misunderstandings; shall we forget everything, and enjoy a sail on the water? It is only to drive over to Crossthwaite cove, where my yacht is berthed—most comfortable, I assure you—and the weather is so mild, the air so clear, I am persuaded it will do all of us good to cruise for an hour or two before dining."

He had been prepared with a number of additional cajoleries, but to his astonishment, Araminta was enthusiastic in agreement! "It is what I should enjoy of all things." She sprang to her feet. "How good it is in you to think of it!"

If the baron had not been so weary, he might have been suspicious of the ease with which Araminta agreed, but it had been an even longer and duller day of travel and misunderstandings for him. He was merely grateful that *something* was finding favor. "Oh, I am not such a bad fellow, after all." He patted her hand with ponderous gallantry. "Now, Mrs. Martin shall take you to freshen up, while the coach is made ready, and we'll be off in a trice."

Outside, the boys observed the horses poled up, and luggage being tied on. "They'm getting ready," Alfie said. "You go along to say, and I'll come behind carriage."

Shortly Araminta appeared, and was gallantly handed in by Sir Francis. Mr. Hankins joined them, while Lord Robert climbed up to take the reins, with Martin beside him. Slowly the coach began to move away, along the track to the coast, and Alfie flung himself on his horse to follow. The road was very nearly straight, running along the edge of the baron's holding, and Alfie had no difficulty in keeping them in sight, while staying well back and under the trees.

At first glance, the headland sward appeared deserted as the baron pulled up. He looked about with satisfaction and a certain mild astonishment, before handing the reins to Martin. By Jove, how many years since he'd been out here! A very pretty spot, with roses running wild along the rim of the cove, and some noble trees shading the grass; but he thought poorly of his son's choice of a honeymoon ship. The *Jolly Joan* looked like a smuggler. Oh, well, Francis could afford to buy a proper yacht as soon as they'd got Araminta's money. . . .

Lord Robert clambered down, Hankins was already opening the door, and Francis was assisting Minta to descend, after which a great many things seemed to happen at once. The headland was suddenly crowded with people, among whom a tall young man with coppery curls appeared the leader. Several other men in sedate black suits closed in about the carriage, and a boy trotted up on a cream-colored horse.

"What is this?" the baron demanded angrily. "Who are you? I'll have no gypsies on my land. Be off with you!"

"All in good time," said the tall young man, "but first we'll have the law search your son for a certain paper that is not his property."

The voice was cultivated; there was a definite air about his lazy stroll forward; Lord Robert did not need Araminta's heartfelt cry, "Giles!" to deduce he faced the Marquis of Bishton, but he attempted a bluster anyway. "What the devil's the meaning of this outrage? This is private property, I am taking my ward for a sea voyage to recuperate after recent illness, and I'll have no interference, young man!"

"A sea voyage is certainly advisable, and the longer the better," Giles agreed courteously, "but for *you,* milord. You are not taking Araminta anywhere. Neither is your son. The paper, Sir Francis, if you please. . . ."

The black-clad men moved forward, and Francis recoiled, white-faced. Thrusting Araminta away from him, he whipped the sword from his stick and snarled, "Hold your ground! You'll not search a peer on his own land."

"We'll search a spy anywhere," said Giles coldly, and with the utmost calmness raised a pistol from his side to shoot Francis' sword shoulder. "Search him! It is probably sewn into his coat, but if you have to undress him for his trousers, do so."

Before the baron's starting eyes, two law agents swiftly secured Sir Francis, while two more patted and felt in pockets. "What is this, what are you doing?" he stuttered. "Who are you, where's your authority? I'll not have this . . . this *brigandage.*" He moved to fumble in the coach pistol holsters. "Martin, come down —Hankins, help Sir Francis."

"Jack, Ted, hold him," Giles said curtly. "Alfie, get Araminta out of the way. I regret, Lord Eddystone—I realize the shock must be severe—but your son has been augmenting his income as a common Bonapartist spy. As for my authority, I am the Marquis of Bishton, empowered by Lord Denning, his Majesty's home secretary, to take whatever measures may be needed to recover that paper before it leaves the country. Ah," as one of the agents slit the lining of Sir Francis's coat, "I fancy they have found it."

Lord Robert sagged speechlessly in the grip of Black Jack and the lion tamer, while a folded sheet was pulled out. "Good God!" he muttered hollowly.

"Exactly so," said Giles politely, examining the paper, "but take heart in that you were in no way suspected of complicity, milord. I would still advise a sea voyage. It cannot be other than painful to be present in these next weeks of trial and sentence for your heir. Dr. Alling, attend to the wound, if you please, but I fancy I placed the shot for the minimum of discomfort; and that, I think, is all. Alfie, take Araminta up with you pillion; Joe, go with them to be sure she is comfortable; Sam, see if you can identify her luggage and bring it along. . . ."

"Do nothing of the sort!" Lord Robert roused himself firmly, shaking off Jack and Ted. "My ward remains with *me;* it will be time enough for you to issue orders when the betrothal is announced. Araminta, come back here."

The Marquis of Bishton certainly blinked, and looked involuntarily at Minta, standing beside Alfie. Her immense gray eyes were agonized, pleading, and Giles chuckled to himself. *Little minx!* "Must I put a bullet through you, too, milord?" He raised his eyebrows at Lord Robert's empurpled face. "Your guardianship ends in two days. Whatever you'd planned to gain a share of her fortune—aside from a forced marriage to your son—I fancy you won't wish to answer questions on these next two days, Lord Eddystone. In view of Sir Francis' arrest as a French spy, any judge must be extremely critical of papers signed at this moment.

"Oh, are you worrying for her good name, milord?" Giles's quick eyes had caught sight of a familiar equipage slowly approaching along the bumpy road. "I assure you I am as concerned for it as yourself, and you may safely leave Araminta in my grandmother's care." He strode forward as the dowager's carriage was reined in, with her anxious face at the window. "All's well, but *bless you* for coming, ma'am!" he said in an undertone.

"Lady Bishton!" Araminta darted around Alfie's protective arm and ran forward tearfully. "Oh, I knew —I knew you would come!" With her foot on the carriage step, she turned to Giles. "I am sorry, milord. You will not regard it, if you please, but I could think of nothing else to say," she stammered apologetically, "when it seemed I was going to be forced to marry Francis. I thought you would not mind such a tiny fib, for no one heard it but Lord Robert, you know."

"I do not mind it at all, it was extremely clever in you to think of it." Giles smiled. "And now, you must go back to Transome for a few days, until all is settled.

Araminta will tell you all that has occurred, ma'am, and here is Baron Eddystone approaching us. May I introduce him to your notice, ma'am."

The dowager Marchioness of Bishton eyed the corseted paunch walking toward her carriage, and said succinctly, "No."

Giles grinned at her and closed the door. "I shall see you when all's finished, ma'am, or you may choose to return to London. You'll send me word?"

"Of course. Tell them to turn the carriage, and let us be off."

By the time Lord Robert had reached the spot, he saw only the rear sides of two liveried footmen moving away on the carriage. "Who was that; what have you done with Araminta?" he demanded, breathing heavily. "I do not believe it was Lady Bishton, sirrah! She would not have left so hastily, without allowing me to assure myself of my ward's safety."

"On the contrary, it *was* my grandmother, and she left because she had no wish for your acquaintance, milord. Neither," said the Marquis of Bishton with steely politeness, "have I."

The baron drew himself up with a furious glare at the insult. "You will answer for this, milord! There will be questions raised in the House on your *authority* to deliberately shoot a peer." His voice shook with rage. "I am not without influence, I'll have you know!"

"I am aware"—Giles bowed courteously—"but in view of Mary Anne Clarke, I should not rely upon the Duke of York, if I were you. She was merely selling commissions. Sir Francis has been systematically selling military information with the aid of Louis de Saumont, in the forlorn hope of inducing Bonaparte to return him the French estates of your wife."

Lord Robert paled. "I cannot believe it," he muttered. "It *must* be a mistake. . . ."

"There was no mistake in the paper you observed for yourself was sewn into his coat."

"Yes, yes, it must be a mistake," the baron insisted. "The boy had no knowledge, he was only a cat's paw, Francis would never . . . it is entirely De Saumont, I have ever distrusted him. You will see that was the way of it: Louis has given him some tale or other, and Francis has supposed himself merely to be aiding a friend, had no notion that what he carried was treasonable."

"Well, it is a possible defense," Giles reflected. "You can try, and probably he did not know the *exact* contents of sealed envelopes, but if they had to be sewn into coat linings, he must certainly have *suspected* they were something more than love letters, unless he is the ninnyhammer of all time."

"No, no, but it is true there is a certain . . . *innocence* in his mind on, uh, the devious motives of others. He is not exactly gullible, but from his own honesty takes it for granted in others. Poor lad." Lord Robert sighed. "I must stand by his side with my full support and counsel."

"Just so," Giles agreed dryly. "The agents will be removing him direct to London, for house arrest—you may yet be thankful for my wound. Coupled with his rank, it should prevent a remand to Newgate. I should make haste to follow, Lord Eddystone; you can return Araminta's coach at the same time; she will have no need of it at Transome. Yes, Alling?" as the doctor came up to them.

"A very pretty shot, milord," he said approvingly. "Came out easily as you please, clean as a whistle. There'll be some slight discomfort for a day or two, but I anticipate no delay in healing. They are bringing up the carriage now."

"Good! Thank you, Alling." With a polite nod to

the baron, Giles walked away to Araminta's coach, where both Martin and Hankins were standing uneasily.

"Pardon me for addressing your lordship," Hankins said anxiously, "but I have not entirely comprehended . . . that is, I apprehend there has been some difficulty with Sir Francis. We will not, then, be taking ship? And since his fiancée has gone away, I shall not be needed for the ceremony at this present . . ."

"Nor at all." Giles smiled.

"Well, I am glad on't," the minister remarked unexpectedly, "for marriage is a blessed sacrement, milord, and with the young lady so wholly out of her wits, I could not have been happy to have performed my part, despite Lord Robert's assurance that it was merely a nervous affliction to which she is subject. But what am I to do now?"

"Return to London, where you may wait upon me at Bishton House two days hence, if you please. I wish to hear your detailed observations on the young lady's illness," Giles said grimly.

"As a guide for medical attention." Hankins nodded. "Anything I can tell your lordship, I shall be happy, although I believe Sir Henry Halford has been attending her."

"Ah? He will be grateful for your assistance, then." Giles turned to the servant. "Martin, is it?" He smiled warmly. "If you will turn the carriage ready for Crossthwaite, and Mr. Hankins get inside, the baron will join you shortly, and here is something for your trouble." He dropped a satisfying *chink* of coins into Martin's palm. "The coach must be readied for travel, and his lordship's luggage packed—all as swiftly as may be. I fear it will be a bustle!"

"Aye, milord; thank you, milord."

It was still some minutes before the carriages had moved away: Francis with three of the agents, followed by Martin with Hankins and the baron. The remaining two agents eyed the *Jolly Joan* thoughtfully. At sound of the commotion atop the cliff, she had quickly broken out her sails and headed for sea, to be blocked by the accommodating *Saucy Sukey,* anchored neatly in her path. "I think we'd best take a look at 'er, could we get aboard."

"*Sukey*'ll send dinghy, I'll come with you," said Ted briskly. "Sam, Rob, Luke—come along."

Giles would have given much to go with them, but he had still to get back to London as quickly as possible, for there was no doubt in his mind that Eddystone and De Saumont were Boney's valued spies he'd been trailing these past months. "Ted, tell *Sukey*'s captain I shan't need her again," he murmured regretfully, "but I hope he'll take me on once in a while for old time's sake."

"Of course he will," said Ted, surprised. "He's me brother."

"Good God, and I never knew!" Giles roared with laughter, and lingered long enough to enjoy the shouted epithets being exchanged between the two ships' crews. With a sigh, he turned to Jack. "We'll go along, if Tam's poor horses can still stand. It's all over; we did it . . . but the women'll want to hear."

"Sally'll tell 'em," Jack said succinctly. "Aye, she were here—you'd not keep her away when little miss were concerned. Soon's t' girl were off in carriage, Sal went back to circus. She allus wanted a daughter," he added obliquely. "Alfie, come up behind me; leave your horse for someone else. . . ."

Slowly, the remaining circus people sorted themselves out, with the youngsters riding pillion, and ambled home in a flood of satisfied accomplishment. "We did it! We got yon spy, our lads'll be safe—nobody's safe in a war—well, them Frenchies won't be *sure* where to look for 'un. . . ."

The Marquis of Bishton rode a bit apart from the main stream, not from snobbery, but because he was thinking.

Araminta was a beautiful child, but no simpering little miss; another gently bred young female would have swooned and had the vapors upon discovering her guardian's wicked plot. Not Minta! She'd fought all the way with such weapons as she had—a game little pullet with quick wits. He chuckled to himself at her invention of a betrothal to one of the first peers of the realm!

And chuckled again at her anxious apology, "I thought you would not object to a tiny fib . . ." What a sweet child it was!

The dowager Marchioness of Bishton loved her. She had come in person to do what she could—that meant much. His grandmother would have been instantly alive to the responsibility of Araminta, but had she not loved the girl, she would have sent couriers to rouse constables and country justices. Oh, she'd have made a monumental tow-row, but she would not, at her age, have forthwith traveled twenty-five or more miles to *save* Araminta, with a further exhausting trip for return to Transome.

It would be interesting to see what developed. Giles speculated to himself, and thought Grandie might well set herself to sponsor Miss Surtaine, which would be good all around. His sisters were perfectly self-sufficient in marrying off their daughters; there was very little for the dowager to do. His mother still led an active social life, delighting in routs and balls. It occurred to Giles (not for the first time) that his grandmother was not *happy;* she was not precisely *unhappy,* but she did not *enjoy* widowhood. With the dimmest recollection of his grandfather, Giles yet had a certainty that Grandie had been supremely well suited, and with old Ludo's death, had ever after been rather at loose ends. To sponsor Araminta would give her an interest, perk the old lady up. "Good!" said Giles to himself. "If she doesn't think of it herself, I will suggest it!"

The dowager Marchioness of Bishton (as we know) was way ahead of her grandson. She was admittedly fatigued by the time they had reached Transome; so was Araminta, but she had put Lady Bishton in possession of all the thrilling events of the day. Descending somewhat stiffly from her carriage, the dowager said, "We will have the *simplest* meal, Royle—whatever Jean-Louis can give us in fifteen minutes, hot or cold, with no formality tonight. We are too tired for service and courses; put everything on the table, and we will eat as soon as we have washed our hands."

It was still delectable, for Lady Bishton's chef was devoted to her, and upon learning she *hoped* to return with little mees that day, had prepared for all eventualities of hunger, or weariness, or lateness of hour. A cup of strengthening bouillon, omelets with a mushroom sauce, a succulent slice of roast duckling, a dish of well-buttered new peas, and a basket piled high with delicate pastries, flanked by a small apple tart, appeared likely to please; and as the emptied plates were returned to the kitchen, Jean-Louis preened himself almost insufferably on his superior knowledge of what milady would enjoy.

"They don't wish a tea tray," Royle informed him sourly, and was further annoyed when the chef nodded smugly. "I thought they would not. *Alors,* tomorrow will be different, and I shall prepare *un gâteau St. Honoré.*"

The ladies—one old, one young—slept exhaustedly, but arose in fine fettle for a late breakfast. "I have been thinking, my love," said the dowager, "and the day after tomorrow will be your birthday. I wonder if we should not make it a festive occasion, by returning to London? Were we to rest today, and travel tomorrow, there would be another night in which to regain our strength, and I fancy we might be in good frame for a celebration. What do you think?"

"It would of all things be delightful, ma'am, but is it not too great a strain for you?" Araminta asked anxiously. "I should have liked to be with Mrs. Hobson, for I fear she must be distraught with worry at my absence, and she has ever been kind to me. It seems hard if she were, by chance, not present for my coming of age."

"Indeed it would, and she shall not be. It is decided: we will allow today to regain our strength; tomorrow we will make an early start, but with an easy pace and frequent rests at the posting inns, we shall reach London in time for a late dinner; and on the following day, we shall have our party in the evening," Lady Bishton said firmly. "Oh, Royle, we shall be returning to London tomorrow. You may send the fourgon, we will be quite content with simple fare tonight, and send word I shall need couriers to deliver letters in town today."

The butler gulped, and stammered faintly, "Very good, milady . . . and Thomas is inquiring what you wish done with Master Alfred's horse."

Her ladyship arose from the table. "Have someone return it to Black Jack's Traveling Circus," she said calmly. "Minta, do you mind to act as secretary for a while? We must write our invitations; whom shall you like to be present?"

"Giles, of course," Minta said absently, "but I

should *like* Miss Benbridge, and Alfie, and Sally, and Jack, and Joe . . . but I doubt it could be contrived."

"Miss Benbridge, by all means if possible, but do you know," Lady Bishton reflected, "I fancy it might be more satisfactory to have a second, special party *at* the circus, do not you?"

"Could I?" Araminta breathed hopefully. "For they were all so kind to me, you know, and I should not like anyone to feel slighted."

"Exactly! Giles will know how to arrange for it."

Araminta flushed faintly and lowered her gaze. "You *really* think he did not mind my lying to the baron?" she murmured.

"You know he did not, he told you himself it was clever in you to think of it. Now, who else shall come to your birthday? Mrs. Hobson, of course, and Lady Urbaugh?"

"Yes, please, and Jane . . ."

At length the guest list was made up, the notes were written and dispatched. "Do you think Giles will come?"

"I am *sure* of it," said Lady Bishton firmly, "if only for a few minutes; he may have other engagements, but he will not fail to wish you a happy birthday."

By superhuman efforts, Royle managed to dispatch the fourgon; Miss Crims packed the ladies' luggage; Jean-Louis devised a suitable birthday menu for little mees and was more passionately Gallic than usual, until he was dispatched in advance by separate post chaise, "and good riddance," Royle muttered wearily. "I tell you, Miss Crims, I'm at a loss—this packing and unpacking, moving and removing. I do not scruple to tell *you,* after our long association, I cannot understand it."

Miss Crims took pity on him. "Strictly between us, Mr. Royle," she said, "I believe there's a match in the making—and I'll say, if I'm right, we'll find it to our liking. It's time the marquis set up his nursery, and where's a sweeter young lady than Miss Surtaine?"

London was, briefly, electrified by the arrest of Louis de Saumont and Sir Francis Eddystone as Bonapartist spies, but no one was more devastated than Mrs. Illington. "Good God!" she muttered, scanning the *Gazette* with popping eyes. Despite her suspicions of the association between the two men, she had not supposed it to have gone so far as to set government agents on the trail. Now it was no longer an ace up her sleeve, but apt to ruin her forever. Pacing back and forth in her morning room, her mind squirreled frantically this way and that, and she was unable to see her course. She *must* be drawn into it; it was she who had introduced Louis to Francis—not with any original motive, but upon observing their increasing friendliness, it was Mrs. Illington who had fostered everything. They often spoke French for an entire evening, "to increase my fluency—it is a golden opportunity for Francis, as well, or he may forget what his mother taught him." When Louis spoke of his property in France, Clara had brought out the map and persuaded Francis to outline his mother's estates. "Such a pity they are lost," she sighed.

"Perhaps not forever," said Louis. "Napoleon cannot last. If he is not killed in his wars, he will die— he has the pox, you know."

If only she knew how deeply involved Francis was —whether he was forever disgraced, or might prove still acceptable socially. After all, the Duke of York had been cleared of complicity with the Clarke woman; Francis, too, would have to be tried in the House of Lords; it might be that Clara could testify in his behalf; but if he were to remain under a cloud, of what use to marry him? Such few slim footholds as she had would be lost. She was under no illusions with respect to her *ton* relatives: they asked her to something unimportant each season, and would like nothing better than to drop her entirely.

Late in the afternoon Baron Eddystone was announced. This, she had not anticipated. With swift decision, "Show him into the salon; bring brandy and Madeira, and tea for me."

Lord Robert looked what he felt: old. These last two weeks had undone him, with the constant search for Araminta, culminating in his son's disgrace; and there was still no money. "My dear Mrs. Illington, it is kind in you to receive me," he said brokenly. "I was prepared for your refusal, in view of the news."

"A friend waits to see," she said smoothly. "I beg you will be seated, milord, and tell me how I may serve you. It seems impossible that Sir Francis should be involved in such a matter; I cannot credit it! Is it very bad?"

"Yes, and no." He shrugged. "De Saumont naturally tries to throw all upon Francis, but it is not so. Already it is proven that Louis has been obtaining secret information from a friend at the Horse Guards—a Captain Rogers, who is notorious for gambling debts . . . but equally proven that Francis has never met the man. Louis insists that Francis has repeatedly taken the information across the channel, but that is merely to protect his other messengers who have yet to be uncovered. Francis says that he has upon two occasions—one a number of months past and this time— agreed to deliver sealed envelopes in France, believing them to be only private letters from Louis to an old family servant, concerning the De Saumont property.

"Naturally, Francis had no distrust—he is heartbroken, finds it impossible to believe Louis could so have abused their friendship!" Lord Robert sighed deeply and refilled his glass with Madeira.

"It is quite shocking," Mrs. Illington agreed, "and the more so in that *I*, too, have been equally deceived in Louis de Saumont, for you must know that he was forever in my house, milord—quite one of our private cronies, no scheme complete without him. Sir Francis always insisted, 'Let us ask Louis first, to be sure he has no prior engagement!' "

"My dear Mrs. Illington, I knew you must feel it, as I do." The baron smiled sadly. "I would have come sooner, but I have all this while been going about to learn what I could, and thought better to bring you the latest word. Francis was most anxious I should do so. 'Clara will be so worried,' he said, and, 'You must not fail me in this, Father, for all my dependence is upon you.' "

"Indeed, I *thank* you, milord," she said earnestly. "I collect you have been permitted to see Sir Francis?"

"Oh, yes—it is house arrest, you know. Louis was taken to Newgate, but for a peer, it is different. Yes, they allowed me to be present during the magistrate's questioning—I will say that he was most courteous, entirely realized what was due to an English peer—and I have retained Sir Godfrey Salterton for defense. It may pass over, but in view of Louis' accusations, we fear it may be forced to a trial in the House, unless additional evidence can be found to clear Francis."

"Ah? What evidence will be required?"

"Rogers has given dates when he transferred information to Louis, who in turn claims Francis carried *all* messages to France on the following day. Unluckily, my son does not keep an engagement book—merely notes for a week or two, which are discarded. I have come to you, Mrs. Illington, or may I be allowed to call you Clara?" Lord Robert inserted affectionately, "for I have long expected also to call you 'daughter.' "

"Oh, milord!" Mrs. Illington summoned up a very

creditable blush of confusion. "It is true that . . . that there is a deep tenderness between your son and myself; indeed, who could not be fond of Sir Francis?"

"Or of you!" the baron beamed heartily. "Well, I have come to you, *Clara,* in the hope that you do have an engagement book, and that on at least some of the dates in question, it can be proved Francis was a part of some scheme or other—either here or in company elsewhere."

Hmmmm! What to say: yes, or no? "Yes, for it commits me to nothing; should the outcome be bad, I do not *have* to marry him. . . ." "Yes, I do have an engagement book." She smiled. "And what is more, I keep them for several years, milord, for you must know it is the habit of females to put a great many other things in their calendars! The address of a seamstress, or the date of a godchild's birth . . . one is forever hunting back for some such note. So if you will give me the questionable dates, I doubt not I shall find something helpful, for an accusation of spying is the greatest nonsense. It cannot be allowed that Louis shall cause deliberate difficulties."

Lord Robert was already eagerly withdrawing a paper from his coat pocket. "My dear Clara, you cannot know! The relief to a father's heart and mind," he exclaimed, "but Francis said it would be so."

"Indeed, he knows me well." She lowered her eyes coyly. "I must have gone instantly to see him, but that I feared it would be an embarrassment, for you must know I have no standing, no right, aside from devoted friendship."

"That in itself is the greatest right, if there were nothing more! Well"—he drew a long breath of relief —"I cannot say how delighted I am that we have had this small opportunity to advance our acquaintance— something I have long desired, my dear, but you know how it is like to be between father and son: different generations, different pursuits, different friends. But however, all that is at an end, and I shall hope to be as much your friend as Francis."

"Most certainly! I shall depend upon you to bring me word how all goes on, and to assure Sir Francis of any aid I can give."

When the baron had bowed himself away, she took the list of dates to the morning room and disinterred the engagement books, for that much was true: Mrs. Illington did keep them. In fact, she had every year since Joe's death; they were specially bound in white leather, tooled in gold, and contained any amount of extraneous notes. Hunting out the particular dates, she sighed with satisfaction: on only two had she had other appointments, nor had she used too much of any other entry spaces to prevent an addition. Very cunningly, cleverly, carefully, Clara Illington set to work, using watered ink that would appear faded to match the rest of the page. . . .

Spying the Marquis of Bishton strolling down Bond Street, his sister Louisa waited for him at the door of her carriage. *"Who* is Araminta Surtaine?" she inquired, ignoring his courteous bow.

"Oh, are you asked, too?"

"To a birthday party 'for a young friend whom I wish you to know,'" said Louisa, "but *who* is she, Giles?"

"A ravishing eighteen-year-old heiress of nabob ancestry and unexceptionable manners. I shall see you there?"

"Naturally—when Grandie commands? Do I apprehend *you* will be present? Good *God!*" Louisa eyed him severely. "Never tell me you're caught at last."

"Dear Louisa, your imagination is as fertile as your

womb," Giles said irrepressibly, and guffawed at her flush and the faint twitch of her lips. "Oh, *no!* Never tell me there's another in the basket? What a man Oliver is!"

She chuckled. "A pity you're not his equal!"

Continuing his stroll when her carriage had rolled away, Giles met his other brother-in-law studying the betting book at White's. "Hallo, Tony, I trust I see you well?"

"Very well, but what about you? Eleanor will have it we're asked to meet your bride-to-be. Can it be true?"

"Oh, devil take it!" Giles snorted. "No, of course not! It's merely the granddaughter of some old coze of Grandie's—not that Minta isn't a beauty to set London by its ears, with a fortune to match."

"Oh. Old lady thinkin' of bringin' her out?" The Earl of Wycombe pursed his lips. "Be a good thing, give her ladyship some amusement; often thought she was moped to death, and bein' gallant about it. I say, that was a bang-up speech in the House, Giles—never knew you were interested in such things."

The Marquis of Bishton might smile to himself at the eagerness with which his family wished to marry him off, but on the morning of Araminta's birthday, he found time to select an exquisitely lacy bouquetière of gold, and further, personally, to direct the components of a nosegay to fit. He then wrote "Happy Birthday!" across his visiting card, and dispatched the whole by a footman to Miss Surtaine in Mount Street. On second thought, he ordered another nosegay and scrawled, "Happy birthday to you, too!" on a card—to be delivered to the dowager Marchioness of Bishton. He then went about his business, which occupied him in various government offices until late afternoon, when he returned home to find Mr. Fogg awaiting him.

"Miss Surtaine's guardianship has been formally ended," he said. "The case was very late on the docket, Baron Eddystone was not present, but the financial trustees—Messrs. Reston and Reston, *most* respectable!—expressed themselves satisfied with the final accounting, although between us, milord, they were *not*. However, as Mr. Reston senior told me later, they considered *anything* was wise to be rid of the baron. 'It's the last he'll get, and not enough to fight over,' was Reston's comment. I thought I would tell you in person, milord—being so late in the day, and all, on the way home. Will there be anything more you would wish me to oversee?"

"I think not," Giles said slowly, "although you might drop a word to the Restons to beware of any later allegation of mental illness in Miss Surtaine. It would appear that Baron Eddystone has set this about in certain quarters to further a marriage between her and his son. There is no truth in it, but it might reach their ears and cause uneasiness. Should anything arise, you will come to me for additional information. And thank you, Fogg!" The marquis smiled and shook hands warmly.

"There is no need of thanks, milord; it is my sincere pleasure to serve you, quite apart from fees!" Mr. Fogg assured him. "I have few clients who understand the ramifications of *management* so well; it is a *joy* to work with your lordship!"

"And an equal pleasure to work with you, Fogg," the marquis told him soberly. "Of course, there are many excellent businessmen in the City, but I have long known there are few with your probity. I count myself fortunate."

While Mr. Fogg was being shown out—in a glow of satisfaction—Lord Bishton was ascending to his chamber for evening garb. Via George Graham's meticulous list of invitations, Giles was aware of no less than two dinner parties, four balls, and a musicale bringing up the rear; but cynicism and the knowledge of London *haut ton* told him that whosoever had been bidden to his grandmother's home would be there. So, too, would the Marquis of Bishton, in impeccable court dress. He admitted to a curiosity to see Araminta as herself, in correct clothing; hitherto, he'd seen only a girl in a night shift with a bandage on her head, and a young lady in a bedraggled pink muslin.

Almost, he did not recognize her. He was aware of a female form descending the stairs as he stripped off his topcoat into Royle's hands, but when he looked up, he took two steps and stood transfixed.

She was unquestionably the most beautiful young woman he had ever beheld. She needed no rouge, no patch, no dusting of powder. Her silky black hair had been cleverly arranged to conceal the inches where it had been cut beneath the bandage. She wore a gown of deepest rose crepe, opened over an underdress of palest pink, with pearl clasps. More pearls hung from her ears, and a magnificent double collar of pink pearls circled her throat. She was minding her steps, but when she saw him . . . "She smiled all over," was Giles's reaction.

He had often—far too often—been greeted with melting flattery, but here was honest delight. "Giles!" she cried, picking up her skirts and flying down the final steps, to catch his hand in a squeeze. "Grandie said you would come, if only for a moment—and thank you, *thank you,* for the bouquetière and nosegay. It was the very nicest present, for I had not one, you know." She was dragging him into the salon. "Here he is, Grandie! I did not believe it above half, but here is!"

"So I see." Her ladyship was resplendent with diamonds. "Do you stay, or go?" extending her hand regally, but as he bent to kiss it, he observed she was carrying his nosegay.

"Go?" he said, bewildered. "I understood I was invited to dine, ma'am—or was that a polite fiction, and you have not enough covers for the occasion?"

"Phoo, nonsense!" Lady Bishton waved her hand toward a lady seated beside her. "Mrs. Hobson, make you acquainted with my grandson, the Marquis of Bishton. The only 'polite fiction' is that Araminta is the granddaughter of my girlhood friend, long deceased, and upon learning that her come-out must be delayed a year for lack of a current sponsor, I have decided to undertake that office immediately."

"I thought you might," Giles observed, straight-faced. "I had nearly entered it in the betting book at White's, but Tony distracted me, and I had come away before I remembered."

"Is it not the kindest, dearest thing!" Minta exclaimed. "I feared it might be too tiring, but Grandie declares she can and will. Oh," she confided to Giles, "Lady Bishton permits the familiarity, because . . ."

"Because you have not one of these, either," Giles finished, laughing.

"Well, I have not, and it is altogether more comfortable to feel, in some sense, one has relatives. Oh, *Benny!*" she squealed, and ran forward to hug a handsome youngish woman being announced as "Miss Benbridge."

"As for all the rest of it," Lady Bishton said under cover of the arriving guests, "we are agreed it is best ignored, Giles."

"My sentiments exactly, ma'am," Giles returned warmly. "The guardianship was terminated this afternoon, Fogg attended as observer on my behalf, and I believe we may now forget the Eddystones. Minta's financial trustees are very sound, Fogg knows them well, and it would seem unnecessary to mention any previous guardian—particularly at this moment."

"No, indeed," Mrs. Hobson added unexpectedly, "for it could ruin all! One knows the tittle-tattle in the *ton,* exaggerated beyond permission; the mere acquaintance could raise a question on Minta, for she speaks excellent French, you know. Ah, Miss Benbridge! How delightful it is to meet again. . . ."

The entire evening was delightful, for the Ormeraux were one of those rare families who liked each other and possessed an easy manner with their fellow men and women. In a twinkling it seemed all were comfortable old friends. Jean-Louis's birthday menu was a triumph of subtleties. Giles's mother (the "Intermediate Marchioness") was *enchanted* to learn she could assist in introducing Araminta; Louisa and Eleanor were brimming with suggestions for seamstresses, and their husbands were equally discussing the horses and carriages that would be proper. From her superior knowledge of the season, Elinor was offering every help to Araminta and Jane, "for it is all very easy, once one knows how to go on—is it not, Miss Benbridge?"

Despite all previous commitments, nobody left before it was absolutely essential. "Oh, dear, we *must* show ourselves at least for a look-in at Anna's ball. Mama, why do you not take Lady Rivers—it is all on your way—and Eleanor can represent us for Lady Coombs. Well, what a delicious party it was, to be sure! And we shall see you tomorrow, Araminta, for breakfast; we shall see you for tea. . . . I will send a note to the seamstress to wait on you, Mrs. Hobson . . . Miss Benbridge, *happy* to make your acquaintance, and *yours,* Lady Urbaugh . . . good night, good night!"

In a spate of loving pats and kisses, smiling bows and "Your servant, ma'am," the Ormeraux were gone, but for Giles. Araminta swallowed, controlling the tears in her eyes. "It was all so . . . so *beautiful,*" she murmured, "so good and kind. They never saw me before, but I felt . . . I felt part of the family. It was particularly pleasant, because . . ."

"You never had one before." Giles laughed.

"No," she said soberly, "but I fancy yours is exceptional. They all *like* each other. It is something I had not previously observed in the families of my acquaintance, which is why I had not previously repined on the lack of relations, and I do not know that I repine even now," she added reflectively, "for who knows but my blood kin might have been odious? I would far rather be a part of the Ormereaux."

"Obviously, they are more than willing to include you." He smiled. "Happy birthday, Minta, and many happy returns!"

Oddly enough, the Eddystones (and Mrs. Illington) owed a debt of gratitude to Araminta Surtaine. The baron might not have got her money, but in the excitement of her presentation to the *ton* by the dowager Marchioness of Bishton, the trial of Sir Francis for espionage was submerged. He had never been the first stare, anyway—he was an English peer, heir to a baronage a good many people had never heard of before consulting *Burke's Peerage.* From the *Gazette* report of the trial, it was really all Louis de Saumont; society wrote Sir Francis Eddystone off as a stupid fool for making friends with a Frenchie, and forgot him.

Much more titillating was the new Incomparable, bursting into mid-season like a floodtide in a Scottish burn, and carrying all before her! On Araminta's first appearance at Almack's, flanked by a united front of

Ormeraux, success was assured, and reinsured when Beau Brummell was observed to be seated beside Miss Surtaine for the duration of a waltz. Chatting, smiling, laughing—he might have been an old friend! Even more sensational: Mr. Brummell wheedled the patroness approval for Miss Surtaine to waltz with him—on her *first* evening!

All London made haste to send invitation cards to its forthcoming entertainments. Every beau on the toddle pleaded for an introduction; so did all the Corinthians after observing Miss Surtaine riding beside the Marquis of Bishton in the park. The gazetted fortune hunters sighed wistfully. "Fifty thousand pounds—but of what use to waste any blunt? She's bespoke for Bishton."

It had rapidly become evident to the *ton* that Giles was catched at last! This increased the excitement to firework proportions: would Arminta, or would she not, have him? The ladies could not agree; their lords said, "Phoo, nonsense, of course she'll have him—never saw a clearer case!"

Giles himself would have been glad to be equally sure. At the outset, he had laid himself out to assist his grandmother's scheme to present Araminta; with Boney's spies laid by the heels, he was free to accept whatever frivolity was offered by London hostesses, and it struck him that however gallant, Lady Bishton *was* an elderly lady. Accordingly, he appointed himself her escort for all evening parties, but by the week's end, he found himself stiffening unconsciously at some of the young sprigs thronging about Minta. It took another week before he admitted to himself that Araminta was the one girl he'd ever wanted.

Subsequently he began pursuit in earnest, but could not be sure Minta was aware that it *was* pursuit. She wrote charming thanks for his gifts—a leather collar and gold bell for El Cid, a fan delicately painted by Angelica Kauffman, a novel fresh from the Minerva Press, a basket of immense strawberries with a jug of thick cream sent by special messenger from his estate at Rushley, together with a tangle of wild roses—all were acknowledged with delight (on unscented stationery). She was prompt to the minute, if they were to ride or join the Promenade in his high-perch phaeton. If he sent flowers before a ball or Almack's evening, Araminta always carried *them* in his birthday bouquetière.

She told him *everything* of her days, confided (with chuckles) every absurd flowery compliment of a beau, asked his advice upon this or that Corinthian who had asked her to join a party for Richmond—"Grandie is not entirely *sure* he is the thing, she bade me inquire from you, Giles, but I own I should like to go."

All the same, he had a dismal feeling that Minta was looking upon him as an older brother!

He could not fail to be cognizant of the *haut ton*'s delicious amusement at his predicament; he no longer gave a tinker's curse! After three weeks, he was beginning to be frantic; there were *five* suitors who could not possibly be rejected by Baron Eddystone (who still had to approve her marriage before she was twenty-five). "Isn't it *fun!*" Araminta chuckled. "I never thought to have so many!"

"I am surprised at so few," Giles returned flatteringly. "Which shall you choose?"

"Oh, heavens—none of them, of course," she said airily, and proceeded to detail their disqualifications so impishly that Giles was roaring with mirth.

In the middle of the fourth week, George Graham picked up the letters signed by Lord Bishton, and smiled at his employer. "Wish me happy, milord? Elinor accepts, her father agrees—you'll read the announcement in the *Gazette* tomorrow."

"I wish you happy, indeed!" Giles clapped the secretary heartily on his shoulder. "Does this mean I shall lose you, George? I would keep you as long as may be."

"We are agreed on it until my godfather dies, from whom I have some expectations, but Elinor sees no loss of dignity in my working for her uncle, milord."

"Uncle? Good God, are you to be my *nephew?"* The marquis snorted with laughter again. "Well, I still wish you happy, George, but do not expect a rise in salary through relationship!"

"No, of course not—I shall have my wife's fortune, after all," George returned blandly, "but do not you suggest that I shall work for *nothing,* milord. Your niece would never agree."

"Oh, what a little money-grubber it is!" Giles complained. "Well, what shall I give for an engagement present?"

"The news of your own? Elinor quite longs for an aunt of her own age." To George's astonishment, his employer's face flushed, and he swung away, "as conscious as a boy teased for his first love," George said to himself. "I beg pardon, milord," he stammered. "I'd no intention of impertinence."

"No, no, it is not." Giles shook his head with a rueful smile. "Merely, I had not thought my heart so obviously on my sleeve. I am well served, am I not? How the family will laugh! Grandie warned me that if I did not make haste, I should be at my last prayers—like poor old Florizel."

"What d'you mean? Are you about in your head?" George demanded, quite forgetting all formality. "Good God, milord—*Uncle Giles!"* with a grin, "do you really not know Araminta is going through the season purely to become a suitable wife for a marquis? You once told me to take pluck and *ask* for what I wanted; I will tell you the same."

Giles shook his head again. "The case is not similar. Elinor grew to love you out of long acquaintance, George. Araminta thinks of me as an older brother."

George stared at him, and uttered a sudden snort of hilarity. "The devil she does! Pray when does a *sister* ruthlessly cancel her engagements in order to ride with a brother? What *sister* excuses herself at Almack's from *Beau Brummell* in order to waltz with a *brother?* Damme, if ever I saw a faint heart! Here's the entire family and all of London waiting for the announcement, to say nothing of Minta—and you're prosing on about being her brother! I didn't think it of you, *Uncle Giles!*"

"You really think . . . ?"

"I really think," George said firmly, "and so does Elinor, *and* your mother, *and* your sisters, *and* your grandmother. It's been in the betting book at White's for the past three weeks—not will she or won't you, but *when.* You've already cost Lord Jersey a monkey; he bet it'd be in the *Gazette* within ten days. For God's sake, set about it, man!"

A country dance at Almack's is not the best place for a proposal, but with Araminta's hand in his and her eyes smiling at him, the Marquis of Bishton said earnestly, "Araminta—will you do me the honor of becoming my wife?"

"Yes, please—I should like it of all things!" she breathed, before the figures required her to move away; but when the steps brought them together once more, her face was anxious. "That is, if you are certain I will suit? Benny thought perhaps I should have another season, or some special studies, although it would be very hard to wait a year."

"It would be *impossible,*" said his lordship firmly. "I won't consent to it!"

Again the dance parted them, but by now everyone in the set was aware of a Situation, and correspondingly agog for every word possible to overhear. By Araminta's radiant face and the gleam in Lord Bishton's eye, it was obviously *now*. "Good God," George Graham murmured to his Elinor, "I told him to set about it, but I never meant him to plunge in the middle of the dancing floor!"

"You might have known he would, if the notion struck him," she returned calmly. "It is what one most particularly likes about Uncle Giles—he is never stuffy." Moving away from him, she faced the marquis for the next figure. "I wish you happy, Uncle Giles," she said demurely. "When is it to be?"

"Over the anvil, if I had my way—but that demmed governess has Minta convinced she needs another season and a course of study to be prepared," he snorted wrathfully.

"Oh, pay no attention to it." Elinor flicked her eyes up and down wickedly. "I feel sure you can teach Araminta whatever she needs to know, uncle."

"Minx!" He grinned, and was once more facing Minta. "My dearest, beautiful darling," he murmured, "I won't wait a minute longer than needed for the banns. To the devil with bride clothes, we'll get 'em later."

"Well, one can do a great deal in three weeks," she returned practically, "and I dare say you are not so completely acquainted with my existing wardrobe that I cannot contrive to surprise you."

"I feel sure you can; you always have, and probably always will."

"Should you like that?" she asked doubtfully.

"Very much! I love you to distraction, my sweeting."

"You *do?* Oh, so do I," she breathed, stopping dead in the middle of the floor. "That is, I cannot *envision* any other man but you, Giles. It has been quite *dreadful,* from fearing you only thought of me as another sister or niece."

"While I was afraid you were thinking of me as an older brother, or uncle." Giles clasped her hands warmly, perfectly indifferent to the other dancers tactfully stepping around them. "My love, I fancy we are in the way—let us go over to tell Grandie?"

The announcement of Miss Araminta Surtaine's engagement to Giles Edward Andrew Ormeraux, Marquis of Bishton, duly appeared in the *Gazette.*

Directly beneath it was the announcement of the marriage of Sir Francis Eddystone to Mrs. Clara Illington. The happy pair were understood to have removed to Crossthwaite Hall for an indefinite stay.

Elsewhere in the *Gazette* it was reported that two Bonapartist spies had been hanged yesterday.

"Where shall we honeymoon, my love?" The Marquis of Bishton nibbled his fiancée's ear agreeably. "There is Transome, and Desmond, and Rushley—or shall we inspect Surtaine Manor? Tony would gladly lend us Wycombe Towers, which is a hideously uncomfortable pile in Cumberland, but we could tour the Lake District, or I've a shooting box in Leicestershire that would put us close to George and Elinor. Oliver's lending them his shooting box." His lordship's lips had moved around from ear to cheek to nose to mouth. "Mmmmm, you've only to say, dearest, and it's as good as done."

"Mmmmm," said Araminta dreamily. "Kissing is delightful, isn't it, when you have the right person? Well"
—she stared into space briefly—"what I should really *like,* if it were possible, would be a week with the circus in a caravan—I *think* I could cook well enough, or Sally would help me—and perhaps another week on the *Saucy Sukey.* It sounds such fun, to wear old clothes and not worry if you're clean or not . . . and putting a net over the side to catch your dinner, or rowing over to look in the lobster pots. That is what I should like, but I suppose it isn't very practical."

"Well, it is certainly *unusual,* but I fancy it could be managed, if you are certain you will enjoy it."

And that is why, to this day, no one in the *haut ton* has ever known where the Marquis and Marchioness of Bishton spent the first two weeks of their marriage before arriving at Transome with one basket of mussels, one basket of clams, one basket of fresh fish, and four baskets of lobsters. . . .